A DETECTIVE CHIEF INSF

A POCKET FULL OF POSIES

NEW YORK TIMES #1 BESTSELLER **TONY LEE** WRITING AS

JACK GATLAND

Hooded Man MEDIA
INSPIRATION • PRODUCTION • PUBLICATION

Published by Hooded Man Media.

First Edition: September 2024

PRAISE FOR JACK GATLAND

'Fast-paced and action packed, Jack Gatland's thrillers always deliver a punch.'

'This is one of those books that will keep you up past your bedtime, as each chapter lures you into reading just one more.'

'This book was excellent! A great plot which kept you guessing until the end.'

'Couldn't put it down, fast paced with twists and turns.'

'The story was captivating, good plot, twists you never saw and really likeable characters. Can't wait for the next one!'

'Totally addictive. Thoroughly recommend.'

'Moves at a fast pace and carries you along with it.'

'Just couldn't put this book down, from the first page to the last one it kept you wondering what would happen next.'

Before LETTER FROM THE DEAD...
There was

LIQUIDATE THE PROFITS

Learn the story of what *really* happened to DI Declan Walsh, while at Mile End!

An EXCLUSIVE PREQUEL, completely free to anyone who joins the Declan Walsh Reader's Club!

Join at bit.ly/jackgatlandVIP

Also by Jack Gatland

DI DECLAN WALSH BOOKS

LETTER FROM THE DEAD

MURDER OF ANGELS

HUNTER HUNTED

WHISPER FOR THE REAPER

TO HUNT A MAGPIE

A RITUAL FOR THE DYING

KILLING THE MUSIC

A DINNER TO DIE FOR

BEHIND THE WIRE

HEAVY IS THE CROWN

STALKING THE RIPPER

A QUIVER OF SORROWS

MURDER BY MISTLETOE

BENEATH THE BODIES

KILL YOUR DARLINGS

KISSING A KILLER

PRETEND TO BE DEAD

HARVEST FOR THE REAPER

CROOKED WAS HIS CANE

A POCKET FULL OF POSIES

CHEATING MY DESTINY

TOM MARLOWE BOOKS

SLEEPING SOLDIERS

TARGET LOCKED

COVERT ACTION

COUNTER ATTACK

STEALTH STRIKE

BROAD SWORD

ROGUE SIGNAL

SNIPER ALLEY

ELLIE RECKLESS BOOKS

PAINT THE DEAD

STEAL THE GOLD

HUNT THE PREY

FIND THE LADY

BURN THE DEBT

DAMIAN LUCAS BOOKS

THE LIONHEART CURSE

STANDALONE BOOKS

THE BOARDROOM

As Tony Lee

STANDALONE

TWELVE TASKS

THE PLAYING CARD WAR

KNAVE OF SPADES

For Mum, who inspired me to write.

For Tracy, who inspires me to write.

CONTENTS

PROLOGUE

THEN.

When the call came through, Anjli Kapoor was in the middle of an argument.

It hadn't been her fault. Unfortunately, DCI Ford, her commanding officer in Mile End, had learned something Anjli had been trying to keep secret for the last six months and had decided that *now* was the exact time to chew her out.

They were standing in Ford's office, with Ford, a mildly terrifying and definitely intimidating woman in her fifties with close-cropped grey hair and a matching grey suit, glaring at her with an almost impotent fury. If she was being brutally honest though, as intimidating as the scene was, Anjli had had enough. She'd expected, and was happy to take, the reprimand on this; as far as she was concerned, she was doing a good thing. Her mother had been diagnosed with breast cancer, and the NHS had said it would take months to get her onto the list, but a benefactor had offered to help with the payments if she went private.

The problem was, as the benefactor was Johnny or Jackie Lucas, the "Twins" of the East End, it effectively meant that Anjli now owed them. But as far as she was concerned, it was a small price to pay to look after her mum. They'd explored the other options; Anjli couldn't remortgage, and her Mum rented, so there was no money from that direction. The costs for the treatments were a major chunk of her yearly wage if they went away from the NHS, and to Anjli, this was a loan she intended to repay.

DCI Ford, however, was not as impressed with what the Detective Constable standing in front of her had done as much as Anjli was.

'You've let yourself be taken by a gangster,' she growled. 'They'll own you.'

Anjli knew Ford was right – it was very much an act of desperation; but this attitude from Ford – a woman known to be on the take as well – was taking the piss here, and Anjli finally reached her limit.

'So you think I should have asked for more?' she asked.

Ford paused, frowning.

'What the hell is that supposed to mean?'

'Maybe I should have asked for the "DCI Marie Ford special" when I sold my soul and career to some gangsters,' Anjli snapped. 'Because, *DCI Ford*, you are in no position to tell me about owing Johnny Lucas anything. Or is it Jackie who pays your gambling debts?'

She waved around the room, effectively indicating the entire bullpen on the other side of the window.

'We all know; it's not exactly a closed secret, no matter what the official record is. You're in hock to him for what, sixty, seventy grand? Yet nobody's turning up to break *your* legs. So I'm guessing that you're probably giving him way more information than I might be asked to do. And, if I'm being utterly brutally honest, Jackie or Johnny Lucas, whoever he was at the bloody time, has actually helped me with more cases before this, even without me owing anything. If you recall, Ma'am, we wouldn't have caught Connelly without him.'

'The only reason he helped you with Connelly, was because the prick was going onto his turf,' Ford replied, now rising from her chair, facing Anjli angrily across the office. 'And don't for one second think that I won't forget that you're insinuating that I work with gangsters.'

'I'm not insinuating at all,' Anjli replied coldly. 'I'm stating it as a cold hard fact. Got a problem with it? Fine. Prove to me I'm wrong.'

'Say *what?*'

Anjli shrugged.

'I know the rule is usually that you're innocent until proven guilty, but the guilt's pretty much all over the place. So, let's go the other way, yeah? Let's go talk to Johnny himself, get the official statement from the source.'

DCI Ford looked as if she was about to say something else or maybe even launch an attack on Anjli, her face reddening with fury, but as she was about to speak, DC Sonya Hart, the unit's resident cyber expert, started waving her hand to gain their attention as she stood up beside her desk, across the office.

'Guv, you need to see this!' she shouted.

Ford glared at Anjli.

'This isn't over,' she said. 'You need to think about your future in this place.'

'Sounds to me I don't have one,' Anjli jutted out her chin. 'I dunno, you always say I need to be more like you, and then when I do something you've done, you chew me out. You can't pretend to be the Queen of the Unit, and all powerful white knight when you're as deep in the dirt as everyone else. Deeper, even.'

Ignoring the barbed comment, DCI Ford left her office, walking past Anjli. As she followed her out to see what Sonya Hart was shouting about, she also knew that her future had to be somewhere else. Mile End was a good place to work, but there were too many temptations, and too many people around her who'd already been tempted.

As they walked over to Hart's desk, Anjli could see she had *Holmes2* open on her screen. *Holmes2* was an advanced AI-driven crime analysis system used by the British police that processed vast data, including past crime records and real-time surveillance, to identify patterns and predict criminal activity. This allowed law enforcement to allocate resources more effectively and solve complex cases with greater efficiency.

Currently, it showed a *crime in progress* report.

'What's the problem?' Ford asked as she stopped at the desk, checking the screen.

'Just received this pop up from Stratford Police,' Hart replied. 'They've got the Posies Killer.'

'You what?' Ford's face reddened in anger. 'That's our case. How dare they?'

'I don't think they walked into it deliberately, boss,' Hart replied carefully. 'It was a drive-by. Police officer was curious about a van driving north down the A12. Probably a brake light was off or something like that. Asked the van to pull over.'

'Who was driving the van?' Anjli asked.

'Thomas Blackthorne.'

'And did he pull over?'

At the question, Hart chuckled.

'The hell he didn't,' she replied. 'Now he's holed up in a house in Leyton, near the station, with a shotgun and a hostage.'

'Hostage?'

'Young boy. That's all we know.'

'How the hell did he get a bloody shotgun?' Anjli frowned. 'He's a florist.'

'He's a florist who works in the East End of London,' Ford replied, glaring back at her. 'It's not exactly the hardest thing to do around here.'

'It isn't if you know the gangsters around here, I suppose,' Hart looked up at Anjli as she spoke, and Anjli almost responded, knowing if there was anything that DCI Ford was involved in, it probably involved Sonya Hart, as well. She was, after all, the mini-me to the DCI, the sycophantic little cow.

'Blackthorne was my case,' she said, looking back at Ford. 'I should be there.'

'Blackthorne was your case, but you didn't solve it,' Ford replied.

'We knew it was him,' Anjli shook her head. 'I'm not having that. The fact that we hadn't brought him in yet and that this has happened now doesn't mean that we weren't going to do it this week. In fact, I was about to arrange the warrant when you decided to call me in and have a go.'

'Don't throw this on me,' Ford growled menacingly. 'You want to finish this? Grab your jacket, go to wherever this is in Leyton and see what's going on.'

Her expression darkened.

'And, when you come back, we'll carry on discussing your future.'

'Can't wait,' Anjli replied. She nodded to Hart, walked over to her desk and grabbed her jacket.

'Shall I take a uniform?'

'From the sounds of things, there's already enough bloody uniforms there at the scene,' Ford smiled. 'And, as you've always said, you do prefer to work alone.'

THE JOURNEY TO LEYTON FROM THE MILE END CRIME UNIT was less than fifteen minutes. As Anjli drove there at speed, her car's siren blaring as she weaved her way through the Mile End and Stratford traffic, she considered the last four weeks.

DCI Ford had been correct when she insinuated Anjli had dropped the ball.

She *had.*

She might have been a recently promoted Detective Sergeant, but in her mind she was still a Detective Constable, further down the chain than she currently was and, if she was being brutally honest, she shouldn't have been running this case. It should have been DI Petrova. He had been seconded over during the transitional phase, but Ford had pushed for Anjli, mainly because she was one of the longest-serving officers there. It was a good suggestion, too, as Petrova transferred out after a few weeks.

He saw the writing on the wall, even then.

However, over the last few weeks, with her mother's cancer diagnosis and the relevant issues with treatment, frustration with the NHS, and the guardian angel-ship of the

Lucas twins causing her concerns, Anjli hadn't really stepped up as much as she knew she could have, even if they had pretty much worked out who the killer was.

It had all started four weeks earlier when Sarah Thompson, eight years old, had been abducted one night while coming home from Brownies. There had been no CCTV, no witnesses; a van had been seen, but it was white and, well, asking to locate a white van in London is like asking to find a guy called John Smith. There was a press call, a reward, all the usuals, but nothing had been heard.

Then three days later, Sarah's body had been found by the Regent's Canal, laid out, arms folded over her chest as if lying in repose, with flowers scattered around her.

It was Rajesh Khanna, the forensic examiner from Mile End, who had noticed that they were a posy of blue pansies and red poppies. And when the body had been checked, they found she'd been poisoned, and that her pockets were stuffed with the same flowers.

Of course, it had come out in the press and the poem "*Ring-a-Ring-a-Roses*" had been thrown everywhere. The "children's rhyme killer", the "posies killer", nobody could decide who he or she was for the headlines.

But, before they could go too far with the names, another child, Mia Chen, disappeared. This time, Mia had been taken while waiting outside the Stratford Westfield; only nine years old, she was apparently going to see a film with her older brother and her parents ... but never made it to the venue.

The press had a field day with that one – never mind the fact the parents were mortified their child was gone, let's kick off on them about how they're shitty parents for letting a nine-year-old wander off around a shopping mall alone – however, now, the police knew that this wasn't some kind of prank or ransom; this was a crazed killer who wanted to murder, and the clock was ticking.

They knew if this was the same abductor, then they'd probably keep to the same schedule; within three days, Sarah Thompson had been found dead, and that meant there was every chance of Mia being found dead as well within the same timeframe. And three days later, with no clues and realistically no further investigations moving on, Mia Chen's body had also been found laid out in the same way, on a different part of the Regent's Canal, with the same flowers around her.

By the time the body had been found, Anjli and her team had narrowed down to one suspect: Thomas Blackthorne, a local florist with a preference for rare flowers like celestial blue pansies, rather than the more ornate orchids and lilies his rivals sold. It had been noted that both times the girls had been taken, more poppies and pansies would appear in his windows, as if he was subconsciously alerting the police, or perhaps mocking them. There was a connection to Sarah Thompson's family through an event at her school and, after checking, Anjli found that Blackthorne also had had a connection to the Chens; a birthday bouquet given to the victim by her mother, days before her abduction, and delivered by Blackthorne's shop assistant.

Blackthorne had been brought in and questioned, but for some reason it hadn't got any further. He had a good solicitor, kept quiet when needed, and more importantly, claimed to have alibis for the two times when the girls were abducted, one of which could be proven. This didn't mean he wasn't working alone, however, and Anjli, absolutely convinced it was Blackthorne, had carried on investigating him, following him, and harassing him on the off chance he'd make a mistake. She didn't care if she got into trouble for this; she knew without a bloody doubt that Blackthorne was the killer. His posies even came from the same source location as those found on the victims, although he pointed out that *many* people's posies and flowers came from the same sources.

And then, two days earlier, Blackthorne had filled his windows with posies once more.

If the rumours were to be believed, it was time for another child, likely a girl, to disappear.

Anjli, knowing that the police couldn't do anything with Ford trying to cut corners, had taken things into her own hands and had spoken to the Lucas twins. She had hoped to speak to Johnny, but it was Jackie who arrived, wearing a black shirt, blue suit, and an expression that looked like he would kill you if you stepped out of line. Luckily for Anjli, Jackie often seemed to like her more than Johnny did. She explained the problems they had, and how they couldn't do much without the still-lacking evidence; Jackie thanked her and said he would *fix* the problem. Anjli felt bad asking, but she knew that nothing else could be done. The unit had failed twice to stop the murders. Ford was as corrupt as she could be, Sonya Hart was working on whatever Ford wanted to do, and half of the unit were just waiting for their pensions. The officers who wanted to solve this properly, like Anjli was, seemed to be left in the dark.

She didn't want the Lucas twins to solve the crime; she just wanted them as informants. *Him* as an informant. It was still hard to claim one man as two people, or two people as one. To Anjli, fixing it meant arresting the culprit.

Of course, it wasn't a foolproof plan, and it derailed pretty quickly. Through her *own* connections with the Lucas brothers, DCI Ford had found out about the deal, and had decided to chew out Anjli because of it.

By now, she was pulling up at Leyton Station, near the semi-detached house Blackthorne had holed up in, and could see the police vans and cars outside, flashing lights and officers exiting. She walked over to the line, flashing her ID to one of the constables passing through, and heading towards Rajesh Khanna, who was standing to the side, waiting. He wasn't in his usual forensic PPE uniform, but he was still visible by his police-issue black turban and pince-nez glasses.

'Shouldn't you be here after something's found?' she asked.

'I'm waiting for them to allow us to get in,' he said. 'We need to find out what's going on as quickly as possible, so I thought I might as well get here early.'

He shrugged.

'I didn't expect him to have a sawn-off shotgun in his hands so I decided I'd let the police deal with that first.'

Anjli nodded, looking back at the house.

'Do we have anything else?'

'No,' Rajesh pointed over to an armed officer to the side. 'SCO19 are waiting. They're trying to defuse it, but they don't think it's going to end well.'

Anjli nodded. She didn't think it was going to end well either, as if everything was true and the suspect was indeed the killer, and the man in the building with the shotgun knew he was about to be arrested and charged with the murder of two girls, possibly a third, as he already had a boy in the house with him, which didn't fit the MO at all ...

She walked over to the SCO captain, showed her warrant card, and introduced herself as he gave his own in response. His name was Mercer. Tall and skinny, he had the look of a scarecrow who had been given a combat suit and an assault rifle, with straw-coloured, spiky hair peeking out from underneath his checkered cap, more in the style of a baseball cap than the usual police issue headwear.

'We've asked for demands. He's not replying,' he muttered irritably. 'We've cut the power, the water, the internet. He's alone in there; the house was empty when he broke in through the door.'

'Apart from the boy.'

'Well, of course, the boy,' Mercer, irritated at being questioned, looked around. 'It's believed he went to the house of a nearby friend, but they're at work. We've called and got confirmation Blackthorne's alone in there with the boy; the so-called friend even gave us the Wi-Fi details so, before we cut the power, we could check through the baby camera in the living room. He's just pacing back and forth, and hitting his head with the barrel while the kid watches from the corner. Maybe he'll accidentally shoot himself. That'd be good.'

'Or maybe he'll accidentally shoot the boy?'

'Yeah. That'd be bad,' Mercer looked to the crowd, now building. 'That said, the press are turning up. It's becoming a bit of a shit show.'

Anjli was about to reply when there was a sudden sound of a gunshot. Or rather, the sound of a shotgun echoing through the street.

The sort of sound made by a *sawn-off shotgun.*

Immediately there was chaos in the street as Anjli and the SCO19 officers charged the building. However, at the now smashed in front door, Mercer held her back.

'Let us clear this first,' he said commandingly. Knowing there was at least one crazy man with a rifle in there whose status of alive or dead still wasn't known, and possibly a now dead child to match, Anjli nodded.

It was a minute later that Mercer came back out.

'Blackthorne shot himself,' he said. 'Decided he'd rather end it.'

'The boy?'

'Alive, in care. Shaken up, but unhurt.'

Anjli considered entering the house, checking for herself, but currently the thought of seeing Blackthorne's mashed skull didn't fill her with interest, Instead, allowing Rajesh to finally enter the house, she walked away, noticing a black SUV parked on the other side of the road.

There was a young man with tracksuit bottoms on, trainers, and a hoodie. He looked like one of Johnny Lucas's boxers, and as most of them ended up being some of his muscle, the chances were it was Lucas himself inside the car.

As she started walking towards it, the door opened, and Johnny Lucas emerged, his hair set as ever.

No, the shirt was the wrong colour. It wasn't Johnny; it was Jackie.

Anjli paused and then realised that he was waiting for her, so she carried on across.

'I heard what happened to the child killer,' he stated. 'Terrible shame.'

Anjli could tell from his tone that he really didn't mean what he was saying.

'Interesting how he found himself a sawn-off shotgun,' she replied. 'Florists in East London don't usually tool up.'

'I know,' Jackie shook his head sadly. 'Place is going downhill, especially in the world of shoddy weaponry.'

'What do you mean?'

Jackie shrugged, and Anjli felt the motion was a little too over-theatrical.

'I heard the sawn-off shotgun had a bit of a hair trigger. If you were to place it against your chin, for example, and consider killing yourself, you might not get the chance to change your mind.'

'Are you saying you gave Blackthorne a gun purely to kill himself with?' Anjli's tone darkened, and Jackie's face darkened to match. 'In a house with a bloody *child* as hostage?'

'Are you questioning me, DS Kapoor?' Jackie eventually asked. 'Cos if I recall, you're the one who asked for my help.'

'To get information, not to kill a bloody suspect,' Anjli snapped. 'Jesus, Jackie—'

'You seem to forget who you're talking to,' Jackie Lucas shook his head, interrupting as he turned to walk back to the car. 'Maybe next time you don't ask me for a favour, yeah? Maybe next time you keep yourself to yourself.'

'Fine,' Anjli snapped back, annoyed, frustrated and furious that her suspect killed himself thanks to the weaponry provided by Johnny or Jackie Lucas. 'If you need me, you can go through your gopher.'

'My gopher?'

'Yeah, DCI Ford. "Go for this, go for that." *Gopher.* She's one of yours, isn't she? And I'm sure if she's busy, there's half a dozen others in Mile End.'

'If I recall, you *too* owe me,' Jackie's face showed he was not enjoying this conversation.

Angie shook her head angrily.

'I'm not going to be one of your kept women, Johnny-Jackie-whoever the hell you want to be right now. I'm a police officer and a bloody good one, and I will not be dragged down by gutter scum like you.'

'Is it really me you should be angry at, DS Kapoor?' Jackie asked coldly. 'It sounds more like you're angry at yourself for what happened here. Maybe you should be cleaning up your own act, and not jumping to judgements like that ...'

Anjli went to answer, but couldn't. *Jackie was right.* Instead, she shook her head, turned, and stormed off.

As she did so, Jackie Lucas started laughing.

'You know what?' he said to the boxer beside him. 'I actually like that one. She might have a future.'

1

FARMERS' MARKET

NOW.

Anjli Kapoor enjoyed living in Hurley. It was an idyllic little village within easy driving distance to most cosmopolitan towns and locations, a long but easy commute into London, and it also meant that every day upon leaving the city, she could leave everything behind and return to a place where, during the summer, she could sit by the Thames and watch the world go by.

The one thing Anjli Kapoor would have liked more of, however, *was* the city. In particular, she missed the convenience of being able to leave her house and, within a minute or two, find a supermarket or at least some kind of large shop that would sell the groceries she needed at a moment's notice. *Uber Eats* or *Deliveroo* weren't sure where Hurley was half the time when she contacted them. Fast food was a thing of the past; most meals were bought at the local pub. When Anjli found herself, as she did on this morning, needing to buy a pint of milk for her cereal before work, there was only one option for her.

Well, there were two options, but one of them involved getting into the car and driving for a substantial amount of time to get to the nearest retail park superstore or grabbing something from a service station. But right now, if Anjli wanted some milk for her coffee or breakfast cereal, she would have to go to the *village store.*

This was a hybrid creation: part corner shop and part organic farm store. Anjli liked the shop if she was being honest. Much of the food there was locally sourced, organic, and as far from the processed rubbish you'd find at the superstores as anything else. Sure, it was more expensive, but it supported local businesses, and Anjli liked the fact she was helping them.

The one thing she wasn't as much a fan of was *Trudy*.

Trudy was the woman who sometimes ran the shop.

In fact, every time Anjli had been there in the two years or so since she'd started living in Hurley, Trudy had been behind that counter each time she'd arrived. It was almost as if Trudy had no house to live in, and she kept a sleeping bag hidden behind the counter.

Trudy was a *Hurleyan, Hurleyite,* or whatever they called themselves. Village born and bred, seventh-generation Hurley resident, and proud of it as well. Her family had been around since Hall Place was built in the seventeen hundreds, probably even longer. Anjli knew all this because Trudy repeatedly told her. Anjli was aware that, as somebody who had recently moved to Hurley, and didn't have the social village standing of the legacy families, she wasn't high up on Trudy's friends' list.

At least, that's what she hoped it was. The last thing Anjli wanted was to find out that Trudy the storekeeper didn't like her because she was *Indian*.

There was enough diversity in the village to make that kind of thinking a thing of the past, but there was still a hierarchy for people who lived there, were born there, and often died there. Anjli was also pretty convinced the only reason she was tolerated by Trudy was because she was a Detective Inspector. After all, Detective Inspector meant rank, rank meant privileges, importance, and even though Trudy believed she was some kind of de facto mayor of the village, Anjli was tolerated more than some of the other people who had moved to Hurley over the last couple of years. People who Trudy would quite happily mention in hushed tones to Anjli and Declan whenever they visited, as if they *too* were part of this sneaky conspiracy.

It was late morning now; the Bally case's final report was due in the night before, and after finishing it they'd not arrived back until way after three in the morning, with Monroe telling everyone to come in for noon. As Anjli entered the store, walking over to the fridge section and grabbing a half-pint of semi-skimmed milk, glancing around the shop and wondering whether she needed to pick up some bread and maybe some eggs to go with this – the thoughts of a breakfast cereal being replaced by scrambled egg on toast – she realised that Trudy, usually happy to start an argument or complain about something, hadn't yet spoken a word.

Turning back to look at the woman, wondering if she was busy writing out stock or doing the crossword she often did, Anjli saw that Trudy was staring directly at her, her face a mask of fury.

'You okay?' Anjli asked. If she was being honest, she expected some kind of response, but none came forth. Trudy continued to stare at her. Anjli went to ask for more, but then paused. She realised that possibly for the first time in her conversations with the older woman, this might not actually have been about *her*.

A week earlier, it had been released in the national press that Detective Chief Inspector Declan Walsh of the City of London Police had been left everything in serial killer Karl Schnitter's last will and testament. There had been outrage and an outcry, and Declan had wisely kept his head down. However, in Hurley, where Schnitter had lived for many years, this had become a more personal issue. There had been graffiti written on the side of Declan's house, although it was the paint that washed off in the rain – after all, nobody wanted graffitied walls to lower the housing prices here. There had been jokes passed around that maybe Declan and Schnitter had been in some kind of secret relationship. People loved to gossip, and gossip was ripe.

Anjli, however, seemed to be caught in the crossfire. So, once more, Anjli looked at Trudy.

'I asked if everything was okay,' she repeated, walking over and placing six eggs, a small loaf of farmhouse bread, sliced, and the milk on the counter. 'I'll take these to go.'

Trudy scrunched her face in anger.

'How long did he know?' she asked.

Anjli realised this was possibly the first time she'd been in the shop since the news had broken and wondered how long Trudy had been waiting to ask the questions.

'I'm sorry—'

'I asked *how long did he know?*' The tone was dark, the words spoken slowly and clearly. Trudy was well spoken at the best of times, but this was almost as if she wanted to make sure that every single word was enunciated correctly.

'How long did he know *what?*' Anjli asked, realising that she was about to have a fight no matter what she wanted. 'That Karl Schnitter was a killer?'

Anjli placed the palms of her hands on the counter, facing Trudy.

'How long did *you* know?' she asked, conversationally.

At this, Trudy's face darkened.

'You *what?*' she asked.

Anjli shrugged, looking around the store.

'Well, let's be honest,' she replied. 'The garage is what, a five-minute walk from here? Karl and his team would probably have been coming in a couple of times a week, picking up their lunch, coffee, tea, milk, all that kind of stuff. All those years he's been coming into this shop and you've been serving him. How many times have you sent your car in to be repaired at his garage?'

'That's not the point,' Trudy shook her head. 'I didn't—'

'Yeah, you *didn't*,' Anjli interrupted angrily. 'Look, you can be pissed at me and I get that, but you knew him for years, and didn't see the real him. Why do you think Declan did? He only moved back a couple of years ago.'

Trudy's face crunched up as she sneered back at Anjli.

'I knew some of the victims.'

'I know,' Anjli replied. She didn't know which victims Trudy was talking about, but there could have been many, as Schnitter had kept quite local in his murders. 'And I'm sure that when you talk about the *victims* you're lecturing me in your *holier than thou way* about, you're also including Declan's mother and father, who were *also both victims*.'

Her voice was rising in volume and pitch, but the last phrase seemed to punch Trudy in the face.

Trudy blinked, her eyes widening.

'No, I didn't mean ...'

'I know exactly what you mean,' Anjli leant closer now, ready for a fight. She'd dealt with bigger and badder than Trudy, and she was waiting for an opportunity to shout back. 'Do you think the papers are true? Do you think Declan made some kind of deal with a serial killer? A man who killed his own parents.'

'He gained the house when they died,' Trudy muttered, almost apologetically.

'Yeah, sure, he gained a house. Whoop-de-doo, he would have gained it anyway,' Anjli shook her head. 'I deal with murders every day, and I can tell you now, there is nothing to gain in what the newspapers have said.'

'Then why did he get everything in the will?'

'Because Schnitter played a stupid game,' Anjli replied. 'He wanted one final screw-you to Declan. Do you know what *actually* happened that night, when we found out he was the killer, when we learned his daughter had been involved in Declan's father's murder, when Rolf Muller was murdered in the crypts just down the road from here?'

'You let him go,' Trudy replied. 'The newspapers said so.'

'The newspapers weren't there!' Anjli shouted.

'And neither were you!' Trudy replied. Anjli had to give her that because she wasn't. She'd been arresting Ilse Muller at the time.

'Karl Schnitter escaped our custody,' she explained, 'because he went to the American Embassy and asked for sanctuary. When he was in the East German police, he spied for America, gave them information that, when the wall came down, kept him out of prison. They knew he had information they still wanted, that he could contact people they needed, and so when he realised there was nothing left for him, he fled to America and gained himself a new identity.'

She held up a hand to pause Trudy's next response.

'And yes, he came back. But when he came back, we went after him once more, and Declan ended him.'

Trudy's eyes widened like saucers, and Anjli quietly berated herself. The last thing she'd wanted to do was give any impression Declan had been part of any kind of vigilante murder, but the facts of the matter were that Declan and Anjli had been on top of a building with Schnitter, and within moments of them arriving, Schnitter was dead on the pavement in front.

No one seemed to believe that Schnitter deliberately jumped, believing it the only opportunity for himself to gain redemption, and the stories had been rife. Declan had thrown him off the top; Schnitter had run and slipped and fallen; Schnitter wasn't actually dead, and this was somebody else who had been thrown off the roof to look like it had happened ...

It didn't matter what had happened, people could decide what they wanted. The truth was the truth. Karl Schnitter had taken his own life. The will made things more complicated.

Trudy, however, seemed to accept that Declan had somehow redeemed himself by murdering Schnitter, and her expression softened slightly.

'I don't want to fight,' Anjli said. 'Especially with the only bloody shop around here. But the fact of the matter is, Trudy, Karl Schnitter was a serial killer, and all of you let him live here for decades without realising.'

Trudy nodded.

'We all let ourselves down,' she said.

Anjli wanted to snap back, point out that this wasn't a case of letting people down, this was a case of letting people get murdered, but instead she tapped her Apple Watch on the cardless reader, allowed it to beep in approval, grabbed her items, and without saying anything else, stormed out of the shop.

THIS WASN'T THE FIRST TIME SHE'D HAD TO FACE SOMETHING LIKE this. Declan and Anjli had been in the pub a couple of days earlier and one of the drinkers, an old regular who often nodded or tipped a hat but barely ever spoke to Declan walked up to him, and simply pointed out that his father would have been ashamed of what Declan had done. There was nothing Declan could do about this, either. The will had been left to him, all he could do was get rid of it as quickly as he could. He'd immediately started making arrangements to have everything Karl Schnitter had owned sold, the profits donated to a victim support charity, but as everybody was convinced that there was no smoke without fire, people kept walking around looking for the flames.

In fact, as Anjli arrived back at the house, she saw Declan outside, soap and water in his hand as he wiped down the latest piece of graffiti that had been sprayed on.

'At least they use organics,' he said. 'Something that could be washed off in the rain.'

'Of course they do,' she said, looking at the words. All that was left was "iller," from the word "killer."

Declan saw the groceries in her hand.

'Problems?'

'Small-minded and short-sighted ones, but nothing

major,' Anjli said. 'But we will have to decide what to do about this.'

Declan nodded.

'I was kind of hoping we could just hide and then eventually it would go away. Once the will is passed on to victim support groups, maybe people might realise that I wasn't as involved as they think.'

'The problem is, Declan, there are no official details on what happened that night,' Anjli walked past, into the kitchen, placing the items on the counter. 'If we could say, "if you looked at item five, you'll see here that Declan actually punched him in the face and he ran off into the woods" then that'd be fine, but ...'

She shrugged.

'All we have is that MI5 took him to a black site, where months later, he escaped.'

'Maybe we can do something with that,' Declan said.

'What, you think Emelia Wintergreen's going to be helping you anytime soon, now she pretty much runs the place?'

'Stranger things have happened,' Declan shrugged. 'I'm willing to give it a go.'

Anjli went to reply, but paused as her phone started to buzz. Glancing down at it, she frowned.

'It's DCI Esposito,' she said. Esposito was the DCI of Mile End, and had worked with both Anjli and Declan multiple times over the years.

Answering it, she held it on speaker.

'Guv?' she asked.

'Anjli,' Esposito's voice was tight, stressed. 'Sorry to call you, I'm hoping I'm not interrupting?'

'Just erasing organic graffiti, if I'm being honest, Guv. What's up?'

There was a pause.

'I ... I need you to come to Mile End today.'

'Is there a problem?'

'It's in relation to unsolved murders and killers who reach out from beyond the grave.'

'Unsolved murders and killers who reach out from beyond the grave, sure,' Anjli grimaced. 'Guv, if this is about Schnitter, we've literally had enough—'

'I'm not talking about Declan,' Esposito snapped. 'This is about Thomas Blackthorne.'

Anjli looked up at Declan in horror as she replied to the phone.

'He's dead. He died when he blew his head off with a sawn-off shotgun.'

'I know,' Esposito replied. 'But the problem is, we've had a girl kidnapped, and it fits his MO exactly.'

Anjli shuddered.

'Sir, if you send me the information—'

'I think you need to come and see this,' Esposito interrupted. 'I've sent you an image. It might change your mind.'

Anjli checked her phone and saw that an attachment was indeed flashing. Opening it up, she saw one single written line:

Ring-a-Ring-a-Roses, a pocketful of posies, ashes, ashes.
Kap0Or falls down.

Anjli felt terror slide down her spine.

'He's dead,' she said, as if trying to convince herself. 'He's dead.'

'I know,' Esposito said. 'I've checked the records. But unfortunately, we don't really have anybody here who was around at that time, what with Declan making sure most of them were arrested. And, well, I could really do with your help.'

Anjli looked over at Declan, who nodded, before returning to the call.

'We'll go to Temple Inn to confirm with D Supt Monroe, and then we'll be there as quick as we can, sir,' she said.

As she placed the eggs away, Declan walked up, placing a hand on her shoulder.

'You've never mentioned Blackthorne before,' he said. 'Is everything okay?'

'Blackthorne's dead,' Anjli said, looking back at him. What she didn't say was that not only was Blackthorne dead, but so were two other children in his wake, a case that had never been fully closed.

And now she wondered whether she'd been wrong when she believed the case had ended with his death. Somewhere out there, another child had been taken, and the nursery rhyme the press had been so fond of ... was about to start all over again.

2

OLD CASES

By the time Declan and Anjli reached the Temple Inn offices, Detective Superintendent Monroe was already waiting for them, with a scowl on his face that looked like it had been etched in stone.

'I'm guessing you've heard about the call then,' Declan said as they walked into his office after being waved unceremoniously in.

Monroe walked to his desk, sitting down behind it.

'Aye,' he replied. 'Esposito gave me a call before he phoned you, or maybe afterwards. Probably thought it was better to apologise than to ask permission.'

He shook his head, muttering to himself. Declan couldn't quite hear what he was saying.

'The fact of the matter is that Mile End isn't our jurisdiction at the moment, and we can't take on their case.'

'With all due respect, sir, I don't think he wanted us to take on the case,' Anjli said. 'I think he wanted me to come in and give him an idea of what happened last time.'

'Aye, and what *did* happen last time?' Monroe asked. 'Because it sounds to me like a complete screw up in Leyton.'

'The prime suspect shot himself in the head,' Anjli snapped back. 'Thanks to a rather dodgy shotgun possibly sold to him by our Member of Parliament for Bethnal Green and Bow.'

'Aye, and if he blew his head off, how is he still around to kidnap another wee lassie then?'

Anjli shrugged.

'Copycat,' she replied. 'It's the obvious answer.'

Monroe leant back in the chair, and for a second the scowl faded.

'Aye, you might have something there,' he replied.

Sighing, he stared at the ceiling.

'Look,' he said, 'I agree with what you're saying, and if it was me, I'd let you go. Christ, when Declan there was a DI, the amount of bloody things he was allowed to wander off on ... the list's too long to think of. The first case we even brought him on with was a cold case just like this, albeit a lot older, anyway.'

He looked back at Anjli, and his eyes pierced straight into her.

'But right now we've got a microscope on us thanks to that man there,' he said, nodding at Declan again. 'Everybody's waiting for us to do something bad, the press are looking for the next story. How do you think they'll react when they find out that his Detective Inspector, who also shares his bed, is now in the midst of *another* case where a serial killer seems to have gone free, only to return years later?'

'Technically, he wasn't a serial killer,' Declan interjected.

'Serial killers usually kill three people, and Blackthorne only killed two before he ...'

He trailed off as Monroe stared menacingly at him.

'If it *is* Blackthorne, this third potential victim would make three, so he's on the verge of becoming a serial killer,' Monroe snapped. 'Look, we can take this case on, but you can't be front and centre, Anjli. I know you want to, I would be exactly the same, and if you want us to take down this bastard, we can do it, but it's a Mile End case.'

He rubbed at his eyes. It wasn't even lunchtime yet, but Monroe looked like he'd already worked a full shift.

'Okay,' he said, his voice softening. 'When was it? Three, four years ago? I had left by that point, and DCI Ford had replaced me. A year later, you turned up, full of anger and a need to prove yourself ...'

He glanced at Declan.

'... with a work ethic that puts this lad to shame. But you took on a double murder, with children being killed, with a woman who was corrupt and owned by the Twins, and with a cybercrime expert that was helping her hide bodies. The moment you return and start working this case, you're opening up all of that. Esposito's done a lot to rebuild Mile End since Declan brought the house down a couple of years ago—'

'That's unfair,' Declan snapped. 'DCI Ford tried to frame me for murder.'

'Aye, she did,' Monroe nodded. 'But she's not here and you are, and how's that working out for you?'

Declan grimaced; he knew exactly what Monroe meant.

Monroe, meanwhile, hadn't finished.

'Esposito's coming here,' he said. 'I convinced him it was a better idea for him to turn up and visit us, rather than for us to bring the carnival to him. At least that way, if we are going to have paparazzi and press asking every question and following our every move, we're not dragging any other wee buggers into it.'

He rose from the chair, stretching as he did so.

'As soon as he arrives, we'll have a briefing, catch the team up on what's happened in the past and we'll learn what this new situation is. Until then, I'd get your facts straight about what happened three years ago, because if we're doing one investigation, we're doing both and I, for one, do not want to have this hanging over my head.'

He glanced back at Declan.

'We've got enough of that going on here, too.'

'Look, Guv,' Declan said, his tone becoming a little more belligerent now, angry he was being blamed for things he felt weren't his fault and for situations out of his control. 'I didn't ask for Schnitter's items and possessions, and I'm sorry that we're getting shit for it. But if we can find a way out of this mess, this case might be it. Be seen to be doing some good for a change.'

'For a change?' Monroe asked.

Declan winced.

'You know what I mean,' he replied. 'When I came here, the Last Chance Saloon was the *Botany Bay* of the police force, the place where the screw-ups they couldn't fire, the people too good to be removed, were dumped. Well, since then, we've made a bloody good case of being one of the best units in the police. And I'm not just talking about the city, I'm talking about the country, everyone. Every time we save a life, we get patted on the back and told how good we are. But every time we screw up, everybody wants to give us a kicking.'

He pursed his lips.

'I'll do whatever it takes to remove this problem,' he said. 'But the first thing we need to do is accept the fact that it *is* my problem and not a problem that I created.'

Monroe watched Declan for a long minute before speaking.

'But we did create it, laddie,' he said. 'You, me, Bullman, all of us. We let MI5 take him, and then we let the CIA take him. And then *you* let gravity take him.'

He turned and walked past Declan, leaving the office.

Declan frowned as he did so.

'That's a bit harsh, don't you think?' he muttered.

Anjli, standing beside him, nodded.

'You good?' Declan glanced back at her.

'No,' Anjli shook her head. 'I'm going to honestly tell you, for the first time in a long while, I am definitely *not* okay.'

DCI ESPOSITO WAS AS GOOD AS HIS WORD AND, WITHIN THE hour, both he and DS McAlroy arrived at the Temple Inn offices.

'Thanks for allowing us to come to your house,' he said as he shook Monroe's hand.

'Because you really didn't want to have us in *your* house?' Declan asked grumpily from his seat in the briefing room.

Esposito said nothing, but McAlroy turned and smiled.

'Why yes,' she said, 'that's exactly the problem, Detective Chief Inspector.'

Declan gave a lazy wave of acceptance. He liked the DS. She didn't suffer fools and, unfortunately, at the moment, that meant that Declan was smack bang in the middle of her crosshairs.

DCI Esposito cleared his throat.

'I contacted Detective Inspector Kapoor out of courtesy—'

'Not because she's named in the evidence?' Declan offered.

'That too,' Esposito said reluctantly as he turned and faced the briefing room. As ever, it was a full house. Billy sat by his laptop, Cooper, De'Geer, and Doctor Marcos sat at the back. Anjli sat next to Declan, and Monroe stood beside Esposito as McAlroy wandered over to find a seat. 'We've had an abduction: Debbie Watson. It was in Central London, but it links to the Posies' Killer, so we've been passed it. However, it was before my time, and all I have are notes from the case ... and, well, the DCI who was running it at the time was, shall we say, a little lax in the note-taking department.'

'That's an understatement,' Declan muttered. 'DCI Ford was less likely to write down what had happened in various cases because half the time she was probably doing something illegal during them.'

Esposito gave a rueful smile.

'We wanted to speak to Anjli here, because we hoped she could tell us a bit more about what was going on,' he said. 'I will point out right now this isn't a call for help, and we don't want you swooping in to take our case from us.'

'They've made it personal, put her name in the evidence,' Monroe said. 'You know how it goes.'

He nodded to Billy, who pressed a button and, on the plasma screen behind them connected to Billy's laptop, the image that had been sent to Anjli appeared on the screen.

'Ring-a-Ring-a-Roses, a pocket full of posies. Ashes, ashes, Kapoor falls down,' Monroe said. 'A children's rhyme that's hundreds of years old.'

He shrugged.

'I'm sorry, Esposito, but you know how this works.'

Esposito shook his head.

'On a normal day, I'd accept your help,' he said. 'But you guys are toxic right now. I believe you could actively hinder the operation.'

'And I believe you are absolutely correct,' Monroe replied with a smile. 'So, let's see what we can work on together.'

Billy raised a hand, frowning.

'I get it's a message to DI Kapoor, Guv ... Guvs, but it's wrong,' he said. 'They spell her name with two zeroes instead of "o's".'

'Maybe they were in a hurry?' Monroe replied.

'To change two characters?' Billy pursed his lips. 'Nobody's in that much of a hurry.'

'Look into it,' Monroe suggested as he stepped back, looking at Anjli. 'Tell us what happened all those years ago.'

Anjli rose now, walking to the front of the room as Monroe took her seat, and Esposito leant against the door-frame. Billy helpfully placed up two images of the two young victims on the plasma screen behind her. Both were girls, both were between the ages of eight and ten years old.

'Two girls who were taken over a two-month period,' she said. 'Sarah Thompson, and Mia Chen, both aged nine, but we believed that was just by chance. Sarah was abducted after coming home from Brownies. A van had been seen, but no reg was ever taken. Then three days later, Sarah's body was found by the Regent's Canal, near the Old Ford Lock and Victoria Park, arms folded over her chest and with flowers scattered around.'

Billy pressed another button and now an image, a crime

scene photo of Sarah Thompson appeared; a young girl, dead, and with her arms folded.

'Manner of death?'

'Poisoning,' Anjli replied coldly, her eyes tight. 'We think it was something like Wolfsbane or Belladonna. Then a couple weeks later, Mia Chen disappeared from outside the Stratford Westfield shopping centre, found three days later by another part of the canal. Same pose, same sodding flowers, same poison.'

There was a moment of silence as Anjli regained her composure.

'To start with, we had no link between the two. The only thing that we knew that held them together was the fact that where both had been left, a posy of flowers, both poppies and pansies had been left on the floor.'

'Posy?' Cooper looked up from her notes. 'As in the poem?'

Anjli nodded.

'They'd both had the poem, written on notepaper, placed with the petals. "Ring-a-Ring-a-Roses, a pocket full of posies, a-tishoo, a-tishoo, we all fall down." However, it'd been altered to say "they" all fall down. Anyway, we looked into it. We couldn't find anything that worked on giving us some kind of connection together. There were a few things where they overlapped; they went to the same Brownies group but were in different year groups. Their families never really met or hung out with each other. But they both lived within half a mile of each other, on either side of a high street. We wondered if there was a location, perhaps, that could link the two together. Meanwhile, forensics – Rajesh Khanna, who we all know here – examined the petals.'

Doctor Marcos made wolfing noises and fist-pumped into the sky.

'Sorry, I'm just stoked to shout out for one of my own,' she said, reddening. 'Please go ahead.'

'Rajesh Khanna realised the pansies were called Celestial Blue, and were a rare strain of pansy, that led to a particular flower market, the New Covent Garden one,' Anjli replied. 'When we looked into it, there were three florists who were all within the area who used it, and who could all have bought posies with the same chemical residue.'

'Did the families use florists?'

'Mia's family were known to have flowers all the time, and received a bouquet a week before Mia disappeared,' Anjli nodded. 'As for Sarah, her mum, Stephanie Thompson worked in a shop on weekends two doors away from one of the florists, and that was where we started our investigation. The florist himself was named Thomas Blackthorne.'

As she said the name, Billy tapped another button, and an image appeared on the screen. It was of a man in his late forties, slightly overweight, with a jowly chin and a head almost shaved, allowing the stubble to come through. But this wasn't a hairstyle choice; this was because he was rapidly balding, and the hair only just about nicked into temples. The one thing about the man that Declan noted was that he didn't look sinister. It was hard to explain, but the man simply looked worried.

Although, when he was having his photo taken, he might have had a dozen fresh worries on his mind at the time.

'Tell us more about Blackthorne,' Esposito said.

Anjli shrugged.

'Kept himself to himself, no wife or children. Three years ago, we said he had a germ fetish and was a bit OCD. Nowadays we'd be saying he's neurodivergent and on the spectrum. Had a thing about being clean, both inside and out. Possibly came from dealing with flowers all the time, and germ pesticides and stuff like that, but when we met him his shop was, well, overpowering.'

'Strength-wise?'

'No.' Anjli shook her head. 'He wore cologne, but it was more like dosing himself in toilet duck. The man was terrified of catching something, of being ill. Wore a mask when on London Transport, even before it became popular. His hands were constantly dry because of hand sanitiser, and he would flip from hand sanitiser to moisturiser and back again. It was believed that he'd decided that both of these girls were unclean.'

'And how exactly is a wee bloody bairn unclean?' Monroe muttered.

Anjli looked at him.

'We think it was to do with the mothers,' she said. 'Sarah's mother had, in her late teens and early twenties, worked as a prostitute. She'd spent days in a house in Birmingham, one of those places where you'd turn up and for fifty quid you went into a room, and eventually a woman would come in, satisfy you, and you'd leave. Nobody knew about it, but when it came out during the case that Sarah Thompson's mother had been a prostitute, she didn't shy away from it and explained that it was a mistake, and something forced upon her years earlier by an abusive boyfriend. She'd escaped it and got clean, and fifteen years later, she was standing in front of me, having built her way up from that to part-time manager of a tanning shop, terrified that people would find out about her past. But it seemed that Blackthorne already had.'

'So, he thought the child was unclean because the mother was unclean?'

'Spiritually and morally, yes,' Anjli nodded. 'As for Mia, well, her mother worked for a hedge fund. I don't know how high up she was or what she did, but I believe Blackthorne decided that she was morally bankrupt as well.'

'And again, the child needed to be cleansed.'

Anjli pulled out a piece of paper from the notebook and read from it.

'This was what a psychologist we had spoken to came up with,' she replied. 'He believed that Blackthorne had a distorted view of cleanliness and morality, seeing himself as a purifier; a literal plague doctor.'

'What happened next?' De'Geer asked.

Anjli went to speak and then paused, shaking her head sadly as she did so.

'We screwed up,' she replied. 'We thought we'd keep an eye on him. We wanted to be one hundred percent sure before anything happened. The bastard put posies in his shop window. He was either goading us, or informing us he was about to kill again. And, somehow, he found out we were on to him.'

'And then he found himself a sawn-off shotgun from some dodgy East End gangster,' Doctor Marcos muttered.

'He claimed, anonymously and through a letter sent to the unit, he was going to kill another if we didn't back off,' Anjli nodded. 'This time it was a boy, Michael Ashton. He'd been picked up after school; Blackthorne had promised him sweets and puppies to stroke or something like that. It was definitely something clichéd; I remember noting it down. Poor bloody Ashton was terrified. He found himself stuck in a broken-down semi-detached house in Leyton. A friend of

Blackthorne owned it and during the day it was empty so Blackthorne had managed to get hold of the keys. Once there, Ashton was tied up and dumped in a corner. Meanwhile, desperate while still trying to stay anonymous, Blackthorne told the police that if we didn't drop the case, say everything was fine and forget everything that happened, he'd kill Ashton as well.'

'Had he chosen Ashton deliberately or was there a …?' Monroe trailed off, knowing Anjli had the question.

'We never looked into it,' Anjli replied. 'We should have, I know, especially with him changing his MO, but before we could things took a slightly darker turn. The police were closing in. SCO19 turned up, doing their best to make a scene. There was a lot of screaming and a lot of shouting. Blackthorne was yelling at us to leave him alone and then, shortly after I arrived, there was a terrible accident, and Blackthorne shot himself in the face.'

'Are we sure it was an accident, lassie?' Monroe asked.

At the comment Anjli shrugged.

'I'm told that the sawn-off shotgun had a hair trigger,' she replied. 'That nervously, he had held the weapon under his chin to make the police back off, had clenched a little too tightly and blew the entire back of his head off.'

She looked around the room.

'He was dead. Ashton was free. The fact he'd effectively confessed to the murders by demanding we stop the case and then killed himself tidied up the case with a nice little bow. It wasn't how I would have done it, but DCI Ford had her own plans.'

'I bet she did,' Declan muttered.

'And with the case closed, we didn't really follow any other avenues. The family were informed of what had happened and as far as they were concerned, justice had been served, even if it didn't bring their children back.'

'Did Blackthorne work with anyone?' Billy asked.

'We saw nothing that suggested that,' Anjli replied, but Billy shook his head.

'No, sorry, I meant in the florist?'

'Oh, there was a shop assistant who did the deliveries, Antony Morgan, but he was cleared when we checked into it; he wasn't even in the country when Mia disappeared. And when Blackthorne killed himself he came to the police offering any help. Ford basically told him to go back to work, but with his boss dead, he pretty much didn't have a job to go back to.'

'Was Morgan a suspect?'

'No, not at the time,' Anjli admitted. 'Everything aimed directly at Blackthorne and we ... well, just left it.'

She let out a breath, and Declan realised that she'd spent most of the talk incredibly tense, as if holding a breath half in while speaking.

'Murder is never the best of cases to have,' she said. 'There's always a victim and there are always others who suffer because of it. But when it's a child ...'

She trailed off, looking over at Esposito.

'So now it's your turn,' she said. 'What do we know about Debbie Watson and this copycat?'

'Well,' Esposito replied, 'for a start, we're not so sure they *are* a copycat.'

With that, he began to explain.

3

EGYPTIAN EXHIBIT

After Esposito had finished his briefing, he wandered off into the office with Monroe to discuss what to do next. After twenty minutes of either deep negotiation, or, more likely, Monroe deciding that actually they wanted the case after all, accompanied by providing Esposito with a large amount of whisky to lessen the blow, they emerged back into the office, Monroe leading the way.

'After speaking to DCI Esposito and reminding him of my superior rank, it was decided that we would assist Mile End with this case,' he said.

Declan grinned. It was known that although they were a City of London unit, they had been given a remit to take on whatever cases they wanted. This had given them investigations in Milton Keynes, Hurley, the Peak District and Scotland, among other places. He had expected Esposito to be annoyed about this, but at the same time, he wondered whether Esposito had actually come here *hoping* this would happen. Cynically, Declan knew that if the case wasn't solved or something bad happened, Esposito could lay the blame at the feet of the Last Chance Saloon, claiming that Monroe's intervention and constant interruptions had caused the problems, keeping his hands clean in the process. If the case was solved, then he could claim credit alongside Monroe.

For Esposito and Mile End, it was a win-win.

For Monroe, it was a case of making sure Anjli could get closure.

Debbie Watson, the most recent child, had been at the British Museum and had been taken directly after opening on an eight am earlybird open day. Declan was impressed, as this was a ballsy move. The place was covered in cameras, and anybody walking out with a child would have been seen. However, as he and Anjli arrived at the museum to check the scene of the crime, he found that the building was under extensive renovation, with closed-off corridors and scaffolding to the side.

Dan Lewis, one of the curating team and the administrator assigned to speak to them, made sure it was the first thing he commented on as he met them in the main lobby.

'Bloody workmen,' he said, irritated. 'They've come in and out, and turned the bloody cameras off half the time.'

'I didn't think you could turn cameras off,' Declan frowned. 'You know, if you're a workman. Are they some kind of specialised spy workmen or something?'

'I don't know,' Dan shrugged. 'All I know is that near where the Egyptian display is, they managed to short out some circuits and the cameras went off. It always happens before the doors open. Unfortunately, because we opened at eight-thirty instead of ten today, this was at the same time as the kidnapping.'

They started heading away from the main doors and into the vast, airy expanse of the Great Court, crowned by a stunning glass and steel roof, the background sound a gentle buzz of excitement, made by visitors from around the world.

'Sounds convenient,' Declan replied as they walked across the court.

'It does until you realise they've done the same bloody thing each day for two weeks,' Dan muttered. 'I think they go for a sneaky hip flask breakfast around that time, you know?'

By now they'd arrived in the northern part of the museum, in particular the Egyptian Sculpture Gallery. Stepping into "Room 4", Declan marvelled at the colossal stone sculptures that loomed over the gallery, relics of ancient Egyptian grandeur. He could understand why, to a small child, these were incredible, and wondered how long before somebody demanded that the British Museum gave it back.

However, much of the corridor had scaffolding against it.

'So, what exactly's going on?' Declan asked, looking around. 'Rejuvenation?'

'This is an old building,' Dan replied. 'And yeah, I know we did it a little while back, but every ten, fifteen years or so, this place falls apart. With the amount of footfall we have, well, let's just say, every time we do it, we could have done it a lot better if we had more money.'

Declan understood that.

'Do we know what happened?' he asked, looking back at De'Geer, who had followed them into the room and was currently reading the notes passed to him by one of the officers from Mile End who'd been there earlier.

'Debbie was here with her parents, part of a family birthday for a friend of hers,' De'Geer said. 'They were walking through on their own, no tour or anything like that, just taking their time, from what the parents said. The early bird ticket meant they could be in and out by mid-morning,

Debbie has always been a fan of Egyptian history and had pushed to come here first. At some point, her mum realised she wasn't around, thought she was playing about, hiding in a sarcophagus or something, and started looking for her. It was only ten minutes later that she realised she was gone. She spent another ten minutes looking for Debbie, before realising she might have been taken.'

Anjli frowned.

'Why would she think that someone had taken her?'

De'Geer looked up and shrugged as Dan carried on into the room.

'Paranoia in this current climate, I suppose.'

'And why were they here on a school day?'

'We get that a lot,' Dan shrugged. 'People don't worry too much about taking kids out of class these days. And with today being an early doors, we had quite a few parents with kids. They could have them in and out by mid morning, back at school by lunch. I suppose it's less of an issue to miss half a day than a full one.'

'If I was leaving this room,' Declan said, changing the subject slightly, 'and wanted to get out quietly, what's the quickest way?'

Dan scratched at his head for a second.

'Honestly, there's only one good way out,' he said. 'They would have to head out into Room Three, the King's Library. We do have some security footage.'

Dan now pulled a pad out of his messenger bag and opened it up. He started tapping on it as he continued.

'We have a camera up there,' he said, nodding upwards. Declan turned and saw a small and unobtrusive CCTV camera watching them. 'They caught the figure—'

'Figure? That's vague.'

'Figure's all we have,' Dan admitted ruefully. 'Large, baseball cap, big coat on, which is surprising because it's quite warm for September. Short hair. Can't tell the sex.'

He scrolled through some posts, and then eventually stopped at video footage. On it, they could see Debbie and her family walking, Debbie and another girl playing as they ran around looking at things. She was laughing, wearing a light cotton dress, a lanyard around her neck with a card on the end, and her waist was cinched with a thin belt; part of the dress, tied in a bow.

Ten or fifteen feet behind them, hunched over, keeping their head down, was a large, unimposing figure.

Declan squinted.

'I see what you mean, that could be either sex,' he muttered. 'We'd need something better than this.'

He looked hopefully at Dan, who shook his head.

'Unfortunately, this is all we have,' he said. 'Well, almost.'

He pointed towards the King's Library.

'We know they went that way because we have video footage that shows them in the background,' he said. 'We know that Debbie seemingly went with her kidnapper without arguing. There's every chance that the jacket they're wearing could be branded. Maybe she thought they worked at the museum. Maybe they'd realised that she knew a lot about the Egyptian side and offered to show her something different.'

He showed another video. On this, Debbie turned, seeing the figure, still positioned to obscure their identity. She walked over and the two of them left.

'Okay, so where did they go?' Anjli asked.

Dan scrolled, showing a variety of images, including a set of stairs.

'Once in the King's Library, they walked into the Enlightenment Gallery. The lighting's dim there and it doesn't really go anywhere outside, but they slipped through one of the staff entrances and into a corridor, away from the public. Then they can take the North Stairs, through the security checkpoint and out of the north entrance. You can see here that Debbie and the kidnapper are making their way up.'

Declan watched the video. It was a camera positioned at a junction on the stairwell. As he watched, the two figures turned and walked past. Again, he wasn't able to see the kidnapper's face. Also, the body language suggested that Debbie Watson didn't in any way think she was under attack or under threat.

'The security checkpoint; is that why she had the lanyard?' he asked.

'No, Guv, that's a lanyard she had for herself,' De'Geer read from his notes. 'Apparently, the lanyard was from *Harry Potter.* Ravenclaw, I believe. You'd have to ask her parents why she was wearing it.'

Declan nodded, putting aside the information; it wasn't relevant for the moment.

'Cameras?'

Dan shook his head.

'The checkpoint?'

'Only for people going in. People going out ...'

'Are expected to have already gone through it,' Declan muttered. 'Okay, so if you're going out that way, where would you escape?'

Dan considered this.

'You'd come out on the corner of Malet Street and Montage Place,' he replied after a moment. 'It's a small exit, but leads out onto a large road. There's probably security cameras there.'

Declan scratched at the scruff of beard under his chin. He had shaved a while back after Anjli had commented on the fact that more of the hairs coming out of his chin had been grey than brown, but recently he had decided to have another go. He had visions of a thick, bushy beard for winter, but already he was getting irritated by the itching as he straightened.

'And there's no other CCTV footage?' he asked.

'We don't know what happened,' Dan shook his head. 'As I said, we think a workman shorted a wire; it happens. We don't like to tell people but, half the time we're here, the security's not fully on. You find that in a dozen different museums. Maybe if they gave us more budget ...'

Declan made a *hmm* noise and nodded, hoping that this wouldn't turn into a diatribe about government funding.

'Can we grab copies of what you have, the video of where Debbie goes with the stranger?' Anjli asked. 'Also, can I see the moment Debbie and the stranger walk off again?'

'Oh, of course, yes,' Dan nodded, swiping on his pad and flicking through a list of files. He looked up as he waited for the file to load.

'You won't get anything from it, I'm afraid,' he continued. 'As I said, whoever this was, well, they were very clever at keeping their head away from us.'

'It's not the head I want to see,' Anjli said, as Dan found the requisite video and played it. On the screen, they could see the same shot of Debbie and her family in the Egyptian Sculpture Gallery. In the bottom left-hand corner, the mysterious capped figure was standing, watching them, facing away from the camera itself. Debbie turned to look at a sarcophagus and must have caught the attention of the baseball-hatted stranger. There was no sound, so Declan couldn't tell if there'd been any noise made to attract the attention, but Debbie had looked around, seen the stranger, and then walked over.

'There,' Anjli tapped the screen. 'Can you zoom in?'

'It's not like ...'

Anjli held her hand up.

'I know, it's not like it is in the movies,' she said. 'I just want to see Debbie's face when she spies our mysterious figure.'

'Sure, I can do that,' Dan replied, pinching his fingers and then widening the screen. The picture was blurred and slightly pixelated, but as he zoomed in, they could see Debbie Watson as she turned to face the new arrival.

Declan saw immediately what Anjli had spied on the full screen. As she saw the stranger, Debbie's face had broken out into the smallest of smiles.

'She recognises them,' he said.

Anjli nodded. It was a small, brief smile, but it *was* a smile.

'That's someone she not only knows, but she's happy to see,' she replied. 'But that they're keeping away from everybody else means they don't want the parents to know who they are or that they're there. They only waited until Debbie was on her own before taking her away.'

She tapped again, and the video continued.

'Watch. The moment she sees the new person, she walks over. They say hello. And then, almost as if it was prearranged, they walk off.'

On the screen, the figure and Debbie turned and walked

away. The figure held Debbie's shoulder, possibly guiding them as they walked off.

'From there, they go directly to the exit,' Dan said. 'They make one stop at the bottom of the North Stairs, on the ground floor.'

He looked back to Anjli.

'That's where the flowers were found.'

'The posy?'

'And the note.'

Anjli's face tightened at this. Declan saw the pain in her eyes. Whoever did this knew who she was. Whoever did this had left a message for her.

'Can we see the place the posy was left?'

'Sure.' Dan motioned for them to follow him. 'Although you won't find much.'

'Well, I'm hoping it's a crime scene and you've kept it locked off.'

Dan started laughing.

'I wish,' he said. 'It's a museum and a construction site. We hadn't realised she'd disappeared for a good hour. When the parents realised their daughter had disappeared, they started hunting, thinking she'd wandered off into another area. By the time they actually found somebody to ask, it was half an hour since Debbie had disappeared. By the time we got to the CCTV and saw she was walking off with someone, we're talking forty-five, fifty minutes. By the time we worked it out, she'd gone through the construction area ...'

'And how busy is the construction area?'

Dan shook his head.

'I couldn't tell you,' he said. 'And that's not me being flippant. I genuinely don't know. With the construction workers walking in and out and the bloody cameras on and off all the time, there's dusty feet, there's brick dust, there's plaster ...'

'Do you have a list of which contractors would have been walking through?' Anjli asked. 'We can interview them, see which ones we can remove from forensics. Cut down their false clues.'

'Maybe one of them also saw Debbie leave,' Declan added. 'We have a rough timeline now.'

By now they had walked through the Enlightenment Gallery, through the staff entrance, and were heading down the back corridors. These were filled with doors leading to administration rooms. Declan pointed at them as they walked.

'Anybody working in here?' he asked. 'Maybe they could have seen something?'

Again, Dan shook his head.

'I'm really sorry,' he replied. 'Because of the noise, a lot of the administrators are working from home or have doubled up in other offices. This corridor is pretty much unmonitored.'

'Who would have known that?' Declan asked.

'How do you mean?'

'Who would have known about this corridor being unmonitored?' Declan paused in the middle of the corridor, hands on hips, as he surveyed the scene, imagining the child and stranger walking down. 'I mean, let's be honest here, this is a particular corridor from a particular area, with a particular problem with the CCTV and a particular list of people who aren't there. Whoever this person is, they *knew*. Which means they had to either have been involved or know someone that was.'

Dan considered this.

'We can get you a list,' he replied, nodding as he did so. 'Here, around this corner.'

As they turned the corner, Declan saw the familiar face of Doctor Rosanna Marcos. Surprisingly, she wasn't in her usual custom-made grey PPE forensics kit, wearing latex gloves and booties, and she was grumbling to herself as she looked up and saw them.

'Bloody idiots. Didn't even bother locking it down after she'd gone,' she muttered. 'Took them an hour to realise she'd gone this way. And even then, they didn't stop people from coming down here for a good three hours. By the time the police turned up, this could have been like Piccadilly Bloody Circus. Even when Mile End turned up and took over a couple of hours back, this has been completely ruined.'

Declan nodded; he understood her irritation.

'I know we've got a lot of things we have to remove, but what do we have that we know for sure?' he asked.

Doctor Marcos shrugged.

'We've got the flowers and we're examining them. The printer ink people are checking the letter. There were no fingerprints that we can find, and obviously, we're dealing with a different police department and a different unit, even if I do "Stan" Rajesh.

'Stan?'

'It's what the cool kids say,' Doctor Marcos shrugged. 'I rate him. Like him. Think he's extra.'

'Another thing the cool kids say?'

'Apparently. I have a niece coming to visit next month so I'm boning up on this. See? I'm using them like a native already.'

She paused as she realised Declan and Anjli were both waiting.

'So, anyway, we're trying to find out what they found out before we turned up.'

She looked over at Anjli.

'We can't confirm or deny yet if it's the same person.'

Anjli nodded, her expression still tight.

'The person we believed did it is dead,' she replied. 'So if it is the same person, there's a bloody weird story coming out there, because they're either a zombie or they're some kind of spectral ghost.'

She stared back at Dan as if imagining that he was the figure for a moment. It was such an intense glare that the curator himself started to shuffle on the spot, uncomfortable under the gaze.

'Anjli?' Declan asked.

As if being thrown out of a dream, Anjli jerked back to life, looking at him.

'Sorry,' she apologised, looking back at Dan. 'Sorry. Blackthorne was about the same size and shape as the figure we got on the image. That can't be a coincidence. But it can't be Blackthorne, he blew his head off.'

She was staring back at the corridor.

'Or did he?' she asked.

At this, Doctor Marcos held a hand up to pause this rabbit hole that Anjli was about to jump down.

'Just because the head might have been missing doesn't mean he faked his death,' she explained. 'The DNA matched, the fingerprints matched. That was Thomas Blackthorne that died in Leyton.'

Anjli looked at her.

'Then how is he back?' she asked. 'How has he done this again? How does he know my name? I wasn't on the press reports. The only people who knew I was involved in this were the police—'

She stopped.

'I need to speak to DCI Ford,' she muttered, but then paused, staring at Dan.

'Show me the video again,' she said commandingly. 'The one where Debbie sees the stranger.'

Once more Dan pulled up his pad and played through the meeting, and Anjli stabbed at the screen to pause it as the stranger started to lead Debbie away from her parents.

'There,' she tapped at the screen again, making sure to touch a spot which wouldn't restart the video. 'The finger.'

Declan looked down at the screen. The capped stranger was walking away, but their hand, resting on Debbie's back to guide her along, was making a pointing gesture, down and to the right of the camera.

'Have we checked that area yet?' Anjli looked at Doctor Marcos, who shook her head.

'It was a busy abduction scene, and we've focused more on where the pansies and poppies, and the message were left as there were, believe it or not, fewer points of contamination,' she replied, peering at the image. 'I know where that is. De'Geer? Now you're here, be a darling and go examine around. It might be just a coincidence, but if they're pointing to something they've left ...'

She didn't need to finish the comment, and Anjli nodded a thanks, her eyes and lips tight as she looked at Declan.

'Want to bet it's a message for me?' she muttered before turning on her feet and storming out.

Declan glanced back at the scene before looking up at Doctor Marcos.

'Keep us updated?' he asked, before following his partner out of the British Museum and most likely into another fight.

4

HOUSE CALL

Tamsin and Pete Watson lived in a semi-detached house at the end of Rutland Road, close to Victoria Park, and pretty much smack bang in the middle of Monroe's old stomping ground.

He stared up at the building, feeling a wave of nostalgia run over him. When he first arrived from Glasgow, he'd worked in Tottenham with Patrick Walsh, Emilia Wintergreen, and Derek Salmon, among others. But then, after everything had fallen apart, he'd taken a transfer to Mile End for a few years before moving to Vauxhall with his then-protégé Ellie Reckless to clean up *that* crime unit. He had left DI Marie Ford, then-becoming-DCI Ford, in charge after he'd made the transfer and to this day still felt that was one of the biggest mistakes he'd ever made.

He'd known that Ford had her demons; he was aware of her gambling and he knew she had a connection to the twins, Johnny and Jackie Lucas. But he never realised how far it went until a few years later when Declan, shortly after punching a priest and looking for an excuse to hide, was transferred there.

Ford had wanted a patsy. She didn't care who it was, and Declan looked like a man on the way out. That was her biggest and final mistake as a serving police officer.

But, after she'd gone, DCI Esposito had moved into the spot. Alvaro Esposito was a good man; Monroe had never really worked with him, although they'd crossed paths on many occasions. The Twins, after all, were still in Esposito's jurisdiction, and the Last Chance Saloon seemed to find themselves working with Johnny on a regular basis. Anjli had worked with Esposito for a month while the Unit was in limbo, a circumstance that then allowed them to work in Hurley on the Reaper case—

Which, if we hadn't, wouldn't have left us in so much shite, he thought to himself, before adding *which, if we hadn't, would have left more dead bodies on the floor.*

Shaking the morose thoughts away as he looked up at the house in front of them, he turned to face Esposito.

'Do you think this is a little bit of overkill?' he asked. 'I mean, it's a missing child, and they're getting two DCIs.'

'Oh, it's absolutely overkill,' Esposito said. 'But at the same time, it's also a statement being made. We're showing that this is important to us. We're showing that it's linked to the previous case.'

'We're showing we haven't got a bloody clue, laddie,' Monroe muttered.

Esposito smiled.

'One thing else, Guv,' he said. 'We're not both DCIs anymore. You're a Detective Superintendent now. You keep forgetting.'

'Aye, it's not a case of forgetting,' Monroe said sheepishly.

'I'm aware that I get less chance to go out, the more I rise in the ranks. I like to pretend I'm back in the good old days, as much as things like this are, anyway.'

'You know, you could always do something so terrible they have to demote you,' Esposito suggested, half-jokingly.

'Aye, and you don't think I've been trying to do that for the last couple of years?' Monroe laughed. 'Come on, let's get this over with.'

The door opened to a uniformed female officer. Esposito knew them; they were from Mile End and had been sent to look after the Watsons, at least for the first day, to stop the paparazzi from pressuring them too much. They'd noticed a couple of men in vans nearby, but the weather wasn't great, and they'd probably decided to hide in their vehicles rather than stand outside taking photos.

Monroe knew, however, that as they approached the door and knocked on it, the police officer opening it and facing them, their images would now be plastered all over the local press.

With luck, it would only be that.

'Guv ...' the officer looked confused as she glanced at Monroe.

'Detective Superintendent Monroe, Lassie,' Monroe gave a smile. 'Don't worry, I'm just visiting.'

'This is Constable Sanford,' Esposito nodded to her. 'She might not be as imposing as your Viking, but she can hold her own. Are they in?'

The second part of the comment was to Sanford, and she nodded, waving back into the house.

'They're in the living room,' she said. 'They were told that someone was coming by. I don't think they realised it was going to be royalty.'

'Is this how you allow your officers to speak?' Monroe looked at Esposito with a smile. 'Calling me royalty.'

'Actually, Alex, I think they were talking about me,' Esposito grinned. But the smile faded quickly as they entered the living room.

Tamsin and Pete Watson were in their late thirties to early forties. Monroe had read from the notes that Tamsin worked in a local coffee shop, whereas Pete was a banker in the city, although the term "banker" was quite generic and could have meant a dozen different things. What it also could have meant was that Debbie was a kidnap for ransom, but as yet no money had been asked for.

Tamsin was in a pair of jogging bottoms and a fluffy hoodie, likely having changed since the trip to the museum only a few hours earlier. Likewise, the same could have been said of Pete. He was in a pair of jeans and a t-shirt, his hair unkempt, as if he'd been tearing at it, in frustration.

'Mister Watson, Mrs Watson,' Esposito said, holding a hand up. 'I'm DCI Alvaro Esposito. This is Detective Superintendent Alexander Monroe.'

It was Tamsin who spoke first.

'Why are there two of you?' she asked.

'We wanted to show you how seriously we take this,' Monroe replied, sitting down and facing them. 'Also, there is a connection this may have to a historical case, one that we are currently looking into.'

'You mean Blackthorne, don't you?' Pete asked.

Monroe paused as the name was spoken.

'Aye, and you know about this?'

'We live in Mile End,' Pete replied. 'There's not much we don't hear about. Gangsters turning politicians. Corrupt DCIs.'

This was said as a side view to Esposito.

'No offence.'

'None taken.'

'And Debbie went to the same Brownies group Sarah had been to,' Tamsin continued.

'Aye, she did?' Monroe raised an eyebrow. This hadn't been in the notes.

'Well, she hadn't been for the last few months. It wasn't really her thing. She enjoyed it when she was in Rainbows, but the girls were ...' Pete trailed off.

'Debbie is a little ... different,' Tamsin said, taking up the comment. 'She loves books like *Harry Potter*, and stories about ancient Egyptian Gods, and goes on about them all the time. I think some of the other girls were a little bit more "reality TV", if you know what I mean. They mocked her.'

'She has a lanyard she wears all the time,' Pete added. 'Ravenclaw. That was the house that she was told she was in when we went to the shop in King's Cross. She was very proud of it, teachers even allowed her to wear it at school, because she wouldn't take the bloody thing off.'

At this, Tamsin started to cry, Pete placing an arm around her.

Monroe pulled a tissue out of the box in front of him and passed it over.

'I promise we'll get her back,' he said.

'You don't even know if she's alive.'

'Oh aye, we're pretty much sure she's alive,' Monroe replied. 'We think it's a dance they're doing at the moment, and while they're dancing your daughter is still alive. But until then, we need to look at some things. Is there anybody in your family who could have done this?'

'In our family?' Pete looked horrified.

'We have to ask,' Monroe said.

'Not that I can think of,' Pete said coldly. 'My family aren't serial killers or murderers. We don't hang out with them either, unlike you guys.'

Monroe let the jibe pass. The chances were Pete Watson was one of the millions of people who had read the national news.

If Pete felt apologetic about the line, he didn't show it, instead looking uncomfortable, possibly as he realised what he'd just said.

'I get why you're angry,' Monroe replied. 'But I have to ask the questions. We're speaking to the school later on and all we're looking to do here is help. Can you tell me why you were at the British Museum?'

'It was a friend of Debbie's birthday, Tanya,' Tamsin said. 'We were there because she also loved the Egyptians. It's why they got on so well.'

'And you had this on a weekday because ...?'

'They're off on holiday next week, and this was the only day they could get tickets. Sure, it meant taking her out of school, but it's one day, you know? And it was a special event, so we could get them in and out early, hopefully out by ten, eleven at latest.'

'So you'd only lose a half day at school?'

'Actually, it was more so we'd only lose a half day at work,' Pete muttered sheepishly.

Monroe ignored the fact that Tanya's parents seemed to have a lesser opinion of school terms than the Watsons did and noted this down.

'So, she liked Egyptians, and she liked magic and wizards and things like that,' he said. 'Anything else you can think of?'

'No,' Tamsin replied, shaking her head. 'It actually caused

a bit of a problem. It wasn't Debbie's trip, you see. But Tanya didn't want to go straight to the Egyptian exhibit, Debbie had made a bit of a scene, and I think her mum and dad decided to take us there for a more peaceful life.'

'Tanya's parents?'

'Parents are Kyle and Lily Rhodes,' Pete explained.

'Do they go to the same school?'

'No idea, they met at Brownies ... I think so.'

Monroe noted this down.

'So it was just the two girls?'

'No, there were three families, I think.' Tamsin considered this. 'We didn't know the other lad.'

'Lad?'

'A boy in her class. His parents knew Tanya's parents and you know how these things go.'

Monroe didn't, but he smiled nevertheless.

'So, who decided on the museum?'

'Oh, that would have been Lily,' Pete said. 'And they had free tickets, so ...'

'Free tickets?' It was Esposito who spoke now. 'How did they have free tickets?'

'One of their brothers or in-laws, I think, I don't know,' Tamsin shrugged. 'Why does it matter?'

'Well, it's more a case of working out who knew you were going to the museum, especially on an early morning,' Monroe explained. 'We know that the person who took Debbie was there, so ...'

'Oh, okay, yes, I see,' Tamsin nodded now. 'I think Lily's brother, Steve, got them. He's a workman there and they get passes.'

Monroe wrote this down, noting the fact that the workmen, who had managed to systematically destroy the CCTV and cause problems with forensic data collection happened to be the same people who had provided the tickets.

'Can you tell me more about the day?' he asked.

Tamsin shrugged.

'It was a birthday,' she said. 'We all turned up. The plan was to go around the museum and then probably find a local McDonald's or something for breakfast, before they stopped serving. We got to the Egyptian exhibits and, well, Debbie was over the moon running around looking at things.'

'The problem with Debbie,' Pete added, 'was that she was like a whirlwind. Once she was there and excited, she was chatting to someone by a sarcophagus and then the next minute she's staring up at a statue. You couldn't keep her still. We'd made a joke about sticking an AirTag on her or something like that but ...'

'But what?'

'But we did that, and it didn't work,' Tamsin took over now. 'She loved that lanyard, the Ravenclaw one, and so we gave her a little ID that she could wear on it. She didn't realise that on the back we'd gaffa-taped an AirTag. We thought it'd work like a tracker, but of course they don't. They only work when someone's iPhone is nearby.'

'We assumed that there'd be a dozen iPhones in every room, you know?' Tamsin spoke.

'But when she disappeared,' Pete looked annoyed at Tamsin for interrupting. 'There was no AirTag. It wasn't showing up at all. We were telling a police officer about this and they explained that if you know how to use an AirTag, you can pull the battery out and once the battery's out, you can't be tracked anymore. Therefore, she was last seen next door.'

Monroe nodded. The AirTag could have been removed

and kept on the abductor's person. 'When did you notice she'd gone?'

'About ten minutes after we last saw her,' Tamsin admitted. 'We'd been running around keeping all the kids together because the others were quite useless if I'm being honest, and then we realised Debbie had disappeared. Kyle and Lily didn't really give a shit, Debbie was a bit of a pity invite.'

'We got the impression Tanya had invited about a dozen people and no one had bothered turning up,' Pete continued. 'And well, Debbie had agreed because it was Egyptians and you know, they were reluctant hosts, shall we say.'

'So, ten minutes in, you realise that Debbie's missing, you look around, you can't find her.'

'I tried to find her on the AirTag. The last known location was in the next room,' Pete replied sullenly. 'I ran in there. She wasn't around. We assumed she'd carried on. We knew there's another room with Egyptian artefacts in. Maybe she'd got excited, run there already ... or who knows?'

He looked as if he wanted to punch something. Monroe understood.

'It was around then that we decided to speak to the museum themselves,' Tamsin continued. 'It had been half an hour by the time we found someone, around nine am. We had no way of contacting her. They put a Tannoy out asking for Debbie Watson to go to one of the information desks, but she didn't appear. It was another ten, fifteen minutes before somebody started looking at the CCTV cameras. All they could tell us is nobody had come out of the front, and they knew she was probably still in the museum. But now we know that wasn't the case.'

Monroe nodded.

'By then you'd found out she had left through the north entrance.'

Pete's lip quivered as he held back his tears.

'Just find our daughter,' he said. 'We're not bad people. We've never done anything wrong. We don't understand why we've been picked. She's never hurt a fly. She's an innocent. Please.'

'We'll do everything we can,' Monroe said. 'We'll let PC Sanford take anything else you can think of.'

He paused.

'There's a figure with a baseball cap in the images we've got of the abduction,' he said. 'Did you see them at all?'

'We weren't paying attention to the surrounding people,' Pete said. 'There was ...'

He trailed off.

'We took a photo at the start,' he said, rummaging for his phone before realising he didn't have it on him. 'When we were all in the lobby, kind of a "yay here we go" kind of Facebook post. I hadn't passed it across because it wasn't when the abduction happened, but if someone was following us in, maybe they're ...'

'Send us anything you have,' Esposito leant forward, holding Pete's arm in a reassuring gesture. 'Anything and everything could help us here.'

'I'll get that sorted,' Pete swallowed and nodded, as Monroe passed his business card across.

'Send me that email address and I'll make sure that our cyber expert gets it,' he said as he glanced at Esposito. 'We'll also be sharing it with Mile End, and their cyber experts can work on it too. Double the amount of people means you should find an answer very soon.'

This said, he rose from the chair, and the terrified parents in front of him. There was nothing much more he could get from these people that hadn't already been gained by the police. If anything, he wanted to face them, look them in the eyes and make sure this wasn't something that *they* had planned, harsh as it was to even suggest that.

As they walked outside, Esposito looked at Monroe.

'What are you thinking?' he asked.

Monroe shook his head as he breathed in the outside air, glaring at one of the vans opposite, a zoom lens poking out from the gap at the top of the passenger window.

'I have no idea, laddie,' he said. 'There seems to be no motivation, no reasoning. Why take the child? Why would the child go with him?'

He sighed.

'Let's just hope we have something better to go back to. But first, I'm going to have a chat with the wee scroat with the camera over there.'

5

JON SNOW KNOWS NOTHING

'Well, you were right,' Doctor Marcos said as Declan and Anjli walked into her office. It was less of an office and more of a desk in a pathology morgue with a cold metal slab to the side. Although Doctor Marcos had recently started adding painted pictures and prints to the walls in some attempt to make it feel a little more homely, Declan hadn't wondered too much about why this had happened. He felt it best not to ask. Perhaps it was De'Geer needing a little more colour in the room to move from the utilitarian grey that it had been since they refurbished.

It'd been half an hour after Declan and Anjli had arrived back at the unit, already grabbing a much-needed mid-afternoon coffee, before Doctor Marcos had returned, muttering. Apparently Rajesh Khanna had arrived and pulled rank, this still technically a Mile End case; Declan had the feeling she was less annoyed at being removed, and more that she couldn't watch Rajesh work.

'How do you mean?' he asked, as Doctor Marcos pulled out a clear bag and placed it on the table in front of her.

Inside was a piece of paper and what looked to be part of a flower.

'We followed the finger,' she said. 'We went to the exhibit. We worked out from angles that the stranger was pointing into one of the sarcophagus – Sarcophagi? Sarcophaguses? Whatever it is. Anyway, we had a peek in and found a small piece of paper on the base. I told De'Geer to clamber in, booties and gloves on, of course, and he gingerly picked it up and found these two items.'

'Can we see them?' Anjli asked.

'We're about to send them to be tested, but I've scanned and photographed them,' Doctor Marcos said, opening up the first image on her phone to show them instead. It was a small piece of paper with a poem written on it.

Pump of fatal water,
And cholera to slaughter,
Snow's map! Snow's map!
We all fall ill.

'What the hell does that mean?' Declan asked.

'It's a rhyme,' Doctor Marcos replied. 'In the same "AABA" configuration as "Ring-a-Ring-a-Roses". If you read it in the same style, you'll see it's almost the same. We're guessing that it links to somewhere else, which we're working on now.'

Declan nodded, looking at Anjli.

'Someone's playing with us,' he said.

'Playing with *me*,' Anjli muttered. 'What's the other item?'

Doctor Marcos swiped the screen, showing a zoomed-in photo of what looked to be a thorn from a rose; but there was something slightly off with it.

'We're having it checked but we believe it is a thorn from

the *Rosa gallica officinalis*, the common garden red rose,' Doctor Marcos explained.

'Ring a ring of roses,' Declan muttered, half to himself.

'Indeed. You will, however, notice that this one has been dipped in what looks to be either black food or flower dye, turning it black. Very gothic.'

'A black thorn.' Anjli looked as if she wanted to scream.

Doctor Marcos nodded.

'Somebody here left a black thorn and a clue, and then later on placed another message mentioning your name. I would hazard a guess that by pointing at it, knowing there was a camera behind them, they're sending us on a journey.'

Declan stared at the poem.

'Do we know what this could be?' he asked. 'Perhaps Billy is able to answer it—'

'Actually, I think I already know,' Doctor Marcos smiled. 'How much do you know about the 1854 cholera outbreak?'

'That there was a cholera outbreak in 1854,' Declan replied. 'I know that now because you've just told me.'

Doctor Marcos shook her head.

'And you being a Londoner as well,' she muttered. 'Back in 1854, people were dying of cholera in Soho. Very bad epidemic, hundreds of people died. Nobody knew where it came from, but in hindsight it was obvious. Many cellars had cesspools underneath their floorboards, which formed from the sewers and filth seeping in from the outside. And, with the cesspools overrunning, the government dumped the waste into the Thames, contaminating the water supply. But, to the average punter, it was almost as if a new plague had turned up. Enter John Snow.'

'What, the guy from *Game of Thrones?*'

Doctor Marcos sighed.

'No, Declan, not the guy from *Game of Thrones*. An actual real-life person. John Snow was a surgeon and general practitioner who, when examining where most of the victims of the Soho outbreak had come from, he worked out that nearly every victim had some kind of link to a public water pump on Broad Street – now Broadwick Street – just off Wardour Street in Soho. Back then, it wasn't the cool, trendy place it is now. And on the corner of Broad Street and Little Windmill Street, now Lexington Street, was a single water pump where many people gained their water for the day.'

She looked around, now in full-on lecture mode.

'By closing the pump and stopping people from drinking from it, he was able to make sure that the cholera died off. The pump is still there; well, a replica, anyway. The original location of the pump is marked by a red granite paver. There's a pub named after him right next to it, though.'

She chuckled.

'Funnily enough, it is a go-to pub for fans of *Game of Thrones*. They do like to take photos. For once, it seems that John Snow knew something.'

'Did he never usually know something?' Declan asked.

'"You know nothing, Jon Snow." It's a line from ...'

Doctor Marcos sighed, deciding the conversation thread wasn't worth continuing.

'Anyway, I think this is telling you to go have a look at the pump. I could be wrong, but it does feel that way. Also, "Ring-a-Ring-a-Roses" is erroneously linked to the Great Plague, even though there's no actual proof of that, and this is a poem that could be linked to a cholera outbreak. Two unclean epidemics, which links us back in a way with Blackthorne's fixation with people who were unclean.'

Declan nodded. He could see where that was leading.

'I'll take De'Geer and Will—'

He stopped as Anjli gripped his arm.

'Declan,' she said, her voice quiet, almost pleading. 'I need to do this one. I know you're the DCI, but ...'

Declan understood. He'd had his moments like this.

'Go with De'Geer and Cooper,' he replied. 'See if there's anything on the pump, or the pub, or wherever. If there is, get Cooper to canvass for witnesses. I'll check into the CCTV cameras with Billy, work out if we can get any other clues.'

'Billy actually has something for you,' Doctor Marcos replied. 'I'd check with him first, as I think you might be changing your plans.'

Anjli was already leaving, phoning De'Geer and Cooper, telling them to meet her downstairs as Declan walked over to Billy. He was sitting at his usual bank of computer monitors, scrolling through file after file, while comparing them to other pages on other screens.

'Anything?' Declan asked.

Billy nodded.

'Actually, yes, but I'm not too sure if it's important or not,' he said. 'So, I'm looking into Debbie to find out anything I can, and I realised she goes to the same school that Sarah Thompson went to three years ago.'

'That can't be a coincidence,' Declan frowned, leaning closer. 'What's the name?'

'Kelsey Primary,' Billy replied. 'Although it probably would have been better named as Kelsey Grammar.'

He looked up optimistically at Declan, as if expecting him to get the comment.

'I don't get it,' Declan said.

'Kelsey Grammar, the actor,' Billy replied. 'Plays Frasier Crane in *Cheers*, where everybody knows your name and they're always glad you came.'

Declan stared at Billy.

'Are you trying to make some kind of comparison between a comedy show and a missing child?'

Billy reddened.

'No, Guv, sorry, Guv. I was just ... it's the name, you know.'

Declan leant back, straightening his spine, feeling the knots click out as he did so.

'Well, the next time you need to consider "taking a break from all your worries", as it "sure would help a lot", we'll find you a nice place to do so,' he smiled, letting Billy know that he actually *did* understand where the joke came from. 'So, Kelsey Primary School. That's too big a coincidence. Was the other girl, Mia ...?'

'No, she was at a school about three miles down the road. We've never found a connection between the two, apart from this weird, unclean idea and the after-school groups like Rainbows and Brownies. This feels new.'

Declan pursed his lips.

'If possible, get me a list of everybody who works at that school. Cross-reference it to anybody who was there three years ago as well. If this is somebody that Debbie recognised, a schoolteacher or school assistant would fit the bill nicely, even someone who worked in the Brownies group she was in.'

Billy nodded.

'Anything else?' Declan asked.

Billy grimaced.

'Actually, there is,' he replied. 'Guv, Bradbury wants to see you in his office, in Guildhall.'

Declan sighed. He'd been expecting this for a while.

'Is it about the will?' he asked.

'Yes, sir.'

'Right then,' Declan replied, looking around the office. 'I'll go speak to him, and then I'll have a chat with the school.'

Billy glanced back at his screen.

'I have something else. We found Antony Morgan, the shop assistant. He now works in his own florist, near Chancery Lane.'

'Maybe we should aim Anjli there, rather than the pump,' Declan mused. 'She'd have spoken to him before, and it might help. Also, three officers at one pump becomes quite visible.'

At the comment Billy laughed.

'Guv, have you seen De'Geer?' he asked wolfishly. 'There's no way he won't be visible, no matter who you send with him!'

DECLAN HAD WORKED AND CROSSED SWORDS WITH Commander Bradbury many times over the last few years since arriving at the Last Chance Saloon. In fact, the very first time they'd met was right before Declan was accused of murder and international terrorism, and forced to go on the run. Bradbury had believed Declan's story and had even worked with him in a sting operation that not only revealed the true culprits behind it, but also helped clear his name. Declan had always felt that Bradbury trusted him, understood him even.

That said, to be called to the Guildhall to speak to the now Commander, effectively the head of all City of London Police, did not bode well.

As he arrived and was led through the north entrance of Guildhall, past security and along the corridors, passing offices where various clerks and Chamberlains gave freedom of the city and performed their daily duties, Declan saw Detective Chief Superintendent Sophie Bullman appear at her door. She hadn't come out to meet him; she looked surprised to even see him there, but her expression turned to one of concern as she gave him a curt nod and continued past him down the corridor.

This was more concerning than anything else. Bullman *never* turned down an opportunity to mock Declan, or "Deckers" as she liked to call him. Ever since she'd first turned up, she'd found ways to embarrass him or mock him. Her acerbic sarcasm was actually one of her finer qualities. He knew it was never in anger; it was only ever in jest, and he was fine with it.

To see her staring at him as one would look at a condemned man, though, was unsettling to say the least.

The aide brought Declan to a wooden door, knocked three times, and then opened it. Sitting at an ornate mahogany desk, looking up from his laptop, was Commander David Bradbury. Tall, with short, grey hair over whiter temples, and wearing the white shirt, black epaulettes and black-tie uniform of his rank, he took off his glasses, used mainly for close-up reading and computer work, rose and motioned for Declan to sit down in front of him.

There was no offered handshake, no warm welcome. Declan wondered whether he was about to be fired. It felt like a tribunal rather than a meeting.

'DCI Walsh,' Bradbury said, Declan noting the officiousness of the title. 'I'm glad you came in. We need to have a conversation.'

'From your tone and from Bullman's expression as I passed her in the corridor, I'm guessing it's not a good talk,' Declan replied. 'I'm also guessing this is about Karl Schnitter.'

'It is,' Bradbury said, holding up a hand in a placating gesture to pause Declan from continuing. 'But it's not what you think.'

Declan stopped the reply he was about to give, something about *being set up and how this was all a kangaroo court,* and simply stopped, keeping his mouth shut uncharacteristically as he waited for Bradbury to continue.

'I know Schnitter giving you everything wasn't a plan of yours, and I know it's done nothing but cause you hassle,' Bradbury said. 'I also know that you're working with several charities to sell all of his items, donate everything to victims of domestic violence and murder, and I appreciate that. You could, if you wanted, make quite a lot of money from everything he has.'

He checked a piece of paper, the slightest of smiles now on his lips.

'Apparently though, and unfortunately for you, the garage he used to own is nothing more than a charred wreck, after a strange fire occurred shortly after he died.'

'I know,' Declan replied, keeping his face emotionless. 'I was as shocked as you were to hear about that.'

He wasn't, of course. The fire had been set by him and Anjli the same night as Schnitter's death, a way of finally saying farewell to the bastard – and Declan was pretty sure Bradbury suspected this as well. But everything else Bradbury had said was true. He had intended to remove everything and didn't want the money.

'It's not about the cash,' he continued. 'I wouldn't take a penny from that man. Everything he has is blood money.'

'I get that,' Bradbury leant back in his chair, squinting as if a migraine was starting to appear. He opened and shut his eyes in rapid succession to try to clear whatever was in his view. 'And we'll do what we can to lessen any paparazzi interest. Once they realise that you're not gaining anything from this and that this is one last sick, twisted gift, they'll leave you alone.'

Declan nodded and then waited.

'Sir, if you know this, why am I here?'

'We had a message from DCI Freeman at Maidenhead,' Bradbury replied. 'He'd spoken to Monroe and Monroe had passed it to Bullman, and Bullman passed it to me.'

'I don't understand. Why couldn't Monroe tell me what this message was?'

'It seemed that nobody wanted to tell you about this in fear of what you would do,' Bradbury stated, his voice emotionless and slow, as if trying subconsciously to calm Declan down before he'd even spoken.

He reached across the desk and picked up a file. Opening it up, he took out a photo and passed it across. It was in a clear bag, and Declan realised quickly it was a photograph taken within the last week of Declan and Jess.

Declan wondered immediately whether this was some fallout from the Reaper case they'd recently finished; that had also involved people taking photographs. This, however, was different. It felt different, looked different, and more importantly, it was a photograph taken with a zoom lens.

'What's going on, sir?' Declan asked, his voice tight.

'We believe someone is watching you, Declan,' Bradbury said, his tone grave. 'And whoever it is, they're getting too close for comfort.'

The photo had been tampered with. The eyes of Jess had been burnt through with what looked to be a cigarette. Declan, seen in the picture, had not been touched, but above him, scrawled in what looked to be black marker, was the word "Killer" with a black arrow aimed at him. And above Jess, in similar handwriting, was another word: "Liar".

Declan looked up at Bradbury and immediately wanted to start shouting. He wanted to know who did this, how they did this, and how he could find them, lock them in an interrogation room with him for half an hour, and tear their skin off. Now he understood why nobody under Bradbury wanted to deal with this.

'This was nailed to the remains of the garage,' Bradbury explained. 'There were no fingerprints on it. And forensics are still looking at the original. We gained it last night.'

Declan frowned.

'Surely I would have been told about this! I'm in Hurley! I live down the road from this!'

'It was decided to keep this from you,' Bradbury replied. 'Freeman was given a call telling him to go to the garage at six, that there'd be a message waiting. We're guessing that they turned up shortly before, nailed it to the remains of the door, and then left. When Freeman arrived, it was waiting. Inside the bag was another piece of paper, folded up and typed. We're now trying to work out what ink and paper it is, but that might take a while.'

He leant closer now, resting his arms on the desk.

'Jess, she's at college now, right?'

'Yes sir. She's started her second year,' Declan didn't like the way this was going. 'Why do you ask?'

'I think she might want to home school for a while,' Bradbury replied carefully. 'Just until we work this out, yeah?'

'What's on the note?' Declan now looked back at the photo. 'What did they say?'

Bradbury looked as if he wasn't going to reply, then gave a slight nod and passed another photo over. On this, the note was unfolded and readable.

He murdered our children
Now we murder yours

Declan had unconsciously half-risen from his chair before Bradbury ordered him to sit back down.

'Schnitter murdered no children I can think of, but he did kill some teenagers,' Bradbury continued. 'Never plural from any family, so I'm guessing this is a generic "our" they're mentioning here. But the "yours" is quite specific. You might be able to weather this, but we'd rather we weren't hunting down someone intent on killing, frankly, the best Walsh Detective we've met.'

Declan knew the jibe was to try to defuse the moment, and he appreciated it – but he still wanted blood.

'Who's examining this?'

'Who do you think?' Bradbury grumbled. 'Told me she'd leave my body where nobody could find it if she wasn't given it. I know she's married to the Scot now, so there has to be a heart somewhere, but she scares the shit out of me.'

The confession now given, Bradbury straightened, waving Declan off.

'Find this missing kid, and we'll look after Jess,' he said.

'Bullman's already on her way. Whoever this is, we'll get them. Not you, DCI Walsh, *we*. Understand?'

'Absolutely, sir, thank you, sir,' Declan said as he rose and left the office. He might have acknowledged this, but there was no way anyone was going to stop him from finding the person who wanted his daughter dead.

And there was no way they'd be able to stop him before he was *finished* with them.

6

WATER PUMPS

THE PROBLEM WITH CENTRAL LONDON IN SEPTEMBER, WAS that it was now out of the school holiday season, which meant that couples who wanted to travel to London without the risk of bumping into children would now start turning up. It was also still warm enough to have a holiday; the rain wasn't as strong as it would be in the later months.

As De'Geer and Cooper walked over to the John Snow pub on the junction of Broadwick Street and Lexington Street, although it was a weekday, it felt like it was Saturday trading hours.

With De'Geer striking an imposing figure, easily seven feet tall with short, blond hair and a beard, and Cooper diminutive beside him – although realistically anyone was diminutive beside De'Geer – both in fluorescent jackets over their uniforms, they became a subject of attention with several tourists asking if they could grab photos with them. Although Cooper was absolutely convinced this was more because of De'Geer's stature than his position in the force, De'Geer had politely declined, explaining that they were actually on duty and doing his best to extricate himself from any situations.

Finally left alone, they made their way over to the replica pump.

The Broad Street Pump was a cast-iron water pump with a tall, cylindrical structure that was at one time topped by a handle used for drawing water. It was placed on two eight-sided bases and was beside Broadwick Street, beside the pub.

De'Geer paused, looking around.

'There's a distinct lack of CCTV around here,' he grumbled. 'You'd think for somewhere like this, you'd get a bit more.'

Cooper looked around as well, and then nodded across the street, to the corner of Broadwick Street and Poland Street where a young man, with long straggly hair fashioned into rat tails and a slightly longer beard, leaned against the window of a shopfront. He had a red *Big Issue* bib on that announced him as an official seller of the *Big Issue* magazine, and in fact had several copies in his hands.

'Who needs CCTV when you have witnesses?' she asked. 'But, before we go off on that, let's see if we actually are in the right place. After all, we are relying on Billy's intelligence.'

On first glance, the pump seemed completely normal. There was nothing out of the ordinary, no packages left at the base. But, as they moved around, De'Geer paused, holding up a hand.

'Gloves on,' he said, pulling out his latex forensics gloves and pulling them on quickly. 'Stop anybody coming near this.'

Cooper frowned, moving around to see what De'Geer had seen and then nodding as she noticed the QR code. It was on a sticker, no more than a couple of inches in diameter, a black code on white sticky paper. But it wasn't the sticker or the code that De'Geer had noticed. Stuck underneath it, almost as if placed onto the pump before the sticker had been positioned, were five strands of long blonde hair.

'Debbie Watson was blonde, right?' she asked.

De'Geer nodded, already leaning closer, peering at the QR code and the hair.

'I'm going to try to peel this off,' he said, pulling out his phone first to take photos. As he did so, his phone instantly picked up on the QR code and went to open a page.

'Don't,' Cooper said, before De'Geer did anything.

De'Geer glanced back at her.

'I'm not a rookie,' he said, lowering the phone. 'The QR code would link to a website, but it could link to anything, there's every chance the code itself could link to a virus, some kind of backdoor Trojan, that would allow whoever had sent this access into my phone and even possibly the police network. Far better to take photos and send them to Billy.'

This done, he now pulled out a clear plastic bag and a pair of tweezers, gently easing the five blonde hairs from behind the sticker. It was difficult, but working with the angle, once he started moving the strands, the glue of the sticker lessening on them, he was able to pull all five out and place them into the bag. This done, he now took a second bag and with the same tweezers, gently peeled away the QR code.

It hadn't been stuck on securely. If anything, whoever placed it here likely wanted it to be pulled off, *wanted* the hairs to be removed. This now done, he placed the sticker onto a small piece of plastic from his pocket, as this way the sticking side wouldn't connect to the baggie. With luck, anything that was on that side would be kept. Although, De'Geer didn't expect to find much evidence on the sticky side. If there were fingerprints, they would be on the surface.

By now, they'd gathered a small crowd, people taking photos and looking to upload them. De'Geer turned, pulling out his phone once more, and calling Monroe.

'Guv,' he said. 'It's De'Geer. We think we have something but we're not sure, and it's quite a busy location. I'm going to search around but I don't think we need a police line.'

He glanced around.

'Although, if Billy can pick up any CCTV, it would probably help.'

COOPER, MEANWHILE, HAD WALKED OVER TO THE *BIG ISSUE* seller, pulling out a handful of change as she did so.

'How long have you been here?' she asked.

The *Big Issue* seller smiled.

'Long enough to know what you're looking at,' he said. 'Buy a copy?'

'I'll buy two,' Cooper said, passing him a five-pound note. 'One for you, and one for the information.'

'I think the information's worth more than one issue of the magazine,' the seller smiled still, and Cooper shrugged.

'True,' she replied. 'It probably is. But I'm not giving you more money, and if you carry on being an obstruction, we'll just take you into the station and ask you there. Which, although it'll be a simple job, you *will* spend several hours in there, which is several hours that you won't be able to make any money selling that magazine, on a sunny September afternoon.'

She smiled back at the seller in response.

'So, which would you prefer?' she asked. 'Five pounds now, or lots of earnings later?'

'For someone so sweet and innocent-looking, you're a firebrand,' the man chuckled. 'Alright, I didn't see much, I wasn't paying attention. But I keep an eye on the people. I try to get eye contact with them. Give them a smile. You know, get them to buy my magazine.'

He nodded towards De'Geer, still by the pump.

'There's a lot of people go around that, but there's no point trying to sell around there, because the people in the pub can be absolute pricks, and the people taking photos don't want somebody like me in the background. So I keep to the side.'

He thought for a moment.

'There was somebody over there, though,' he said, 'just buggering around with the pump. Happened about four hours ago.'

'Four hours.' Cooper pulled out her notebook and noted this down. That would have made it after Debbie had been kidnapped, but suitably short enough time enough for anybody who had found the item in the British Museum to arrive to find a code. Whoever was turning up to leave whatever clue this was, though, they were cutting it fine; the police would have been able to pounce on them immediately if they arrived first. Although that wasn't factoring in the time spent working out the riddle.

But why take the risk?

'Are you absolutely sure it was four hours ago?' she asked.

The man nodded.

'Give or take,' he replied. 'I start here before nine, catch the workers as they go past. It wasn't long after that, perhaps ten? So yeah, I'd say maybe four hours, say nine thirty or ten in the morning.'

Cooper pursed her lips as she looked back across the road. It was somewhere between eight-thirty and nine in the morning when the abductor had left the message in the sarcophagus. Enough time to hide the victim, and travel here.

'What's your name?' she asked.

'Scrumpy. You know, like the cider.'

'I somehow don't think your parents named you that,' Cooper frowned.

'They really did,' Scrumpy smiled. 'They were road protesters. Spent a lot of time in a caravan. When I was born, it was because they'd got drunk one night on Scrumpy Jack, and that's how I was conceived.'

He grinned.

'So I'm Scrumpy. Scrumpy Daniels.'

Cooper noted this down.

'I don't envy your school years,' she said.

'Homeschooled,' Scrumpy shrugged. 'Never had a problem. We followed the festivals. People at festivals always have weird names. Never really felt like I was out of place.'

'And now?'

'Now I still follow the festivals,' he said. 'I sell the *Big Issue,* it gives me enough money. I carry on to the next place.'

'You've never wanted to get a house or a job?'

At the words, Scrumpy laughed.

'Why would I want a job or a house?' he said. 'I have everything I want. I'm happy with my life. I have friends, I have family, I'm loved, and I love in return.'

Cooper simply nodded. She didn't really want to have a conversation about the joys of living on the road right now.

'So, this person you saw,' she said. 'Can you describe them?'

'About five foot ten. Quite fat. Or, they were wearing a really bulky jacket and platforms. I mean, they could have been thin underneath it. Those puffers are quite massive. They had a baseball cap on.'

He shrugged.

'I didn't see their face, but, you know, I think they had brown hair. Or, you know, like a dark blond. It was shortish. Unless it was pulled back underneath the collar, which it might have been.'

'Male or female?'

'Shapeless,' Scrumpy replied. 'I don't really work with pronouns anymore. They were whatever they wanted to be.'

'I get what you're saying,' Cooper said, holding back her irritation. 'But we need to find a description of a suspect here. Saying male or female isn't about their personal choice. It's about what the police officers can look for when they're hunting a kidnapper.'

'I get that,' Scrumpy said. 'And I wish I could help. Even though it sounds like I'm profiling, if someone's done something bad, they need to be punished. All I can tell you is—'

'All you can tell me is that they might be fat or thin, depending on the coat they're wearing. They've got brown, possibly blond hair. And it might be short, but could be long, depending on if it's underneath the collar,' Cooper looked up, the irritation finally boiling over. 'Thank you for your help.'

'Sorry,' Scrumpy replied, and then frowned as a thought came to his mind.

'Actually, I do have something,' he said. 'The baseball cap they were wearing. It was navy-blue, but had like a gold crest on the front.'

'Okay. Did you see the crest?'

'No, they walked back across the road and I was only half paying attention. I think it was a duck.'

'A gold duck.'

'Hey,' Scrumpy looked hurt by the comment, stated in a disbelieving manner. 'I didn't see much, but I know a duck when I see one.'

Cooper nodded, noting this down.

'I'm guessing there's no point asking for an address or a phone number?' she asked.

At this, Scrumpy seemed even more offended.

'What, you think just because I don't have a house, I don't have a phone?' he replied. 'I've got a pay as you go. I need to be contactable. I do TikToks.'

'What, of you selling the *Big Issue?*'

'Nah. I'm mainly at the festivals. I do Diablos, Fire Poi and Devil Sticks, things like that. I'm quite a performer. You should check me out.'

He rummaged in his jacket pocket underneath the red *Big Issue* bib and pulled out a card.

'Here you go,' he said. 'It's got my number and my TikTok on it.'

'Appreciated,' Cooper said as she passed her own card across. 'If you think of anything else, please let us know.'

'There was one other thing,' Scrumpy replied. 'I know you're focused on the person in the hat, but there was a young kid, thirteen, fourteen years old, maybe, standing over there by the shop.'

He pointed about twenty yards from the pump.

'All the time the person with the hat was standing there, fiddling about with the pump, he was watching them. Then when they walked off, he followed them.'

'Was he following them, or was he with them?'

'Unsure,' Scrumpy replied. 'I don't think they knew he was there, because while they were buggering around with the pump, he was turning around left and right, keeping out of their sight. But then when they left, he walked over to the pump and took a photo of it.'

Cooper wrote this down. Maybe he was taking a photo to show they'd done it. Or maybe he was checking the QR code to see if it actually worked. Either way, it sounded like it wasn't a solo practitioner they were dealing with anymore.

By now, De'Geer had finished his examination and was walking over.

'All right?' he said, conversationally.

Scrumpy grinned.

'Bloody hell, when they made you, did they break the mould?'

'When they made me, I *ate* the mould,' De'Geer replied pleasantly, looking at Cooper. 'Are you done?'

'Yeah.' Cooper turned and nodded to Scrumpy. 'Thanks, I'll check out your TikToks.'

'You should, they're pretty awesome,' Scrumpy grinned.

De'Geer and Cooper started back towards Poland Street, where their squad car was parked.

'Flirting with the natives?' De'Geer asked.

'Nah, I like my men a little more clean-cut,' Cooper replied, linking her arm with De'Geer's. 'Did you get anything else?'

De'Geer shook his head.

'Whoever turned up, they kept a low profile. Maybe CCTV or whatever your witness there said can give us a bit more.'

He looked around.

'I get the feeling we're being watched.'

Cooper glanced around and saw that many of the tourists were looking at them. Some of them were frowning.

'This doesn't look good,' she said, as one of them, an old woman holding a phone in her hand, stomped up to stand in front of De'Geer, looking up at him and then at her phone.

'You're one of them, aren't you?' she said. 'The people who the serial killer left the money to.'

'I'm sorry?' De'Geer frowned.

The woman turned the phone to show him. It was a recent news piece that had just appeared on the BBC website and pushed the story to anyone who had notifications "on" in their phone's settings. On it was a photo of Declan at a crime scene. It was taken with a zoom lens and it looked like a photo of Declan, from when he had saved Parliament at the Queen's State Dinner. De'Geer was in the background, and unfortunately, he was imposing and quite visible.

'If you are commenting on the will that was left to our Detective Chief Inspector,' he said coldly, 'it was nothing but a sick joke and he is donating everything to victim support charities.'

'Yeah, that's just a guilty conscience, isn't it?' the old woman muttered in reply.

Cooper took the phone without asking and the woman went to complain, but paused as she saw Cooper's furious expression.

'It went up a minute ago,' she said, passing the phone back as she looked at De'Geer. 'That's why people are looking at us. Anyone who has a push notification has just seen a picture of the man they're now looking at here.'

De'Geer sighed.

'Looks like I'm part of the story as well now,' he said,

looking back at the woman. 'I don't know what the article says, but know this now. DCI Declan Walsh is a good man, and he's not in league with any serial killers. So I suggest you go on with your day before I get really angry and start arresting people.'

The woman paled, placed her phone in her pocket, and walked off.

De'Geer let out a long, deep breath.

'Let's get the evidence back to Doctor Marcos,' he said. 'At least at Temple Inn we don't risk finding riots on our doorstep.'

'I don't know,' Cooper said as they walked towards the car. 'If the BBC are now mentioning it, we're rapidly approaching the pitchforks at the doors stage.'

7

FLOWER POWER

Anjli hadn't been happy about being pulled off the Broad Street pump, but she was aware that De'Geer and Cooper alone were more than enough for what was required, and she understood the logic in having her speak to Antony Morgan. After all, she was one of the few people who had actually spoken to him three years earlier.

Morgan seemed to have gone up in the world since the last time she'd spoken to him. No longer a shop assistant in a Mile-End florist, he now had his own small boutique in a set of shops near Chancery Lane Tube Station. It felt no wider than an alleyway, but Anjli assumed that the postcode was a good one. The local businesses likely had good trade, and Morgan probably made a lot more from *Interflora* and online delivery orders than he did from walk-ins.

The shop looked old, even though it was a new design and new business; Morgan had obviously opted to try to give a more traditional, long-standing appearance. The green text above stated that the shop was called the *Green Man*, a title usually given to pubs more than florists. But the term *Green*

Fingers and suchlike had been around flowers for so long Anjli assumed there was a term that related to this.

Entering, she found herself facing Antony Morgan for the first time in three years.

He was on his own, a slim, effeminate man with very short, grey hair left long on top. His face was angular and slim, reminding her of a slightly anaemic David Bowie. He wore a slim-fit white shirt and jeans under what looked to be a dark-green apron. He wore gloves on his hands, but this seemed to be to stop himself from gaining nicks and cuts as he worked a pair of secateurs on a selection of thorned roses.

He looked up as if to greet his latest customer, but then his face darkened, and his eyes narrowed when he saw it was Anjli Kapoor.

'Well, well,' he said, placing the secateurs down and stepping away from them, as if making sure she knew he wasn't going for a weapon, his voice a strange lilt of both British and American. 'If it isn't Detective Inspector Kapoor.'

Anjli raised an eyebrow at this.

'How did you know that?' she asked. 'Last time we met, I was a Detective Sergeant.'

Morgan smiled, pulling off his gloves as he did so, grabbing some antiseptic hand gel and rubbing his hands with it, before placing it away.

'I watch the news,' he said. 'Your City of London unit's made you quite famous. When they mentioned your name, I noticed your rank had changed recently. I suppose congratulations are in order.'

He glanced around the florist shop with an idle gaze, but Anjli wondered if he was trying to find something.

He looked back at her.

'Of course, none of the news pieces have claimed

anything about you arresting the wrong person recently, but maybe that's a habit you've removed.'

Anjli's lips thinned as she glared at Morgan.

'I didn't get the wrong person,' she said. 'Thomas Blackthorne was the killer, and we both know it.'

'I know nothing like that,' Morgan shook his head. 'What I do know, however, is that you worked for a DCI who wanted only to take shortcuts in the case, and who was quite happy to let a case close without a true killer being found or brought to justice.'

He stopped for a moment, and the slightest of vindictive smiles appeared on his lips.

'I see you've not really changed your DCIs as well. What is it in the news right now? Your current DCI is being investigated for receiving money from a serial killer?'

'That's not the case and you know it,' Anjli snarled. 'Declan is an honest man.'

'Oh, I'm sure he is,' Morgan laughed. 'And I'm sure Ford was an honest woman too, until the moment she wasn't, no matter what her friends say.'

He sighed, walking over to where he had looked a moment earlier, picking up a handful of blue pansies and placing them down in front of Anjli.

'This is probably what you want,' he said. 'These are the pansies I sell in my shop. They're called Celestial Blue, and they're incredibly hard to find. Check them against whatever it is you're looking for now. I don't buy from the same place Blackthorne did. In fact, not many places would sell to me for the first two years.'

'And yet here you are.'

Morgan mouth-shrugged.

'I had an uncle pass away back home in Philadelphia,' he

explained as he opened a drawer, pulling out some wipes, and started wiping down the counter. 'Left me enough to start this place. You like it? I spent a fortune on renovations. The neighbouring shops were pissed at me for filling the street with builders.'

He looked down at the flowers.

'Come on, chop-chop, don't forget your evidence.'

Anjli hadn't intended to take the pansies, but the fact that he'd offered them in such a manner made her feel like being more of a jobsworth than she'd intended to be. Carefully, she pulled out a plastic baggie, large enough to place some of the blue pansy petals in, and, pulling on a latex glove, she made a point of gently placing several of the pansies into the bag.

Morgan, watching her, actually started to laugh.

'Tell me you are *not* serious,' he said.

Anjli looked back at him.

'If you're going to treat me like the enemy,' she said, 'then I'm going to do the same to you. If you can, I'd like some of your poppies to check, too.'

She looked around the shop.

'You've done well for yourself, Antony,' she said. 'I wasn't coming here to investigate. It was more looking to you as a witness.'

'And how's that?' Morgan asked, walking over to a small display of poppies, taking one and placing it, sullenly, in front of Anjli.

Anjli placed the additional flower into the bag before returning it to her pocket. She then looked back at him.

'There's a girl missing,' she said. 'As you already know, it seems. She matches the same MO as Blackthorne had.'

'But Thomas Blackthorne is dead,' Morgan replied

matter-of-factly. 'Killed himself after you forced him to take his own life.'

'We didn't force him to do anything,' Anjli replied. 'The flowers he had matched the ones found by the bodies. His cleanliness fetish matched the MO.'

She leant closer, resting her hands on the counter, moving in towards Antony Morgan, who, to his credit, didn't shuffle backwards.

'You worked with him every day,' she said. 'Are you seriously telling me he wasn't the killer? You might not have known at the time, but you've had three years to consider it.'

Morgan glared at Anjli for a long moment and then looked away.

'Thomas Blackthorne was a good man,' he said. 'Did he have problems? Sure. Did he have ghosts? Absolutely. Did he kill those children ...?'

He paused, looking away once more across his small florist shop.

'I couldn't tell you,' he breathed. 'We will never know.'

He took a deep breath, sighing it out, as if releasing pent-up tension.

'Look,' he continued. 'Everything you found out about Thomas made even me think he *could* have been the killer. But if you've now got somebody doing the same thing, maybe he wasn't. If the petals match, then that has to be somebody who knew the original murders, because I don't recall you mentioning the exact types of pansy they used, in the press.'

'Have you spoken to anybody in relation to the case?' Anjli asked. 'Anybody contacted you in the last few months asking about it?'

'No.' Morgan shook his head, but Anjli felt there'd been a pause beforehand, something left unspoken here. 'And if they did, I wouldn't talk to them, anyway. As I said, it took time for me to regain any kind of credibility in the industry. I would contact florists and wholesalers, and as soon as they realised I was someone who had worked with Blackthorne, I was shunned. It didn't help that I couldn't really get a previous employer reference, as my previous employer had blown his head off, and he was forced into doing so by armed police banging on his door.'

By this point, Anjli had had enough.

'Your boss,' she said, 'blew his head off while hiding in a suburban house with a hostage, a young boy tied up beside him. He had a sawn-off shotgun in his hand and had been anonymously demanding that the police close the case rather than focus on him. I get you have loyalty, and I get that at the time you might not have at least believed it, but believe me, Mister Morgan, your previous employer was a killer.'

'Yet it looks like he's killed again. How can that be?' Morgan shook his head sadly. 'And here you are again, trying to close the case without thinking about it, coming to me. Am I your only suspect?'

'You're not a suspect, Mister Morgan,' Anjli snapped. 'I came here out of courtesy, seeing if you knew anything, or if anybody had contacted you. This is a copycat. Blackthorne is dead; he was the only suspect. *I* know he did it. *You* know he did it. So let's not dance around the truth.'

Antony Morgan licked his lips as he watched Anjli across his counter.

'Nobody has come to me and asked about Thomas Blackthorne,' he said. 'If they have asked about him, then it's been to somebody else. Have you spoken to the parents?'

'Of Sarah and Mia?' Anjli frowned. 'What do you know that I don't?'

'I know they weren't happy with how things went,' Morgan shrugged. 'They wanted revenge and retribution and everything else that's in the thesaurus under that word, and you gave them a dead body that couldn't even be identified without a pathologist exam.'

'That wasn't my fault.'

'Of course it was your fault,' Antony Morgan growled, snapping back. 'Who else's fault could it be? You and your DCI. Trying to get home early because of the football, or whatever.'

Now it was his turn to lean forward.

'If you had both done your job better,' he said, 'then a good man would still be alive and you might have realised that Thomas Blackthorne wasn't the man that killed those two children.'

'If it wasn't Blackthorne, then who was it?' Anjli asked. 'Because, believe me, that's a question I've asked myself repeatedly over the last three years.'

'And yet you *still* have never reopened the case,' Morgan said sadly. 'Until someone else has appeared and done it for you.'

He bundled up the roses he'd been working on, passing a small bouquet of them to Anjli.

'Here,' he said, 'a parting gift. Roses. It's believed they used them when the sweating sickness hit London in the fifteen hundreds; rose water and rose oil were common ingredients in medieval medicine, believed to have cooling and calming properties – hence the "Ring of Roses" mentioned in the rhyme, when you hunted Thomas.'

He smiled darkly.

'And I get the feeling some of you guys will be sweating quite a lot over the next few days.'

Anjli took the flowers, more automatically than by choice, and placed her business card on the counter as Morgan wiped his hands once more with the antiseptic gel. It was almost as if he felt dirty being near her.

'You should be careful,' she said, nodding at the wipes. 'You'll get a germ fetish like your boss did.'

'Being clean isn't a sin, DI Kapoor,' Morgan sniffed. 'And these plants often have pesticides on them. I'd rather not eat with that shit on my fingers. It's when unclean things happen that the troubles start. You know, germs wise.'

Anjli thought about this for a moment, looked at the flowers, and then nodded.

'We'll talk again,' she said.

'No, DI Kapoor, the only way *you'll* talk to me from now on is with a solicitor present,' Morgan replied. 'The same solicitor that will now be placing a restraining order on you, keeping you away from me. I won't have you do to me what you did to Thomas.'

'What, find him guilty of murder?' Anjli snapped, and was about to leave when she stopped, mulling over what he'd said.

'I'm sure Ford was an honest woman too, until the moment she wasn't, no matter what her friends say,' she said.

'What?'

'Your own words, just now,' Anji replied. 'What "friends" are saying that she's still an honest woman?'

Morgan looked incredibly uncomfortable.

'I think you need to leave now,' Morgan folded his arms. 'I want—'

'What you *want*, Antony, is to tell me who's been talking to you,' Anjli replied, a little too sweetly. 'Because believe me, I will find out. The kidnapper knows my name, too. I wasn't on the police reports, only people connected to the case, people like you, for example, who met me, would know that. I'd like to think you wouldn't tell someone who wanted to kidnap a small girl to aim this at me, so who spoke to you?'

Morgan looked really uncomfortable now.

'I don't think—'

'Was it DCI Ford?' Anjli asked, watching his expression. 'DC Hart?'

There was a twitch, a poker player's tell. Anjli smiled triumphantly.

'Why have you been talking to DC Hart, Antony?'

Morgan turned and walked to the back door of his shop.

'If you won't go, I will,' he said. 'I never spoke to Ford or Hart. Sure, they both contacted me, but it was because they didn't believe Blackthorne was the killer, said you'd forced your own agenda. They had nobody else to tell apart from the parents.'

Anjli wanted to scream.

'You idiot,' she hissed. 'They signed off on it! They just said that to you because they wanted to get back at me! The DCI you mentioned I now work for? He's the one who had them put away in prison! And people like you just sit back and listen to whatever crap they say. What did they tell you?'

Morgan stared defiantly back.

'Solicitor.'

Knowing this wasn't ending with an answer, Anjli sighed as she walked out of the door to the florists.

'They set people up and watched them fall,' she muttered at the doorway. 'You'd better damn well hope they don't do that with you.'

Morgan said nothing, hurrying up to the door to the

florists and slamming it shut, locking it, and turning the OPEN sign to CLOSED, before hurrying back into the shop.

Anjli watched him, her eyes narrowing. Ford and Hart, or at least one of them, was playing a dangerous game.

But why? Was it to get back at Anjli? To screw over Declan?

Or both?

This was a question Anjli decided she needed to ask right now. She'd seen Ford a few months back, though, and she'd been as arrogant as ever.

Time to bypass the organ grinder and speak to the monkey, then.

'Good afternoon, Mrs Farrow,' Bullman said with a smile as the onetime Liz Walsh opened the door of her Tottenham apartment to face her. 'Do I call you Liz or Bet now?'

'You might as well stick with Liz. I suggested Henry start calling me Bet, but the problem is that so many people get confused and keep calling me by my original name. It seemed a lot easier just to stay with it,' Liz replied. 'Although Declan can sod off, as far as he's concerned, I'm Bet. Or better still, Mrs Farrow. I dealt with enough shit under the name Liz Walsh. I was hoping Bet Farrow would give me a new start.'

'Yeah, about that,' Bullman forced a smile. 'I don't think changing your name is going to stop the shit that comes with being Declan Walsh's ex-wife. Can I come in?'

Liz frowned, nodding as she stepped back, allowing Bullman into the apartment.

'Should I be calling my husband?' she asked.

'I think Henry's about to be called, actually,' Bullman replied. 'By my boss, David Bradbury, the City of London Commander.'

Liz sighed, resting her head against the wall behind her.

'Christ, what's Declan done now?'

'Actually, it's less Declan and more Jess,' Bullman replied. 'Is she here?'

'No, she's on her way back from college.' Liz was getting concerned now. 'What's happened?'

'You know what's happened with the Reaper, right?' Bullman asked. 'The will and all that?'

'Sure,' Liz nodded. 'We've seen the papers. Schnitter left everything to Declan. Dick move, if you ask me, but I can see how it's probably screwed him over.'

'Well, it's a little more far-reaching than that,' Bullman replied. 'Somebody's got a bit of a vendetta against him, and left a note in Hurley saying that because Declan's allied with a man who took children, they're going to do the same to him. And well ...'

She trailed off. She didn't need to explain to Liz anymore what the message meant. Declan only had one child.

'Oh my God,' Liz said. 'Do we have to hide again?'

'I think this is probably nothing more than a crazy with an agenda,' Bullman replied, her voice desperately trying to calm Liz. 'It's probably some weak-willed incel keyboard warrior who just wants to have their five minutes of fame, but we just want to be certain.'

She went to continue, but there was an almighty crack at the window in the room next to them, making them both duck from the echoing sound of what seemed to be a gunshot and breaking glass.

Bullman ran into the side room and saw that one of the

double-glazed windows now had a circular hole expanding out. It wasn't a bullet hole. It was likely something more like a .22 BB gun or airsoft rifle. However, it was still a weapon that, if used at close range, could cause damage.

Bullman pushed past Liz, now rambling to herself as she stared at the window, running to the door, slamming it open and looking out into the street.

It was busy; it was rush hour in Tottenham. But to the left, riding away on what looked to be some kind of electric dirt bike, was a hooded figure; young looking, maybe a teenager, with one hand on the handlebars while the other rummaged in their pocket, possibly replacing an airsoft pistol.

'You son of a bitch!' Bullman screamed, pulling out her phone and taking photo after photo, hoping that it wasn't so far that she couldn't make out any kind of registration number.

That said, if it was an electric bike, it wouldn't have one, anyway.

She turned back to the apartment and saw Liz Farrow standing there, a look of resignation on her face.

'And thus it starts again,' she said. 'I'll call Jess, get her home now.'

'I don't think this is as serious as it looks,' Bullman replied. 'But, until we get things done, I think she needs to stay here.'

Liz walked off, muttering about grabbing a phone and destroying Jess's evening with Prisha. Bullman watched one last time after the mysterious shooter, then texted Monroe.

It was best that Declan heard about this from a friend.

8

SCHOOL VISITS

AFTER SPEAKING WITH BRADBURY, DECLAN HAD TRAVELLED over to Mile End and Kelsey Primary School. He hadn't wanted to; he'd wanted to solve the case of who was burning holes into photos, but he also knew he needed to keep his eyes forward on the case in hand.

At the main reception, he explained who he was, showing his ID, and this led him through to a side room where, after a few minutes, the headteacher, Joanne Linton, appeared. She was tall, slim, and had grey hair cut into a pixie cut. The grey looked premature because, as far as Declan could work out, she was no older than late thirties to early forties, and he did wonder if it was a bottle-dye job, silver hair being quite popular these days.

'Mister Walsh,' she said. 'What do I call you ... Detective Chief Inspector?'

'Declan's fine,' Declan rose, shaking her hand.

'I hope you don't mind,' she said, 'we don't really want to have you walking around the school today. The children aren't aware of what's happened. Seeing a strange man, especially a police detective ...'

'I get that,' Declan replied. 'I was hoping you might be able to give me some information.'

'Of course,' Linton nodded to the chairs, waving him to sit down. 'Would you like some water, a cup of tea, coffee perhaps? They're always quieter after lunch and the mid-afternoon break, so things are a little less chaotic. Until home time, at least. And you really don't want to be around during that.'

'I'm good,' Declan smiled. 'I just want to get some questions answered and then move on. We're kind of against the clock on this one.'

Miss Linton nodded. She settled down opposite him, flattening out the flowered dress that she was wearing, placing her hands on her lap.

'It was such a shock,' she said. 'I wasn't here when the last child was taken.'

Declan looked up from his notes.

'How long have you been here?'

'About a year and a half. I came in at Easter last year, which meant I finished off the Summer term and then started the full year in September. This is the start of my second full year here.'

She smiled.

'School years can be confusing.'

'You said you came in at Easter. I thought most headteachers didn't leave during the terms?'

'Margaret had her own issues,' Miss Linton said. 'She was the previous headteacher. She couldn't get over the fact that she'd had a child die on her watch. I know it wasn't as simple as that. But Sarah was a known student, always helping teachers, always going to after-school activities ...'

She shrugged.

'There are some things you can't really get over.'

'I understand,' Declan replied. 'Hopefully we can make sure that this isn't something that sits over you.'

'I'd appreciate that,' Miss Linton smiled politely. 'I understand she was on a family trip?'

'Yes,' Declan replied. 'We're speaking to her parents. They'd gone to the Egyptian room because she was a big fan of Egypt. And then within a matter of minutes she was gone. Like a ghost.'

'Terrible. I'll call them later.'

'Perhaps you could also explain why you allow parents to take their children out of school during term time?'

'Unfortunately, there's not much I can do about that,' Miss Linton pursed her lips at the question.

'You can't punish the parents?'

'Well, It *is* illegal to take your kids out of school during term-time, and often it can lead to a fine,' Miss Linton explained. 'Unless you have a good reason, that is, and a visit to a museum doesn't really constitute a good enough reason.'

'So you fine them?'

'Yes, but half the time they don't care. We can't, well, *police* them like you might. And, right now, I think they're feeling worse than any punishment we could give – but feel free to ask me anything.'

'Does Debbie have any enemies?' Declan asked.

'Detective – I mean, Declan – she's nine years old,' Miss Linton replied. 'She's just starting Year Five. If she has any enemies, they were just going to shout nasty names at each other.'

'Sorry, I didn't mean it in that respect,' Declan replied. 'Does the family have any problems? Are there any adults in her social circle that have issues? I mean, I remember when I was a kid I'd managed to piss off a few locals.'

'I don't really know what your childhood was like, Mister Walsh,' Miss Linton replied curtly, and Declan got the impression that this question had pushed him away from "friendly Declan" to "officious Detective Chief Inspector Walsh". 'But here we have an open and inclusive group. Debbie was-*is* well-liked. There are no problems that I can know of. Her parents are both members of the school board. They attend after-school activities.'

Declan noted this down in his book. *If the parents were so involved, it could explain why Miss Linton was wary of fining them for taking their child out of class.*

'You mentioned Sarah,' he replied. 'Did Debbie ever meet her? Did they know each other?'

'Not that I can see,' Miss Linton shook her head. 'When Sarah, God rest her soul, passed away, she was also in Year Five, nine or ten years old, and that meant that Debbie would have been in Year One, maybe even Reception at that time. The Key Stages don't really pay much attention to each other. Key Stage One, Two, and Three, when you move from one to the other, it's almost like going to a different world.'

'Thank you.' Declan noted that down as well. 'Are there any teachers that get on with her? With Debbie?'

Miss Linton frowned, thinking back.

'Pretty much all the teachers get on with her. She was a lovely kid. *Is* a lovely kid. Sorry,' she shook her head. 'I'm already envisioning her as dead. I don't mean to, it's just, you know, with the history.'

Declan understood.

'And you've not seen any strange figures around the school?'

Miss Linton laughed at this.

'We're a Mile End Primary School,' she said. 'We *always* have dodgy figures wandering around outside the gates. Most of the time, they're either teachers or parents. But in answer to your question, and on a more serious note, we've not noticed anybody appearing that shouldn't be here. We have quite good security for the school. That comes, in a way, from previous occurrences. As I mentioned, a lot of parents will often help out. School Assistants will make sure that things are okay, and even people like the playground monitors and the dinner ladies pretty much know the children. If somebody was out of the ordinary, it would have been raised.'

Declan placed away his notebook.

'Well, thank you,' he said. 'If I could get a list of the teachers and ...'

'Oh, I've already done that,' Miss Linton said, picking up some headed notepaper. On it was a printed list of names. 'Here are every teacher and support assistant that we have on duty, as well as the ones not around today. If anybody here turns up on your list, then at least I might be able to help.'

'Thank you,' Declan folded the papers, placing them away in his jacket pocket. 'If there's anything else you can think of, please let me know.'

He pulled out his card and passed it to her.

'We're against the clock on this, and we're very much aware that if somebody is pretending to be the same man that took Sarah ...'

He didn't need to say anything else. Miss Linton understood exactly what he was stating.

If they didn't finish fast, Debbie would be dead.

'Whatever we can think of, I'll let you know,' she shook her head. 'So sad.'

Declan nodded and, after saying farewell, exited the school through the main reception and headed towards his car.

As he did so, however, he noticed a woman waiting for him, standing on the kerb near the side of his police issue Audi.

'Are you the detective running the case?' she asked.

Declan paused. There was something mildly confrontational about the woman, but he couldn't quite place what it was. She was in her thirties, stocky built, and bald, with what looked to be a headscarf over her head. She had no eyebrows and an ageless quality to her face that meant that when she grew older, you would never be able to tell what age she was. She also had a mask of fury on her face.

'When you say the case ...' he started.

'The missing girl,' the woman replied. 'Are you here connected to the missing girl?'

'My name is DCI Declan Walsh. We're helping Mile End in the case.'

The woman nodded, almost to herself as he spoke his name.

'I've heard of you,' she said. 'You've been in the press a lot recently, and not for good things.'

Declan forced a smile, wondering if this was where the argument was going.

'Look,' he said, 'we're very busy—'

'I know how busy you are,' the woman interrupted. 'And I'm not talking about all this crap going on at the moment in the press. I've seen you in the news about the things that you've done. You work with her, don't you?'

'Her?'

The woman nodded, her lips tight, as if she didn't want to carry on talking.

'Kapoor,' she replied. 'You work with DS Anjli Kapoor?'

'She's a DI now,' Declan replied. 'And that you know her old rank means that you know something about her past.'

The woman nodded.

'My name's Stephanie,' she said. 'Stephanie Thompson.'

'Thompson,' Declan replied, the pieces now falling into place. 'Of course.'

'Sarah was my daughter,' Stephanie replied. 'My daughter, who was murdered by a man your partner claimed *killed himself.*'

She looked back up at Declan.

'So, tell me, DCI Walsh of the City of London Police, helping Mile End solve a case that people have said was already solved, how the hell is a *dead man taking more people?*'

STEPHANIE SAT ACROSS THE TABLE FROM DECLAN, SIPPING HER herbal tea.

'Alopecia,' she said, the single word stated as some kind of explanation. 'It happened after I lost my daughter. The stress of everything meant that my hair came out in clumps. Some of it went white and patchy and then kind of felt like straw. Within a year, I was completely bald. Eyebrows too.'

She looked up from the cup.

'They gave me wigs to start with,' she said. 'Said it would help with the transition, but honestly, I find it easier just to wear a headscarf or a hat. The biggest problem is to make sure I put sun cream on it. Sunburned heads are really not fun.'

'I'm sorry to hear,' Declan said, sipping his own coffee. After Stephanie had explained who she was, she had pointed out there was a local coffee shop a two-minute walk from the school that would have eased up after the lunchtime rush, and perhaps Declan would like to have a chat with her about what had happened. Declan hadn't really wanted to have a chat with her, but it felt quite insistent, and if this did turn out to be connected to the previous case, he didn't want something landing on his shoulders down the line by *not* having the chat.

He was, however, aware that by having this meeting, he was potentially risking Anjli's anger when she realised he was talking to witnesses from previous cases, one that Anjli now wondered whether she had actually solved or not.

'What can I do for you, Stephanie?' he asked. 'I'm aware you're angry, and I get it, but having read the case notes from three years ago, Blackthorne looked the obvious candidate.'

Stephanie nodded, sipping gently at her cup.

'I get that,' she said. 'But I always felt there was something off, you know? DS Kapoor never solved the case, never gave us closure. She cack-handedly affected it, and Blackthorne escaped.'

'I don't think escape is the term I would have used,' Declan replied. 'He placed a shotgun under his head and pulled the trigger.'

'Okay, escaped justice then, and I don't mean heavenly justice,' Stephanie replied. 'But you've got to see it from my point of view, Mister Walsh. My daughter never got justice, and they just simply closed the case, said it was done, that Blackthorne was obviously the killer, and with him dead, nobody else would die. I thought they were right. I didn't know they were lying to me, covering their tracks.'

'They?'

'DCI Ford and DS Kapoor,' Stephanie muttered. 'They were the only people working on it.'

'And what do you mean by covering tracks—'

'Come on. Ford gets kicked off the force less than a year later? Kapoor's transferred? Something dodgy was going on. They covered it all up.'

She leant forward now, placing an arm on the table, her other hand still holding the cup.

'But it's not the case, now, is it?' she asked bitterly. 'Because now someone else has gone, and they're using the same coloured flowers, and they're using the rhyme. Ring-a-Ring-a-Roses, a pocket full of posies, a-tishoo, a-tishoo, they all fall down.'

'You seem to know a lot about a case that hasn't been passed out to the press,' Declan replied coldly.

'I've got a friend who worked in Mile End,' Stephanie shrugged. 'Someone sympathetic to how I am and what I've had to deal with. She kept me updated on what was going on. It's how I know you came into Mile End and got rid of Ford.'

She held up a hand to stop Declan from talking.

'As far as I'm concerned, that's good riddance. DCI Ford was a bitch, treated us like scum, thought she was "holier than thou". My daughter's death was nothing more than an annoyance, a mark on a career tick sheet that caused her problems. The press might have been happy with the outcome, sold a fair few newspapers, I'm sure, but Ford? She was more than happy to find a way to close it without having to deal with things. But then, I'm guessing you've got a measure of her personality as well, considering what you did to her.'

Declan nodded. He had very much learned about DCI Ford when he'd worked for her. The fact she'd tried to have him accused of murder to clear her own corrupt name was still forefront in his memories.

'I'm angry at Kapoor for not pushing it, but I do get why she didn't,' Stephanie said, 'Though, I won't forgive her. And if this turns out to be the same thing ...'

She shrugged, seemingly out of words for the moment.

'What do you want, Stephanie?' Declan asked. 'Revenge?'

'No,' Stephanie replied, her voice softening slightly. 'I want justice. I want to know that my daughter didn't die in vain. And I want to make sure no other parent has to go through what I did. If that means bringing down anyone who was involved, even tangentially, then so be it, no matter the sacrifice.'

'I understand,' Declan replied. 'We're doing everything we can to find Debbie and bring her home safely. If there's anything you know, anything at all, that can help us, please, tell me.'

Stephanie looked at him for a long moment before speaking.

'There was always something off about Blackthorne's death,' she said finally. 'The way he did it, so suddenly, right after being accused. It felt too convenient, too ... neat. I don't have proof, but my friend at Mile End says they saw Ford move the case aside, that someone helped her cover it up.'

Declan felt a chill run down his spine.

'Do you have any idea who that might be?' he asked.

'No.' Stephanie shook her head.

'I'll look into it,' Declan promised. 'Thank you for talking to me, Stephanie. I'll make sure DI Kapoor knows you're still seeking answers. And if you remember anything else, anything at all, call me.'

Stephanie nodded, her eyes sad but resolute.

'I will. And, Detective, please find her. Find Debbie and bring her back.'

'I'll do everything in my power,' Declan assured her. As he stood up to leave, he felt the weight of the promise he had just made land solidly on his shoulders.

The stakes were higher than ever, and he knew he couldn't afford to fail.

Stephanie, however, hadn't moved, simply staring at him.

'What?' he asked, confused.

'You're just ... different from how I imagined,' she said. 'From what I've heard about you.'

'And what have you heard?'

Stephanie, at this point realising she'd said too much, rose.

'I need to go now,' she said hurriedly. 'Find the girl.'

'No, wait,' Declan held a hand out to stop her. 'Someone told you about me, but I don't fit what they said. Who did you speak to? Was it this person at Mile End? I was only there a couple of days. Maybe they're more recent?'

Stephanie pushed past him, walking out of the coffee shop, and as she did so, Declan realised what had been bugging him about her earlier comment.

'Hey,' he shouted as he walked out of the shop, following her. 'You said you were happy Ford was arrested, but you never mentioned DC Hart. Did you ever speak—'

'I never spoke to her before she was arrested,' Stephanie walked off, back to Declan. 'I'm sorry, I'm running late.'

Declan stared after her.

'I've got a friend who worked in Mile End, someone sympathetic to how I am and what I've had to deal with. She kept me updated on what was going on. It's how I know you came into Mile End and got rid of Ford.'

The "she" could have been DC Hart. Who, according to Stephanie's comment about only dealing with Ford and Kapoor, would have been a name they didn't know much about. But Stephanie had just stated she'd never spoken to her before she was arrested.

Spoken to "her."

Declan had never given the first name or the sex of DC Sonya Hart. So, if Stephanie had never spoken to her, how would she know who Hart was? And if Hart was the friend keeping Stephanie in the loop, how was she getting the information, and why was she doing this?

Declan sighed audibly.

He was going to have to go chat to someone he really didn't want to confront.

9

VISITING HOURS

With Anjli and Declan both having dealt with DCI Ford and DC Sonya Hart in the past, it was decided that they should split their forces for this one. Ford was currently in HM Prison Downview, an hour's drive just outside of Banstead in Surrey, while Sonya, classed as a lesser dangerous subject, her defence having claimed during the trial that she was being forced into her actions by DCI Ford, was now in a more open prison at HM Prison East Sutton Park, near Maidstone in Kent.

Anjli, having seen Ford more recently, had suggested that Declan go in as a new pair of eyes while she spoke to Hart. This was done partly so that she didn't have to face her onetime boss, but Declan knew that this was also because Anjli really wanted to speak to Hart more than Ford right now, especially following the possible fact that Sonya Hart had been interfering with this case.

Upon arriving at Downview, Declan had passed through security with simplistic ease: a warrant card, a signed request form and a scowling expression being all that was needed these days to get what you required. And, even though it was now late afternoon, there was no waiting as Marie Ford, no longer a DCI, walked into the hall; a bare, windowless room filled with plastic chairs welded to tables.

Like the last time Anjli had seen Ford here, the room was empty, deliberately so, as other inmates, seeing Ford talking to police, could actively affect her prison experience. Anjli had hoped at the time that Ford would have been found out, and Declan found he had the same wish as he watched her enter. She was wearing the prison-issue pale-grey sweatshirt and joggers, her grey hair still cut in the same short style she'd worn while serving at Mile End. Anjli had claimed she had a small scar on her cheek, but this was now a faded white scratch.

'Checking the place out before you come and stay?' she asked. 'I hate to remind you, this isn't a mixed prison, Declan, you're going to have to find your own place when they lock you up.'

Declan waited, allowing Marie Ford to get whatever it was out of her system. He knew there was no love lost between the two of them; after all, she had tried to kill him, and he had used a piece of paper she'd given him, telling whoever saw it he was working for her, to his advantage, saving his job but showing her to be the murderer.

It had been before he joined the Last Chance Saloon.

It was hard to believe that so much had happened in the intermediate time.

'How's your dad?' Ford asked, before scrunching her face slightly. 'Oh, I'm sorry. I forgot. He died, didn't he? Terrible thing. Accident, wasn't it? No, wait ... he was killed by a serial killer who's now left you everything in his will.'

She leant back in her chair, smugly staring at Declan.

'How's Monroe doing?' she asked. 'He doesn't owe you anything in his will, does he? Because if he did, I'd be very worried if I were him.'

Declan said nothing. He simply waited it out, knowing eventually Ford's curiosity would gain the better of her, and she'd need to know why he was there.

It took less time than he expected for her to finally lean closer, placing her elbows onto the table between them as she jutted her chin out, facing him.

'The least you could bloody do is speak to me,' she said, 'after what you did.'

'After what I did?' Declan laughed. 'Marie—'

'*DCI* Ford.'

'*Marie*,' Declan insisted. 'You killed people, all for crypto coins. You thought you'd got away with it, even set me up as a patsy, thinking that because nobody wanted me on the force, I was expendable.'

He shook his head.

'You deserve everything you've got.'

'It doesn't matter,' Ford shrugged. 'Eventually I'll get out. I've got a little nest egg waiting for me.'

'I hope you're not thinking about the *Hood* Cryptocurrency,' Declan laughed. 'I don't know if you noticed, but it fell off a cliff. What you thought you had, those millions of pounds' worth of tokens, I think it's worth about seven pounds fifty right now.'

He waggled his finger.

'That's the problem with gambling, Ford. The house always wins.'

Marie Ford glared at Declan.

'I thought it would be Anjli,' she eventually said. 'You know, who came to see me today.'

'Ah, so you *were* expecting one of us.'

Ford said nothing, simply smiling. Declan knew that she'd been waiting for a call in relation to Blackthorne.

'I'm guessing you know about the Posies Killer being back,' he said.

Ford nodded.

'I get told things. I'm quite popular, still. You should try it one day.'

'Try what?'

'Being popular. Does wonders for you. Especially when you're in prison.'

She shrugged.

'Although it's probably a bit too late for you to get popular before they arrest you and put you away for what you've done.'

Declan was wondering whether this was mocking, or whether Marie Ford had actually given herself some kind of persecution complex, where Declan had got away with a ton of things that she felt she wasn't guilty of.

'Have you spoken to anybody in relation to that case?' he asked.

Ford shrugged.

'I'm sure I have, here and there,' she said. 'Prisoners love to hear my wartime stories. Why do you ask?'

The question was given in a mocking way, the kind of way that someone who already knew the answer would ask. Declan decided he'd had enough.

'There's a girl missing, Marie, a nine-year-old girl, and currently everything that's happening is pointing at a man who's dead. Somebody – maybe even you – pressured Anjli, naming her in connection to something Anjli wasn't even officially mentioned in. Yet here she is being targeted by a copycat.'

'Couldn't happen to a nicer person,' Ford smiled. 'So, what exactly is this conversation about, Declan? Are you here to gloat? Are you here to see how the other half lives?'

She leant closer again, licking her lips in anticipation of the answer.

'Why are you here? Are you visiting to make me a deal? Because I have one I want to make.'

SONYA HART HADN'T CHANGED SINCE THE LAST TIME ANJLI SAW her, three years earlier, when she was removed from Mile End's roster after going postal on a wife-batterer. Doing nothing to alter her appearance, she was still short and slim, with mousey-brown hair in a bob, and wide-rimmed glasses. She looked like Velma from *Scooby Doo;* at least if Velma helped cover up murders. In a similar sweatshirt and joggers uniform to the one Anjli had seen Ford wear in Downview the last time she'd seen her, Hart leant back in the chair in the waiting room with a casual arrogance as Anjli sat down opposite her.

'DI Anjli Kapoor, what a surprise,' she said, with the tone of somebody who really didn't mean it.

'I'm sure it is,' Anjli smiled, with the smile of someone who *also* didn't really mean it. 'You know why I'm here, so let's cut the shit.'

Sonya Hart nodded, straightening in the chair.

'Straight to business, I appreciate that,' she said. 'You want to know about Debbie Watson, whether I've been in contact with anybody.'

'Debbie disappeared this morning. How do you know about the case?'

'I have friends. And we can discuss this if you want, but I'm guessing you're on a clock.'

Anjli shifted irritably on her seat.

'I want to know if it was you who spoke to Stephanie Thompson. And I also want to know if it was you who spoke to Antony Morgan. Because currently both of those people are getting information that only you or Ford could tell them,' Anjli snapped back.

'I hope you're not accusing me of manipulating a witness,' Hart smiled casually. 'How could I do such a thing? I'm in prison. Look around, Anjli. I can't phone out privately. I can't send emails.'

Anjli leant forward.

'And yet you know of a case that happened this morning,' she said. 'This isn't the days of Charles Dickens. I know damn well what you can get away with in here. I've seen others do it. And I can tell you now that if you wanted to send an email, I'm sure you could.'

She tried to lower her voice to stop the anger building.

'Antony Morgan as good as told me that either you or Marie Ford has been talking to him.'

Hart made a dismissive shrug.

'Well, maybe you should speak to her then,' she said.

'We are,' Anjli replied. 'DCI Walsh is there right now.'

'DCI Walsh?' Hart shook her head. 'I must have missed that little promotion.'

'Oh, I don't think so,' Anjli replied. 'You always struck me as the one who has the finger on the pulse. You knew I was a DI. You named me as such when I arrived.'

Sonya Hart stared at Anjli for a long moment and then shrugged with a resigned expression on her face.

'You've got me,' she said. 'I do know more about you than you think. I know about your cases. I know about the people who want you out.'

'People want me out? I'm touched,' Anjli replied. 'They can get in line.'

'Brave words,' Hart tutted. 'I seem to recall hearing similar from my own boss back before we were rudely removed from our roles.'

'Rudely removed ...' Anjli shook her head. 'I've read the case report, Sonya. Don't give me any victim blame here. You did the crime, you're doing the time, you know how it works. If you didn't want to be in prison, you shouldn't have tried to steal so much money.'

'Didn't you hear?' Hart replied calmly. 'I was an unwilling patsy, just like Declan. Although I didn't get a magic letter that said that I did everything on behalf of DCI Ford, like he did. Convenient, wasn't it?'

Anjli could feel her gut tightening with anger. She didn't want to be here. In fact, she wanted to shout, to scream.

'Just tell me what you did.'

'Say my name.'

'Tell me what you did, Sonya.'

'Say my *name*.'

'Tell me what you did, *Detective Constable Hart*.'

'There you go,' Hart smiled. 'Oh, it feels good to hear that again. How's your cyber-guy doing? William Fitzwarren, isn't it? Came from money, never needed for anything in his life? I've read about him as well. I wonder if he's up to the challenge with this one?'

'Why wouldn't he be?'

'I don't know. Depends on the level of the suspect he's up against,' Hart continued to smile now, obviously in control for the moment. 'Maybe you could use the woman that betrayed your team, who then became a hacker for MI5.'

Anjli ignored the comment, although noted that if Sonya Hart knew about Trix Preston, she was *definitely* paying attention to what was going on in the Last Chance Saloon, as someone was feeding her intel.

Eventually Sonya Hart shrugged.

'Look, I'd love to help you,' she said. 'I really would, but there's nothing in it for me.'

'And what would you like, then?'

'I don't know,' Hart replied. 'Come back to me tomorrow, and we'll have a think about it.'

'Tomorrow might be too late,' Anjli said. 'Tomorrow, Debbie Watson might be dead.'

'Nah, you've got time,' Sonya leant back in her chair now. 'Debbie Watson wasn't taken until what, nine-thirty?'

Anjli paused Hart from continuing, holding her hand up.

'We haven't made that public,' she said. 'How do you know that?'

'I'm aware of what's going on,' Hart replied casually. 'I'm aware of lots of things. I'm aware, for example, that you found out about this, not while at the office, but while at your Hurley house. With your lover, Declan. Wiping terrible words from his walls at eleven in the morning on a workday. What was it, a late night beforehand? Maybe if you'd been at work earlier, you could have stopped all this.'

She leant closer.

'Good job they used organic materials, isn't it? Easier to wipe clean ...'

Anjli's eyes darkened.

'If I find that you're the one—'

'That I'm the one what?' Hart leant back. 'I'm the one who's caused some kind of public backlash against you? Your boyfriend did that when he accepted a dead man's payout from a serial killer. That I'm the one who took a photo and burned eyeballs out of his teenage kid—'

She stopped as Anjli launched across the table now, grabbing her by the front of her sweatshirt. The guard, seeing this, moved closer.

'Oi!' she shouted.

Anjli let go, still in position, gripping and un-gripping her hands as she forced herself to calm down.

'You've just given your hand,' she hissed. 'Declan only just told me about that. Even the team doesn't know yet.'

'I've done nothing, know nothing,' Hart said. 'Check my records. I've not been in contact with anybody for days. Maybe I'm psychic? I'm a model prisoner, don't you know? Spend my time here helping people pass their computer GCSEs. It's amazing how many women never had a good education before they fell into crime.'

'Let me guess, it's far better to have one, then fall into crime?'

Hart shrugged.

'Currently, I'm on the fence,' she said. 'But again, maybe I *do* know about this. I have friends and of course, I get told lots of things the police don't. I also know a few people in North London, if you need any help to find anyone ...'

She leant back, holding her hands out as if holding a bike's handlebars.

'Beep beep, bang bang,' she said, before rising. Anjli wasn't sure what she was going on about here, but mentally noted it down, anyway.

'I don't feel comfortable in this room anymore,' Sonya Hart now said. 'Guard, you witnessed Detective Inspector Kapoor try to kill me.'

'I grabbed you by the front—'

'She tried to kill me,' Sonya Hart smiled back at her. 'I would like to raise a complaint. I would like this woman to be banned from ever attending this prison. I don't feel safe. She's accusing me of assault, of kidnapping. I've done no such thing. It's harassment.'

She paused, as if she couldn't quite leave it at that.

'And, for the record, I don't know if Marie's been playing games with you as well,' she continued. 'We've never spoken since you dumped us into prisons. Well, maybe once or twice. But these were more ...'

She considered the words carefully.

'Councils of war,' she finished, before walking out of the room, the guard following, leaving Anjli alone.

Anjli leant back in the chair, furious at herself for letting her emotions get the better of her. But then one of the final lines that Sonya had said, when she thought she was on top and when the arrogance was heavy in her voice, came back through.

'Come back to me tomorrow, and we'll have a think about it.'

Not *I'll* have a think. *We.*

'I don't know if Marie's been playing games with you as well.'

As well. As good a confession from Hart that she was playing games as Anjli was likely to get. She knew without a doubt that somehow Sonya Hart was involved, whether in the disappearance, in Jess's attacks, or both. Anjli wasn't sure.

'Hey,' she said, looking back at the door, where another guard waited to take her out. 'I want to see every record, every note, on that inmate right now.'

She stood up, brushing herself down, forcing herself to calm.

'I want to know exactly who Sonya Hart's been talking to over the last week and why.'

THE DEMAND HAD BEEN SIMPLE AND, AFTER ORGANISING IT, Declan now sat back on the chair as he watched ex-DCI Marie Ford devour her large Big Mac and fries, with chocolate milkshake on the side.

'Oh, God,' she said, smiling widely as she finished the burger, pieces of lettuce still in her teeth. 'It's the small things you miss when you're in prison. Genuinely, Declan, I suggest you get as much as you can before they take you in, 'cos they're gonna take you in. You are aware, right?'

Declan ignored the comment, waiting patiently until the food was gone.

'There,' he said. 'I've fulfilled my side, now you fulfil yours.'

Ford wiped down her mouth with a napkin, nodding as she pushed the packaging aside, motioning for the guards to come and pick it up.

The guard ignored her.

'I've been talking to some friends,' she said, unbothered by the ignoring guards. 'Underworld people that are dangerous but who owe me favours. I'm kind of thinking about being a bit more like Ellie Reckless, you know? Someone who can manipulate people, gain favours owed and all that kind of thing, and I've got a few favours that I've built up. I'm willing to burn them all for you, Declan, to find out where this small girl is.'

She leant back, taking a long deep sip of the milkshake, and then burped, laughing as she did so.

'Can I take this back in with me?' she said to the guard, who stared at her icily. 'Nah, didn't think so.'

'Ford,' Declan's voice was cold, commanding. He'd had enough of this. 'There's a girl missing.'

'I know,' Ford replied. 'But don't you worry, okay? You'll find her tomorrow.'

'What do you mean, we'll find her tomorrow?'

Ford sniffed dismissively.

'Look, I'll speak to some people, ask around, put in my favours, and I'll guarantee you that through my work you'll find Debbie Watson by lunchtime – let's say noon – tomorrow.'

'That's too convenient a statement,' Declan said.

'I was a DCI of Mile End,' Ford replied. 'You saw me in action. Let's just say I've got a good feeling, that with my help, I'll find you your girl.'

'And what do you want for this, apart from your banquet in front of you?'

'Bullman, the one who came and saw me with Anjli, when you'd lost PC Mainsworth ... I understand she's shacking up with the Commander of the City of London police now. She's second in charge, Deputy Chief Superintendent or something.'

She shook her head.

'Must really piss you off she was the same rank as you when you first met her. And now she's pretty much running the City of London, because let's face it, I met Bradbury and he's a prick.'

'She was a DCI when we met.'

'Oh, so that's *so* much better for your ego then,' Ford

grinned. 'Look, I just want a good word put in for me. Point out that I helped out when I didn't need to. Solved a crime you couldn't. Helped my old buddy Anjli.'

She rose, and accidentally or not, she knocked the chocolate milkshake to the floor, where the cup burst open, spilling the contents across the ground.

'Whoopsies,' she said. 'I'd clean it up, but I'm guessing you need me to get going quickly on this.'

Declan looked at the guard apologetically.

'If she can get anything that helps us find this child ...' he said.

The guard sighed.

'Come back to me at lunchtime tomorrow,' Ford said as, while the guard led her out of the waiting room, she looked back at him. 'And bring us a KFC, yeah? Like a Zinger burger? I haven't had one of them for ages.'

10

OUIJA BOARDS

'OK, THEN, LADDIES AND LASSIES,' MONROE SAID AS HE STOOD at the front of the briefing room at the end of the day. 'What do we ...'

He trailed off, frowning, and then looked at DCI Esposito standing beside him.

'Sorry,' he continued. 'This should be more your statement, shouldn't it?'

'Well, you do outrank me,' Esposito said, stepping forward, looking at the briefing room.

It was early in the evening, the room was still full. Declan sat with Anjli beside him, both recently arrived from their respective prisons, DS McAlroy sat beside Billy, and at the back, De'Geer, Dr Marcos, and Cooper were in their usual positions. Bullman wasn't there, but apart from that, everybody else was.

'I'd like to say, "what do we have?"' Esposito continued. 'But, first off, I'd like to make a complaint.'

Monroe's face fell slightly, almost as if he was irritated at the comment.

'And what exactly would you like to complain about?' he asked with fake politeness.

'DCI Walsh spoke to Stephanie Thompson,' DS McAlroy read from her notes. 'We would have liked to have been involved in this conversation, as this is not part of the ongoing investigation but is, in fact, a Mile End investigation.'

Esposito looked back at Monroe.

'I think you can understand, Alex, that although we're happy for you guys to help us with this current case, what with Anjli being involved historically, if you're going to start talking about the cold case, then we need to be with you every step.'

'If I may?' Declan held a hand up to halt Monroe's most likely expletive-filled reply. 'I didn't intend to speak to Stephanie. She ambushed me as I left the school.'

'The school that Sarah went to,' Esposito said.

'Yes, and the school that *Debbie* goes to,' Declan replied. 'Which means it's the current investigation, *as well* as the historical one.'

'And Anjli speaking to Blackthorne's old assistant?'

'Crossing "T's" and dotting "I's",' Anjli gave a polite, fake smile. 'You know, Guv. Police work. Although DCI Walsh and I did go speak to ex-DCI Ford and ex-DC Hart today at their respective prisons, in full transparency for the room.'

Esposito went to reply, but before he could, Monroe waved Declan back into his chair and looked at Esposito.

'There's going to be crossover,' he said. 'We both knew that. And the woman did blindside the poor bugger, and they both worked with Hart and Ford, whereas you never did. So let's give them these and just get on with the case. Us arguing about who's got pissing rights isn't exactly going to help the wee girl that has been taken, and I'm sure all the information will come out in the chat.'

Esposito reluctantly nodded.

Monroe, noticing this, placed a hand on his shoulder.

'We're here to help you, Alvaro,' he said. 'You came to us, remember? If you're unhappy at any point, you can take the case back. We can second Anjli over to you if she wants to be involved, but it is a Mile End case whether you want it or not.'

'No, you're right,' Esposito nodded. 'It's just—'

'I get it,' Declan said from the side. 'It's not your case because it was Ford's, and now it feels like it's not your case because Anjli's been involved. We're here to help you, not the other way around. And I apologise if that's the way it feels.'

Monroe gave a small smile to Esposito, as if to say, "Happy now?" And Esposito, in return, gave a small smile back.

'Detective Superintendent, as the ranking officer in the room, I'm happy for you to run the briefing,' he said, taking a seat next to McAlroy.

Monroe seemed surprised by the comment, almost as if he'd expected an argument, but wasn't about to look a gift horse in the mouth.

Declan watched Esposito carefully as he sat.

Was Esposito aware this would collapse around the Last Chance Saloon if it went wrong, and so was allowing them to create the rope they'd hang themselves with?

No longer watching either Esposito or Declan, Monroe now looked back to the briefing room.

'Go on then, tell us what Mile End's pair of dirty secrets wanted,' he said.

It was Anjli who went first here, rising.

'I saw Hart, DCI Walsh went to see Ford.'

'Why?' Monroe looked between them both.

'Because I would probably have killed Ford. Although for transparency's sake, you might get a complaint from Hart's prison, as I did almost strangle her.'

'Christ, I'm glad she's with you now,' Esposito shook his head. 'And to think she almost came to work for me.'

'Go on,' Monroe encouraged, ignoring the comment.

'Hart definitely knew something,' Anjli explained. 'And DCI Walsh got the impression Ford had somehow connected with Stephanie Thompson, while Morgan gave me the impression he'd spoken to either Hart or Ford. Whatever they're doing, it's churning up the waters, maybe even deliberately.'

Esposito looked at Declan now.

'Ford?'

'She knows things, but I got the impression it was more of a fishing exercise,' Declan replied. 'She offered a deal, to speak to her contacts, find Debbie Watson by noon tomorrow for us.'

'Why?'

'The "for us" part seemed to be the clincher,' Declan replied. 'She said she wanted Bullman to put a good word in with Bradbury for her. Point out that she helped out when she didn't need to. Solved a crime we couldn't.'

He looked across at Anjli.

'Help her old buddy Anjli,' he finished, and Anjli barked out a laugh of derision. 'But that was it. There were no threats, no winks, just a woman who knew what was going on, and reckoned she could help.'

'Do you think she can?' Esposito asked.

'No, but I think she wants out of prison and will say anything to get that,' Declan continued.

Monroe looked back at Anjli.

'Hart?'

'There was an arrogance there,' Anjli read from her notes now. 'She wanted me to know she'd heard about the promotions. She didn't confirm if she'd gained it from the press or from someone else. She claimed she doesn't have email access—'

'That's true,' Billy interrupted, checking her prisoner file. 'She's barred from all communication tech outside of phones. She can't have received or sent messages.'

'Unless she has a burner phone.'

'Sure, but that's an obvious answer,' Declan muttered. 'That's not "clever" enough for her, and they'd check someone with her background constantly for that kind of contraband.'

'She did say she was better than Billy,' Anjli admitted. 'But that could just have been to goad him to do something. But she said, and I quote, "Check my records. I've not been in contact with anybody for days. Maybe I'm psychic? I'm a model prisoner, don't you know. Spend my time here helping people pass their computer GCSEs," before moving on.'

Billy frowned and started typing.

'What?' Seeing this, Declan asked, as Billy waved a hand in a "in a minute" gesture.

Sighing, Anjli continued.

'She tipped her hand when she said she didn't know if Ford had been playing with us *as well*, which to me said she'd definitely been ...'

She trailed off, her eyes widening.

'Organic.'

The room was silent, as everyone watched Anjli as her face slowly reddened with anger, turning to Esposito.

'Guv, who was on the phone with you when you called me?'

Esposito frowned.

'What, this morning?'

'Yes. You were on speaker, right?'

Esposito nodded, looking at DS McAlroy.

'McAlroy was there, maybe Sanford, I think, Detective Superintendent Harris was in the room, perhaps a couple of other uniforms ... why?'

'When you called, you asked if you were interrupting anything,' Anjli replied coldly as she remembered the call. 'I said I was just erasing organic graffiti. But in the meeting with Hart, she mentioned I was in Hurley when Debbie was taken.'

She flipped through the notebook, finding the phrase.

'She said, "Good job they used organic materials, isn't it?" as she finished. Which means either she knew who did it ... or someone on the call I had with you told her. And, as I was the only one on my end ...'

Esposito looked at McAlroy, who was already texting.

'I'll grab CCTV,' she said. 'See who was in earshot. It could help work out who's keeping Ford in the loop, too.'

She looked apologetically at the room.

'Unfortunately, there's a lot of old coppers there who owe them,' she explained. 'There's a bit of a loyalty issue going on.'

'Aye, find out what you can,' Monroe growled. 'Anything else?'

'Just that she reckoned, like Ford did, that things would sort out tomorrow,' Anjli replied. 'And, just like Ford, she gave the impression she knew something about Jess's stalker, mentioning the photo, and pretending she was on a bike, saying "Beep beep, bang bang," but I have no clue what she was doing there. Maybe even having a stroke.'

At the sound effects, Monroe paled. Declan noted this, but before he could speak, McAlroy held a hand up.

'Sorry, but Jess Walsh has a stalker? We weren't told anything about this,' she said. 'Is it to do with the case? Is she okay? I only met her briefly, after she broke Molly Delcourt's wrist with a baton. She seemed ... capable.'

'And the rest,' Declan replied, a little smile now on his face. 'You weren't told because I wanted to keep it off books for the moment. Bradbury called me into his office; it looks like there's somebody in Hurley who wants to cause problems, although with Anjli's news, I'm wondering how "local" it is now.'

He nodded to Billy, who put up the image that Bradbury had passed him, of Jess and Declan, the cigarette holes in the eyes.

'Jesus,' Monroe muttered. 'And Hart didn't say how she knew this?'

'She claimed she was psychic, Guv,' Anjli repeated.

'I contacted Henry Farrow, her stepfather, and DCI of Tottenham North, and he's made sure that Jess is out of college,' Declan continued. 'I think Bullman went to speak to Liz. Obviously, following the Reaper issues from a few weeks back, Liz hasn't wanted to speak to me.'

He shook his head.

'This just adds to the shit I've got to deal with, pardon my language. Either way, we've got somebody who has decided that they have a personal vendetta against me, and they want to take it out through my daughter. Again, it felt to me like

Ford already knew about this, and Hart ... well, you know. But anything we can find out would be good.'

'We're already on it,' Billy said. 'I've already spoken to Freeman. He knows he owes us his job after Schnitter screwed him over. Their forensics are already checking into it.'

'Our forensics would like it next,' Doctor Marcos replied. 'Jess might be the unit mascot, but she's one of ours. She's done good work. And I'll be damned if I'm going to let someone like this scare the hell out of her. Besides, she's the only competent Walsh.'

'You're very funny,' Declan said. 'I'm glad that you're able to make light of this terrible situation at my expense. Bradbury made the same joke, too.'

Doctor Marcos frowned.

'Who said *I* was joking?' she asked, but there was a hint of a smile behind it as Declan now returned his attention to Monroe.

'Now, Guv, would you like to explain why you looked like someone had driven over your grave when Anjli talked about Hart making bang bang noises?'

There was a moment of uncomfortable silence, and then Monroe nodded.

'Actually, I got off the phone with Bullman before the briefing,' he replied carefully. 'She did speak to Liz Farrow, but while there, someone shot an airlift weapon at a window. They're fine, and Henry Farrow has one of his team checking the area, but—'

'Someone shot at them?' Declan was half out of his seat.

'It was a BB gun, it was nothing more than a message, and you were in Surrey,' Monroe growled. 'It's in hand. Bullman snapped some shots of the assailant, what looked to be a hoodie on an electric bike. No licence plate. But we'll keep looking, laddie.'

There was a second moment of uncomfortable silence in the briefing room.

'"Beep beep, bang bang,"' Doctor Marcos growled. 'That bitch knows exactly what's going on.'

'She said she knew people in North London, so perhaps that should be where we start?' Declan rose, but again was waved down by Monroe.

'Look, laddie, I get you're angry, but tonight we have a wee lassie still missing,' he replied. 'Jess is under guard, and if it is Hart, she's unlikely to hurt her if it stops her chances of getting out of prison. This is fun and games for her, buggering around inside your head, nothing more. We'll find the culprit, get proof they spoke to Hart, although this could be through a Ouija board, apparently, and then—'

'Actually Guv, sorry to interrupt, but I have something on that,' Billy looked up from some notes. 'Hart was banned from technology—'

'Aye, we know that.'

'Apart from when she was teaching GCSE Computer Science,' Billy continued. 'She has a linked PC, not connected out of the intranet, so unable to send messages or emails.'

'Maybe she does something while pretending to teach the class?'

'Oh, no, she's definitely teaching the class,' Billy read the screen. 'They've had a fifty percent pass rate since she started and reports say she works them hard. But currently, we have nothing on how she gets anything out.'

'So, we now have Sonya Hart somehow contacting the

outside world,' Monroe nodded. 'Park it with the rest of the "inconclusive" data we currently have.'

'Guv—' Declan protested, but Monroe waved him down.

'Priorities, laddie,' he said. 'First, let's find Debbie Watson and put this whole Blackthorne mess to bed.'

11

FOLK-LAW

MONROE GAVE EVERYONE A MOMENT TO SETTLE DOWN.

'For the moment, we ignore Hart and Ford until they become pertinent to the case,' he commanded. 'So, going back to the case itself, what do we have from the pump?'

Doctor Marcos stood.

'Rajesh Khanna, Mile End Forensics, is checking it over as we speak,' she said. 'There's nothing extra there. The DNA in the hair strands does seem to match that of Debbie Watson, and I think we can pretty much state it was left for us as a message.'

'Okay, so we know whoever stuck the sticker on the pump must have had contact with the girl to get the hairs,' Monroe said, crinkling his nose in annoyance. 'We need to work out the sex of this woman – man – whatever, as I am sick to death of calling them *they*. I'd much rather say *he* did this, or *she* did this. It feels better for me.'

'We're working as fast as we can, Guv,' De'Geer said.

'Anything on the sticker?'

'No fingerprints, no DNA,' Doctor Marcos continued. 'It

was definitely printed on some sticky paper and then cut out with a pair of scissors. Perhaps we can work something out if we can match the ink the message was on.'

'What about the witness?'

'Unsure, boss,' Cooper replied now as she read from her notes. 'Scrumpy – the witness – claimed there was one person by the pump. Again, unknown if it was male or female. Bulky jacket, although that could have been done deliberately. Baseball cap over hair, which could have been brown or dirty blond. Second figure was a thirteen, or fourteen-year-old boy, according again to the witness. Black hair, short at the sides.'

'He watched around while the unknown assailant fiddled with the pump,' De'Geer added. 'And then left shortly after they did, after either taking a photo of the item or checking that the QR code worked.'

'Aye. And does the QR code work?' Monroe asked, looking over at Billy. 'Or is it some kind of devious trapdoor Trojan, as De'Geer seems to think?'

'No, it links you to a website,' Billy nodded. 'The domain was created a week ago. It's difficult to find the router, though. Whoever did this is clever enough to understand how to hide their tracks.'

'Or had help by someone with computer knowledge, like Hart,' Anjli muttered.

'Possible, but circumstantial right now,' Monroe looked back at Billy. 'Continue.'

'The domain was bought by a fictitious name through the blockchain.'

'Which means?'

'It means they used crypto coins to pay for it,' Declan looked at Anjli as he spoke, wondering if she was getting the same feeling. 'Guv, both Ford and Hart seem to have been contacting witnesses, and both had access to crypto coins before they were arrested. Hart even spoke at my daughter's school about it.'

'Aye, and as much as I think they're crooked as a twelve-bob note, "having crypto" is something half the bloody country probably has,' Monroe muttered. 'We still need more before we go raiding their cells. Billy, can you hunt the coins?'

Billy shook his head.

'Unfortunately, there's a variety of ways you can do that and stay off the grid these days. The site itself is a free site; anyone can use it. And again, whoever did work on this is very good at hiding their tracks because there's no IPs, no metadata that links to whoever logged on.'

He sighed.

'They're good and it annoys the hell out of me. And yes, this could be Hart. I'll keep looking.'

'So if it is a website, laddie, what does it say?' Monroe asked.

At the question, Billy tapped a button on his keyboard, and a website appeared on the plasma screen behind Monroe; a simple image of girls standing in a circle, looking as if they were wearing some kind of medieval clothing, holding hands and dancing.

'It's an AI-based image,' Billy said. 'Probably from something like MidJourney or one of the others. I think it's supposed to show girls dancing while singing Ring-a-Ring-a-Roses. When you first arrive, it asks for a password, probably so nobody random gets there before us.'

'And do we know a password?'

'Actually, we were told it,' Billy turned to face the others.

'It was a six-letter combination, and the text under said it was a mix of uppercase, lowercase and numbers.'

'Six letters with capitals and numbers,' Anjli paled as she counted on her fingers. 'Kapoor, with the two zeroes?'

'Bingo,' Billy carried on scrolling on his laptop, the mirrored screen showing the website as it went down. 'They knew we had it, and we would be curious about the strange spelling, so we'd be the only people to log in for the moment. So, I logged into the page, scrolled down, saw the image ... and then saw this.'

On the screen, as Billy scrolled down to it, the room leant forward to read as the first poem appeared.

Ring-a-Ring-a-Roses,
A pocketful of posies,
Ashes, ashes,
They all fall down.

'Well, at least it doesn't have my name on it anymore,' Anjli muttered.

'I thought it was "a-tishoo",' Declan asked. 'As in sneezing?'

'It is,' Billy replied. 'But, in America, "ashes" is the term instead when the song is sung. Apart from Anjli's name, this is phonetically exact to the one found first.'

'What about the original poem?'

'Never existed,' Billy replied. 'The press started using it. The bodies never had the poem, just the posy of flowers. This, and the message for DI Kapoor are the first times they're seen.'

He scrolled down further, and now there was an image of

people dancing in the same manner the first picture had shown them, but this time it was around John Snow's cholera pump.

It was created in the same way as the first one, likely some kind of AI graphics program. Underneath it was the poem they'd found at the British Museum.

Pump of fatal water,
And cholera to slaughter,
Snow's map! Snow's map!
We all fall ill.

'This was the one we solved to get the QR code, and that led us to ... this,' Billy carried on scrolling down, and a third poem appeared.

Ring-a-ring of geese,
As they never lie at peace,
The Bishop! The Bishop!
The church stands still.

'Is this some kind of bloody treasure hunt?' Declan asked. 'Are we now supposed to find this as well?'

Billy shrugged.

'Honestly, at the moment, we're at the mercy of whoever wants to do this,' he said. 'All we can really work from is the first two.'

Anjli was already writing the poem down, scribbling it out as she started reading it.

'So, what do we know about this poem?' Declan said.

'We know Blackthorne had a thing about cleanliness,' DS

McAlroy now spoke. 'Based on the notes from the previous case, he'd had some kind of germ fetish or whatever, and it was believed he used the Pocket-Full-of-Posies part when he left the bodies because of uncleanliness, or whatever the term is.'

'Mysophobia is an extreme fear of germs,' Doctor Marcos added from the back. 'Also known as verminophobia, germophobia, germaphobia, bacillophobia and bacteriophobia.'

McAlroy turned to face her.

'And you know that all off by heart?'

Doctor Marcos shrugged.

'It's my kink, I suppose, knowing the Latin terms.'

Shaking her head, McAlroy looked back to the room.

'We know that both parents had situations in their lives that could trigger this – well, what *she* said – in Blackthorne, and we know that the poem itself is about the plague.'

'Actually, that's not quite correct, Sarge,' De'Geer spoke from the back.

'Oh aye,' Monroe smiled. 'Of course, our resident folklore expert would know something about this. Care to share with the class?'

Monroe waved for De'Geer to stand, and De'Geer hesitated, reddening slightly.

'I didn't mean to—'

'No, no,' McAlroy spun around in her chair. 'Genuinely, if you can give me some information that I don't know about this bloody poem, I'm all ears.'

De'Geer smiled slightly.

'Do you want the short story or the long one?'

'Whatever can help us,' Declan said, looking back at him. 'Just hurry up, yeah?'

De'Geer nodded, clearing his throat, and Declan wondered how long he'd known about the poem's history. He could have checked it when he was first looking, but knowing De'Geer, it was probably something he'd known about for years. After all, he did like to dress like Little John and hang around with re-enactors in his spare time.

'Well then,' he said as he opened his notepad and started reading from it, 'the earliest known printed version of the rhyme appeared in Kate Greenaway's "Mother Goose or The Old Nursery Rhymes" in 1881. However, oral traditions likely predate this. Folklorists Iona and Peter Opie suggested the rhyme may have existed in various forms since the eighteenth century.'

'That's not the medieval song I was expecting,' Monroe said.

'Nobody ever said it was, sir,' De'Geer looked almost apologetic at this. 'The song might be about something old, but it's less than a hundred and fifty years, itself.'

'So if it's not about the plague, then what is it?' DS McAlroy frowned.

'It was believed in the mid-twentieth century that the rhyme describes symptoms of the bubonic plague,' De'Geer read from the notes again. 'The song's parts explained it. "Ring a Ring o' Roses" was the circular rash. "A pocket full of posies" were the herbs carried to ward off disease. "A-tishoo, a-tishoo" was sneezing or coughing symptoms, and 'We all fall down"—'

'Meant death,' Doctor Marcos muttered from beside him.

'But that wasn't the only option,' De'Geer continued. 'There's also the religious persecution theory, proposed by some scholars as an allegory for Catholic persecution in

England. "Rosies" are interpreted as Catholic rosary beads, and "all fall down" as a genuflection or execution.'

'That's a bit of a reach,' Declan muttered.

'Oh, they're all like that,' De'Geer smiled. 'We even have springtime rituals, with the "ring" referring to circular dances", and "posies" as flowers gathered for celebration. Many versions exist across English-speaking countries, so for example "Ring a Ring o' Roses" is sung here, while "Ring Around the Rosie" is sung in the US, with "a-tishoo" being a corruption of "ashes" found in some versions, or vice versa.'

'The one with my name said "ashes" but used "roses",' Anjli commented.

'Closing thoughts?' Monroe asked.

De'Geer shrugged.

'Unless the originator of the song appears in a seance, we won't know.'

The lecture now over, Monroe motioned for De'Geer to sit down, which the Viking officer did with relief, while Anjli, no longer listening, was working on the poem once more.

'Ring-a-Ring-a-Roses is about something unclean, whether it be the plague or whatever,' Monroe said. 'The second poem was about a cholera outbreak. I think we can pretty much compare that as unclean, and it fits with this entire plan of unclean locations. What it doesn't tell us is why they're doing it.'

'It's simple,' Anjli replied. 'They're playing with me. They want me to know they're cleverer. They want me to run around chasing my tail while they do whatever they're doing.'

'They being?'

'The abductor, or maybe Ford and Hart. Hart's got less than a year on her sentence now, Ford around eighteen months. Or, they're looking to muddy their criminal pasts, land things on my shoulders, because they can?'

She shook her head, as if to shake away that line of conversation, before changing the subject.

'The hairs, that's proof that Debbie's alive. What do we find at the next location? Teeth?'

'The quicker we can get there, the better,' Declan said.

'Before we go anywhere half-cocked,' Monroe replied to Declan, 'we need to know the rest. What did you find out at the school?'

'There's nobody out of place that can be noticed. The headteacher reckons Debbie and Sarah would never have met because of their ages. If anything, it feels like Debbie was targeted because she went to the same school, but that's hearsay on my part.'

'Do we have anything on a connection between Debbie and the abductor?' Monroe asked. 'We know she seemed to recognise the stranger.'

'There was a duck,' Cooper interjected. 'Sorry, that sounded weird, but the guy, Scrumpy, he claimed that the cap that the mysterious game player was wearing had some kind of gold duck on it.'

'Gold ducks, that could be anything,' Billy added now. 'I'm working through it, but need a better idea of the logo or what it could mean.'

On the screen, Billy now showed scans of the lists of names given over by the school on their headed notepaper.

'DCI Walsh was given these,' he said, 'by the headteacher, Miss Linton. It's a list of everybody who's employed by the school. I'm hoping a name will pop up as I go through it. If there's a connection to Blackthorne ...'

'There's definitely a connection to Blackthorne,' Doctor

Marcos mentioned in the back. 'One thing I forgot to mention is the pansies that were found in the British Museum, they're an exact match for the Celestial Blue strain of pansies that were found three years ago. I'm not saying they're cut from the same branch, but wherever Blackthorne sourced his rare pansies from back then – or wherever whoever it was sourced *their* pansies from – this person knows it and has gone to the same place.'

'Well then, that's something else we can look into,' Monroe said. 'Although I wouldn't hold my breath on that one. I can't see pansies being a minority purchase, no matter how rare. If everybody and their dog buy them, then we've got a bigger game to play than that.'

'True, but if we can find out who buys *those* pansies, the Celestial Blue strain, and then sells them, we might get an idea of some local florists we can keep an eye on,' Doctor Marcos suggested. 'The pansies and poppies had been picked fresh within a day or so, so they would have had to have bought them probably yesterday. A florist's records for pansies being bought yesterday narrows it down quite substantially.'

'Get on that,' Monroe said, looking at Billy. 'Do you need help?'

'I'm good,' Billy replied. 'I don't really want to bring in Jess – as good as she is, this computer expert is better.'

'You could always bring in Hart,' Anjli muttered. 'You might find her skills at unravelling this are miraculous.'

'Right then,' Monroe said, ignoring the comment. 'We keep moving on. The kidnapper has yet to give demands. It seems they want to play a game. If it carries on like what Blackthorne did, we don't have long before she's killed.'

'Excuse me, Guv,' DS McAlroy put her hand up. 'I don't

want to piss on anyone's chips here, but ... are we absolutely *sure* that it was Blackthorne back then?'

Anjli half rose angrily in her chair.

'Are you saying—'

'Sit down, lassie,' Monroe ordered, and his tone was cold and commanding. 'DS McAlroy didn't work the case, but has every right to ask the question. You claimed you had the murderer, but it was never taken to court. It was never proved conclusively. What if you didn't get it? What if this is another Victoria Davis case?'

Anjli stopped, took a breath, and sat back down.

'It was Blackthorne,' she growled. 'I'd swear on my career it was.'

'And I trust your judgment,' McAlroy said, holding her hand up. 'I wasn't having a go at that in any way. What I'm saying is, looking through the notes, Ford hurried the case through because she wanted it removed. You were the only one pushing to get things continued and, well, maybe you didn't have enough help at the time. Maybe Blackthorne worked with someone else? Maybe there was somebody who was doing this that you never found? Maybe someone was looking after them, making sure they were protected. And now they're back, continuing where he left off.'

She looked around the room.

'This might not be somebody trying to get revenge on Anjli. This might be the actual killer returned, and who's decided to have a little more fun at her expense?'

'It's an option and one we need to look into,' Declan said, looking at Anjli. 'I'm not siding against you, but she has a point.'

'I know she does,' Anjli muttered. 'Doesn't mean I have to be happy about it.'

Monroe looked at his watch.

'Right then,' he said. 'It's getting on, we have an hour or two of light yet, and I'd really like to find this lassie before she ends up the same way as the other two. Or, even worse ...'

He grimaced.

'... DCI sodding Ford finds her first.'

12

WINCHESTER GEESE

MONROE HAD ONLY INTENDED TO POP OUT FOR A COUPLE OF minutes. He was hungry; he hadn't eaten for most of the day and close by to the unit's offices, the food shops on Fleet Street were likely to start closing soon. If he wanted to grab something to eat that wasn't from a pub, he had to go quickly.

He'd intended to pop into a *Pret* or *Itsu*, and grab something healthy; he'd been doing his best to avoid pasties in the last couple of months, something that had helped him with a slight weight loss. Not as much as he had hoped, but anything that could keep him fitter – especially in his new situation as a married man. But, as he walked out of Temple Inn, through the Middle Temple Gate, facing The Olde Bank of England pub, he found someone waiting for him.

'Have you been standing there for ages, waiting for me to come out for food?' he asked, as Emilia Wintergreen now walked in step with him onto Fleet Street.

'No, I called ahead,' Emilia replied. 'I was entering the Inns of Court, and I wanted to check you were there. The sergeant on the desk pointed out you'd just left to grab something to eat, so I had two options. You either came out of this exit, or you went out of the closer Temple Lane gate. If I'd missed you here, I would have caught you on the way back, but this was a calculated guess. You're in the middle of a case. You need time to think things over. The walk here is a peaceful one to get your thoughts into order.'

'You know me so well?' Monroe joked, about to make an "ex-wife" joke, but Wintergreen deadpanned him.

'I'm MI5,' she replied. 'We know everything.'

Monroe said nothing to this. Emilia Wintergreen was a very high-up woman, a member of MI5 and Station Head in London, if not higher. He'd lost track of where she was now, but he knew it was something important, because recently she'd had her identity returned to her. She'd gone covert when she ran the off-books Section D in MI5; in fact, it was her return to life, so to speak, that had caused him problems with his marriage to Rosanna Marcos, as when she came back to life, so did his onetime marriage with her.

'If you're here to ask for me back, Emilia,' he smiled, 'I'm afraid I'm a married man now, and I can't.'

'Don't worry,' Wintergreen replied, the slightest of smiles on her lips. 'Remember, you're not exactly my type anymore, and the only beard I have these days is one I have beside me for meetings.'

Monroe let the comments slide.

'Then why are you here?' he said. 'I'll be honest, you've not exactly caused us anything but problems recently.'

'I know,' Wintergreen replied as Monroe paused outside a sandwich shop. 'And that's why I've come here. Your boy's suffering because of what we did.'

'Declan?'

'Yes. We shouldn't have thrown Schnitter into a black cell.'

'He made his decisions,' Monroe contested.

'True, but not without our pressure,' Wintergreen continued. 'We were the ones who pulled him in, gave him the file, showed him what Karl Schnitter had done. At the time we didn't realise the Reaper was him but ...'

She shrugged.

'We needed someone to find and end The Red Reaper, and we knew Declan had a reason – with his father's death at his hands, in a roundabout way. We played it bad, and I apologise.'

'It's not me you should be apologising to,' Monroe snapped. 'We should be apologising to the wee laddie, who not only realised his father and mother had been murdered by a man he'd known for most of his life, but then you took the suspect from us, left him in a room to rot, and then let him go.'

'We didn't exactly let him go,' Wintergreen snapped. 'I lost men when he escaped. And, if I remember correctly, it was because of people with an axe to grind against *your* department that did it.'

'Aye, I know,' Monroe nodded. 'And Tom Marlowe almost lost his life as well. I don't blame you for that. I know you had problems inside the agency at the time but ...'

He looked around, making sure they weren't being listened to.

'We can't exactly tell people that Declan didn't arrest the serial killer because MI5 wanted to take him away from the Americans.'

'No, you can't,' Wintergreen replied. 'But *I* can.'

At this, Monroe's eyes widened in surprise.

'You'd go public?'

'We'd find a way of spinning it, but sure,' Wintergreen nodded. 'Declan's had the blame for too long for this. We're going to put a statement out, explain that he'd been working for us as part of a joint operation with the City of London Police, and that we took Schnitter from you at the end. We'll then fudge how America got him, not mentioning his escape, of course. If anything, it should take the heat away from Declan.'

'The City of London Police will not accept a lie like this,' Monroe replied.

'It's not exactly a lie,' Emilia Wintergreen smirked. 'And Edward Sinclair, the Commander at the time, is waiting for a Peerage to be confirmed and knows we can stop it, so he'll pretty much agree to anything.'

She nodded at the window.

'You should try the BLT,' she said. 'If you go to the back, there's some that are on half-price.'

'How do you know this?' Monroe frowned.

Wintergreen simply gave a mouth shrug as she turned and walked off down Fleet Street, leaving Monroe alone once more.

'Didn't I already say? I'm MI5,' she replied. 'We know everything.'

ANJLI KAPOOR SAT AT HER DESK, STARING AT THE PIECE OF paper in front of her. She'd spent the hour beforehand staring at the same words on the screen, but had felt that maybe by writing it down she'd get a better idea of what it actually meant.

Ring-a-ring of geese,
As they never lie at peace,
The Bishop! The Bishop!
The church stands still.

She leant back on the chair, rubbing at the back of her neck. There was obviously some kind of burial ground. But "never lie in peace" made her worry that she wasn't thinking straight here. A ring of geese? How was that to do with plagues or unclean people? And what did it mean, "The church stands quiet"? What church? Was it a church where the burials were?

Billy emerged from the stairs that led to the canteen with two coffees in his hand and walked over to Anjli, placing one down in front of her. As she gratefully took the coffee, he placed his own down on the table and picked up the piece of paper, staring at it.

'Any clues?'

She shook her head.

'Nature centres and cathedrals are the two primary choices, but we don't seem to have many of those where they work across each other. Also, I haven't yet worked out why it would connect to the theme that game player seems to want.'

Billy sat in the chair.

'Okay, so let's start working through it,' he said. 'There are geese, there's a bishop, there's a church, and they're not lying at peace.'

He started typing on his keyboard, pulling up a variety of different browser windows.

'We know it has to be nearby. They wouldn't be making us run out somewhere distant, so I'm keeping it within the remit of London, maybe even the City as such.'

He closed some browser windows and opened some more, focusing down as he did so.

'The bishop's geese?' Anjli muttered to herself.

'The bishop's what?'

'The bishop's geese.'

As she repeated this, Billy froze, turning, staring at her.

'Oh my god, I think you're right,' he said. 'Of course, I don't know why I didn't think of it earlier.'

He started scrolling through one of his browser windows, hunting for something.

'The Bishop of Winchester,' he said.

'He collected geese?'

'In a way,' Billy smiled. 'So, picture this. Medieval Southwark, just across the river from London. It had a bit of a reputation back then if you know what I mean.'

'It's got a reputation now.'

'True, but back then, the area's full of taverns, theatres, and ... well, brothels. And who's in charge of this den of iniquity? None other than the Bishop of Winchester,' Billy explained. 'Now, these brothels were staffed by women known as the "Winchester Geese," probably because they laid him golden eggs, money wise. The bishop wasn't just turning a blind eye – he was actively regulating the place and raking in the taxes.'

He pulled up a screenshot of the Thames as he continued.

'This whole setup was in an area called the "Liberty of the Clink," outside of London's reach. The bishop had free rein, and he made the most of it. This went on for centuries, if you can believe it, and the party finally ended in 1546, when Henry VIII decided he'd had enough and shut the whole operation down.'

'So, how does the Winchester Geese link to plagues and uncleanliness?' Anjli asked.

Billy was reading from a screen by now.

'Because they weren't buried on consecrated ground,' he explained. 'They were buried in an unconsecrated burial ground in Southwark known as the *Crossbones Graveyard*, in the heart of where all those brothels used to be. It's believed to have been the last resting place for many of the Winchester Geese and other "outcasts" of society. The sad reality was that these women, despite generating income for the church through their work, were considered "sinners" and "unclean", and as such weren't allowed to be buried in consecrated ground, so they were buried in Crossbones.'

He turned and looked back at Anjli.

'"Ring a ring of geese, as they never lie in peace." That's the unconsecrated ground where the prostitutes were buried. "The bishop, the bishop." That's about the actions he took. "The church stands still." That's the fact that the church did nothing about this. Even when they were found, centuries later, during archaeological excavations for the Jubilee Line Extension of the London Underground in the early nineties, they wanted to remove it. Luckily, the graveyard is now a place of remembrance ...'

Anjli was already grabbing her jacket.

'A place for unclean burials? Give me the location,' she said.

'Do you want to take someone with you?'

As he asked this, DS McAlroy walked out of the briefing room, seeing Anjli pulling on a coat.

'Clocking off?' she asked.

'We think we've worked out the rhyme,' Anjli said. 'Care to take a trip to Southwark?'

McAlroy smiled.

'Not really, as I hate south of the Thames,' she said. 'But I'll come anyway.'

THE JOURNEY DOWN TO SOUTHWARK TOOK LONGER THAN ANJLI had expected. Even though they had sirens wailing, it was still a trip to get south of the Thames, especially as the night-time traffic was picking up. Eventually, Anjli and DS McAlroy arrived on Redcross Way, pulling up to the side of the metal gates of what was now known as the *Crossbones Graveyard Garden of Remembrance.*

As Anjli exited the car, she felt a shiver go down her spine. She knew it was her imagination, but she couldn't help feeling like she was being watched.

McAlroy, watching her, smiled.

'You feel that too, do you?' she said. 'That's the weight of history watching us.'

'You believe so?' Anjli asked, walking towards the gates.

'You've worked in Mile End. You know what's buried there,' McAlroy said, following her. 'You get a kind of sixth sense, a kind of "spidey tingle". We're always under scrutiny, and not just by the living.'

The railings that they could see Crossbones Graveyard through were a striking sight. They were red-painted-iron, and completely adorned with colourful ribbons, flowers, trinkets, and mementos left by visitors. Attached to the railings were plaques and signs telling the story of the site, along with personal messages and tributes to the "outcast dead." The overall effect was a vibrant, makeshift shrine that stood in poignant contrast to the grim history it commemorated.

McAlroy continued by rapping the back of her knuckles against one of the railings, the ring that she had on her finger clanging against it. It was almost as if she was knocking on the door to wake the dead.

'These people know what I'm talking about,' she continued. 'Poor buggers.'

'Do you know much about it?'

'I came here years ago,' McAlroy replied. 'There was a women's festival on in Southwark, and they did a ... I want to say a ritual of some kind, but it was more just a kind of gathering of women lighting candles and holding a vigil. The people here were treated badly.'

She looked around.

'So, are we looking for another QR sticker, do you think, or something different?'

Anjli was already checking the coloured pieces of cloth as she investigated the railings.

'I don't know,' she replied. 'These are ribbons and pieces of cloth, each one with a name, I'm guessing, of someone who was buried here and never had a gravestone.'

McAlroy nodded absently, already going through the named cards on the railings as well.

Anjli stepped back, trying to take in the gate as a whole.

'Look for more modern ones,' she said. 'Try to find a ribbon that looks like it's been placed on in the last day or so.'

She turned, doing a full circle of the location. She couldn't see any CCTV cameras, and the road was quite empty, especially for the time of day. The buildings opposite looked modern, or were old buildings that had been scrubbed and cleaned, with each of the terraced buildings three storeys high, with windows facing the garden. There was no movement from any of the curtains; for all intents and purposes, Anjli and McAlroy were alone.

McAlroy was already moving along, checking from top to bottom of each of the railings before moving to the next one. There were a lot of ribbons to check through so, tightening her lips, Anjli started at the opposite end, working back. They'd eventually meet in the middle, but as she was checking her fourth railing, she paused.

'I think I've got it,' she said.

McAlroy looked up, and Anjli tapped at a piece of blue and silver fabric tied to the railing.

'What is it?'

'It's a Ravenclaw lanyard,' Anjli said, looking at it. 'From *Harry Potter.* You can buy them in the tourist shops.'

She was examining it a little closer, but not touching it at the same time.

'When we spoke to Debbie's parents, they said she had a Ravenclaw lanyard on around her neck that held an AirTag in it, so she wouldn't wander off.'

She tapped at the bar, making sure not to touch the ribbon, and with her other hand, she reached into her jacket to pull out a latex glove. Putting it on, and now pulling out a pencil, she used the gloved hand to hold the pencil as she flipped the cut-down lanyard upwards.

Under it was a piece of paper, laminated against the rain.

'What does it say?' McAlroy asked.

However, instead of replying, Anjli stepped back, spinning around on her feet, staring around once more as McAlroy went and, taking the pencil from Anjli's hand, flipped up the lanyard to reveal the message.

Hello, Anjli. I'm watching you.

'They're here,' Anjli muttered, looking around. 'They can bloody see me.'

'But how?' McAlroy asked. 'There's nobody around, and if they're watching through any of these windows, we'd see them. And unless that killer's dead and lying with the ...'

She trailed off.

'There,' she pointed.

Attached to one of the railings at the top, a good eight feet in the air and definitely above the two women, was what looked to be some kind of camera.

'I've got one of those at home,' McAlroy said. 'It's a Ring security camera. You know, the people who do the doorbells? It's battery operated. Motion detected. You can check it on an app.'

'Yeah, I've seen them before,' Anjli, furious, walked up to look at the device and visibly saw a blue light.

'You're watching me now,' she said to it. 'You knew I'd come. Who are you? What do you want?'

She turned back to McAlroy.

'Is there sound on this?' she asked. 'The one my neighbour has, you can hear and speak through it.'

'Should be; if you see someone in your back garden, you can speak through the speaker,' McAlroy nodded. 'You know, ask them what they're doing there. If they're watching you right now, they can hear you. And if they wanted to, we could hear them.'

Anjli spun back around.

'Show yourself, you goddamn coward,' she said. 'How are you connected to Blackthorne? Why are you doing this?'

There was a slight screech of static. And then a voice spoke.

'Reopen the case,' it said, a woman's voice, deep, but also

slightly artificial, as if being changed from something else, deliberately hiding the true identity of the speaker. 'You deserve to pay. You never checked to see if you were right, Kapoor. And now, like the others, you will fall down.'

'This isn't to do with Debbie Watson,' Anjli said. 'It's to do with me. You want revenge on me? Fine. Let Debbie go, and I'll go wherever you want. You can have me instead.'

'I don't want you to be a plaything,' the voice continued, muffled. Not computerised so, but still as if somebody was speaking into a microphone and trying to disguise their voice. 'I want you to suffer, like the parents did, when you failed to do what needed to be done.'

'How do you know I failed?' Anjli shouted. 'The case was closed. Nobody knows what happened.'

'Mile End knows,' the voice continued. 'Mile End knows everything.'

'Mile End doesn't have a bloody clue,' McAlroy shouted now. 'I'm Mile End, and I can tell you right now, you're—'

'Mile End now,' the voice said. 'I don't know you. Or the man who you work for. I know Mile End *then*. I know Ford. I know Hart. I know Kapoor.'

There was a pause, and Anjli wondered whether they'd stopped or lost the connection. But before she could say anything, the voice started one more time.

'They all fall down.'

There was a moment of tense silence as Anjli stared up at the camera.

'You know what? I've had enough of your bullshit,' she said, as she reached into her jacket and pulled out her extendable police baton, clicking it open. 'Whatever bloody stupid game Ford and Hart are playing, it ends now. Do you want to know what else falls down?'

Before the voice on the end of the microphone could speak, she swung hard with the baton, connecting with the base of the camera and sending it clattering to the floor beside them. There was a smashing noise as it landed, the plastic casing of the security camera cracking open. The blue light no longer shone as the battery clattered out of the base.

'Well, if you wanted any fingerprints or anything, that's out the window now,' McAlroy muttered.

'Looking at everything else this bastard has done,' Anjli shrugged. 'We wouldn't have found any fingerprints or DNA on that device. They're too good.'

She gave a smile.

'But one thing we will find is in the software. IP locations of where the connection goes to. The Apple or Android device they were using to watch through the camera, all that techy stuff; that's how it works, right? There'll be somebody at the other end, and if they've not been careful, we've got a chap back at Temple Inn who's really good.'

Straightening, she frowned.

'This doesn't feel right, though,' she said. 'Something should have been here by now. Some next clue. This can't be just so they could stare at us. Whoever's doing this wants me to keep running for their entertainment.'

She glanced back at the bars of the graveyard.

'The lanyard wasn't that long, but maybe Debbie was wearing something else they've put here.'

Pulling out her phone, she started scrolling through images. One of them was a screenshot of the CCTV when Debbie was taken by the stranger in the hat.

'She's wearing a dress with a waistband,' she said. 'It's about an inch thick, a light material. If they've taken the lanyard ...'

She started staring around, narrowing her eyes as she focused in on the bars.

'Look for something that's different from the others,' she said. 'Like the lanyard, but—'

She paused, tapping one piece of cloth.

'This is new,' she said. 'And there's nothing attached to it.'

Using her gloved hand, she untied the loosely attached piece of fabric. Holding it up in her hands, she stared at it.

'Place of sweating fever,' she whispered. 'What the hell does that mean?'

However, McAlroy had already moved to another bar. Carefully, using a pen, she pulled up the second piece.

'Butcher's hook! Butcher's hook!' she looked at Anjli. 'There's four lines in every verse. We've got two of them; I reckon there's two more to find.'

'Great,' Anjli muttered. 'Not only are we now playing hide and seek with a waistband to find a poem we've got to translate, we now have to put the bloody thing together as well.'

13

MAMAS AND PAPAS

ONCE THE POEM HAD BEEN FOUND, MONROE SENT EVERYONE home for the night; it was late, and nothing new was going to be discovered before the next morning at the earliest. Therefore, Declan had spent the night in his Hurley house, staring out of the window, waiting for someone to come by and write more graffiti, or perhaps fire their own airsoft rifle at his windows.

In the end, just after midnight, Anjli had turned up and pulled him away, reminding him that, for all of its faults and small village attitudes, Hurley wasn't the kind of place that was filled with serial killers and murderers, apart from the ones they already knew about.

Declan, however, wasn't sure anymore. The gunshot at his ex-wife's house, even if it was a .22, had shaken him.

Eventually, first thing in the morning, Anjli and Declan drove into work separately. Anjli went to Temple Inn to continue looking at the next poem, found at Crossbones Graveyard;

Place of sweating fever,
Where illness finds deceiver,
Butcher's hook! Butcher's hook!
We all feel ill.

Meanwhile, Declan drove to Tottenham. He'd told Anjli he was going to check on Jess and DCI Farrow, but actually, he had a different person to speak to first.

MAMA DELCOURT RAN THE SEVEN SISTERS, THE CRIMINAL organisation that controlled most of the north of London. Declan and Mama Delcourt had met many times in the past, and the most recent of these had involved both an occasion where she blinded herself with a simunition grenade, thinking she was committing suicide, rather than going to prison, before a second meeting, months later, when her own daughter tried to usurp her.

Mama Delcourt was almost blind thanks to the damage to her eyes from the paint grenade and now had an assistant, a young girl, who would travel with her, make sure she could do what she needed to do. Though, somehow, over those years she had managed to hang on to her role of being a leader of the Seven Sisters.

Her base was a set of purpose-built houses above some shops near Seven Sisters Underground stop; really keeping to the "Seven Sisters" branding.

Declan had been there before but the last time he'd arrived, he'd pissed a lot of people off and ended up being knocked out with a baseball bat after having a gun rammed in his face. This time, understandably, he was trepidatious as he arrived at the Brazilian restaurant that was the actual entry to the building.

It was early in the day, and the restaurant wasn't yet open for business. As Declan walked through the open door, past the tables and chairs, up to the counter at the back, a Brazilian man, wearing a simple white shirt and black trousers, recognised him.

'She's busy,' he said.

'This isn't business,' Declan replied. 'This is personal. Tell her that DCI Declan Walsh is here, and I'm willing to give her anything she needs if she can help me.'

This was not something the man had expected, so he shrugged, made a phone call, and then waved Declan towards a doorway to the side.

'You know where to go,' he muttered sullenly.

Declan gave him a nod and walked upstairs.

The back set of stairs led to an armoured and locked steel door that was usually manned by a young gun for the Seven Sisters. Declan didn't even know if there were Seven Sisters anymore. Anita Taborska had been one of them and, after pretending to be Johnny Lucas's long-dead brother in an attempt to steal his turf, and failing, she had been placed in prison. There had been rumours they were looking for a new seventh sister, and Declan wondered if they had found them yet.

Janelle Delcourt, better known as Mama Delcourt, sat on an expansive and opulent plush leather sofa in an ornate, red, wallpapered lounge. Next to her was a young woman, a notebook in her hand. As Declan entered, Mama Delcourt looked up. He believed she could see better than she made out, like the rumours about Stevie Wonder had always played out, but actively leant into the story about her blindness, if only to see what her rivals would do in her presence.

Declan decided to play it properly.

Stepping close, he leant forward, grabbing her outstretched hand, shaking it with both hands in a familial greeting.

'Thank you for seeing me, Mama Delcourt,' he said, feeling like he was in a *Godfather* movie.

'The great Declan Walsh wants a meeting, and it doesn't sound like I'm in trouble,' Mama Delcourt laughed. 'Of course I'm going to see what this is. What seems to be the problem?'

'I need assistance with a slightly personal matter,' Declan replied.

'Is it assistance in working out what to do with the will?' Mama Delcourt grinned. 'We all know about that, Mister Walsh. I could give some advice.'

Declan shook his head.

'No, but in a way, yes,' he said. 'My daughter, she's in danger.'

'How so?'

'She's being targeted because she's my daughter,' Declan explained. 'Somebody is unhappy with what happened with ... well, you know, as you just mentioned the will. And I know you also know my ex-wife and Jess live in North Tottenham, and that's technically classed as your manor.'

He leant closer.

'I'm sure you *also* remember that your daughter tried to kill my daughter, and I feel that kind of puts you in my debt a little.'

'Oh!' Mama Delcourt smiled. 'So I *don't* get a favour from you. I'm repaying a debt I didn't know I owed.'

'No,' Declan said quickly, straightening. 'I'm just pointing out that you do owe me, but if you do this, I *will* owe you.'

'It's that important to you?'

Declan rummaged through his jacket, pulling out a printout he'd made the previous night. It was the best of Bullman's photos she'd taken.

'Someone fired a .22 BB gun, possibly an airsoft rifle at my ex-wife's apartment,' he said. 'Which was stupid to say the least, because she's married to the DCI of Tottenham North.'

Mama Delcourt smiled gently.

'Yes, we know DCI Farrow well. Interesting that you would come instead of him.'

'It's personal,' Declan said. 'Henry Farrow will do what he can to save the day, find the culprit, but this is a teenage kid in a hoodie. The only thing we have to go on is the electric bike. We spoke to some experts, and we've been told it's a fat-tyre E-bike, most likely a *Hidoes* B6-Electric Mountain Bike, from the looks here, in black and red. Quite expensive, not something you can fold up and hide. You've got people on the streets around here. I was hoping you could put the word out; ask quietly if anybody knows someone who would do this kind of job.'

'You think it was hired?'

Declan shrugged.

'I don't know,' he said. 'But if somebody new is in the area driving around with a BB gun on an electric bike, I'm guessing you guys would know about it. And if it is somebody brought in or somebody local, again ...'

He let the sentence trail off. Mama Delcourt knew what he meant.

The young woman beside Mama Delcourt looked surprised at the description, however.

'Easter rides one of those,' she said.

'Easter?' Declan asked, looking over at the girl. 'As in the holiday?'

Mama Delcourt looked at her assistant at this point, and Declan had seen the glare that came from her. *This was something that Delcourt hadn't wanted to be known.*

'Easter Clarke,' Mama Delcourt eventually replied. 'Named because he was conceived at Easter. He's a bit of a loner, but if you're looking to hire someone to help you, to scare off somebody, he would be one option.'

'And you hadn't considered him before the name was mentioned?' Declan asked, watching for a response.

Mama Delcourt shrugged.

'I can't follow all my lost sheep,' she replied. 'But he's definitely an option. He lives in Tottenham, so I can check into him for you. Some of my lads work on the streets. I won't say what they do there, because even if you're here as a personal request, you're still a DCI, and I don't really want to sour any relationship we might still have. But, if there is somebody in the area who's stepping on my turf, I'd prefer to know. You'll know soon enough.'

'Thank you,' Declan replied, grateful for the help. 'And as I said, if you can do this, I'll owe you—'

'You'll owe me nothing,' Mama Delcourt shook her head. 'I have a daughter too, remember? I know what it's like when you stress about them. And currently everyone I speak to seems to go on about debts, ever since Ellie Reckless took down the Simpsons.'

Declan grinned. He knew Ellie, and she'd been trained by Monroe.

'Then I'm in good company,' he rose from the chair he'd sat on. But before he could move far, Mama Delcourt reached out and grabbed Declan's hand; for a moment he was touched by the gesture ... before realising there was no way she should have known where it was.

He looked down at her, and her slightly milky eyes glittered as she smiled.

Well, well, Mama Delcourt, looks like you see better than you claim after all.

He didn't say the words out loud; he didn't need to. He just gripped her hand back.

'Anything you need,' he said.

Mama Delcourt nodded.

'Now DCI Walsh, if you don't mind, please piss off out of my house,' she said, almost magnanimously, leaning back and throwing her arms out as she raised her voice for all to hear. 'I have a reputation to uphold, and you're really causing me problems by being here.'

Anjli had found Billy in various stages of excitement over the years when she had arrived at Temple Inn. Often though, it was because he'd spent the night hopped up on caffeine trying to solve a dilemma, or some kind of mystery. He would usually be either tired or very agitated, excited at what he'd found. Sometimes he'd whistle, sometimes he'd hum little tunes.

This, however, was the first time she saw him actively speaking the words to poetry.

'"Ducks, ducks, quack, quack. Ducks, ducks, quack, quack,"' he was muttering to himself, as he moved from the printer to his computer. '"Look closer and you may recoil in surprise, at web-footed fascists with mad little eyes—"'

'What are you going on about?' Anjli asked.

Billy jumped; he was so engrossed in what he was doing, he hadn't even noticed that she was in the office.

Calming, he grinned as he looked at her.

'"Ducks, ducks, quack, quack."'

'And I'm supposed to get what you're talking about?' Anjli queried.

'It's a song by the *Sinister Ducks,* sung by Translucia Baboon, who was later outed to be Alan Moore,' Billy explained. 'One of the greatest writers of all time. He did *Watchmen* and *Halo Jones.*'

Anjli knew the name of the first book, and so just smiled and nodded.

'And he hates ducks?'

'Oh, he knows the truth about ducks,' Billy chuckled. '"Dressed in black jackets and horrible shoes, getting divorces and turning to booze." But that's not why I'm singing it.'

He tapped some paper on his desk and Anjli, looking closer, realised it was the list of staff working at Kelsey Primary School.

Anjli took the paper in her hand as she read the names.

'I'm guessing you found something,' she mumbled, 'or else you wouldn't be singing your little song.'

Billy nodded.

'Look at it,' he said. 'What do you see?'

'I see people,' Anjli read down the list. 'Names I don't recognise. Nothing that's come up with the case.'

'I'm not on about the names,' Billy spoke. 'Look at the letter heading. Kelsey Primary.'

'Billy ...' Anjli trailed off as she looked at the logo of the school. 'Is that ...?'

'Yes,' Billy finished. 'It's a stylised image of a duck. Apparently Kelsey Primary School, since it opened in nineteen sixty-two, has had a duck as its logo.'

'It's quite stylised,' Anjli said. 'Almost unrecognisable. I wouldn't have said it was a duck at first view. It's only because you're singing that bloody silly song.'

'True,' Billy nodded, opening up the school's webpage. 'But, once I started down this rabbit hole, I had a look at their photos. Here's one from five years ago.'

Anjli leant closer to the monitor screen, staring at the image.

'I can't see what I'm looking at here,' she muttered.

'It's a school sports day. Banner at the back,' Billy pointed. 'Kelsey School's old logo. This was a far more obvious duck design.'

Anjli nodded as she saw the defined silhouette of a duck facing to the left.

'Well, that's definitely a duck, as you said—'

Her eyes widened as she tapped on the picture.

'The teacher, there.'

'The one wearing the baseball cap?' Billy asked with a smile. 'The one with the gold duck logo on it? Yeah, I thought you'd recognise that.'

'Are you telling me that the person who abducted Debbie Watson was wearing a Kelsey Primary School cap?'

Billy leant back in his chair and placed his hands behind his head in a triumphant expression.

'Looks that way,' he mumbled. 'Now, I've checked, and I've been told that the school stopped selling those caps two years ago, when they changed the style. It may have been because of the publicity the school had after the murder, and they wanted to move away from it, or they just simply wanted a new style. It doesn't matter. Whoever was wearing the hat in the British Museum had to have purchased that baseball cap over two years back. I checked the photo Debbie's parents gave Monroe – the group shot – and in the background is someone wearing the same cap.'

'So now we have a definite school connection between Debbie and Sarah.'

'More importantly,' Billy muttered, tapping the names, 'Debbie recognised the person in the CCTV image and smiled. Remember, if they're wearing a school cap she could've recognised them from the school. Somebody on this list could be the kidnapper.'

Anjli nodded.

'I'll take Cooper. We'll go have a chat with the school, see if they can give us any more advice. Anyone who fits the look, we can then have a chat with.'

'Anjli,' Billy said quickly as she turned to walk away. 'It might not be a teacher or support assistant. You could buy these off the website when they were being sold. It could be a parent, a friend ... anyone.'

'We'll cross that bridge when we come to it,' Anjli replied. 'As I said, currently we know Debbie recognised the figure. Do we have anything on the CCTV at the back of the museum?'

'No,' Billy sighed. 'We're still waiting for some of the ANPR to turn up. But the biggest problem we have is the workmen who were causing such a pain with the CCTV inside, had also managed to pull their vans up and lorries in such a way that—'

'Let me guess, it blocked the CCTV?'

'I don't think it was deliberate,' Billy admitted. 'I genuinely think it was a mistake, but whoever did this definitely realised and worked it to their advantage. Builders rarely give a shit about where they park, no matter how much it pisses the neighbours off.'

Anjli went to reply, but something in his words paused her.

'What did you just say?' she asked, but Billy didn't answer; his phone beeped, and he glanced down at it.

'Doctor Marcos wants to speak to you if you're still here,' he said. 'Before you go, that is. She's downstairs in her office.'

'Tell Cooper to meet me there,' Anjli mumbled, grabbing her jacket and leaving as quickly as she arrived. 'Why didn't she text me?'

'Maybe she knows I answer my texts quicker?' Billy suggested with a smile as Anjli left through the main doors and headed to the morgue.

DOCTOR MARCOS WAS AT HER DESK, WORKING ON HER LAPTOP, when Anjli knocked on the door.

'You asked to speak to me, Doc?' Anjli asked.

Doctor Marcos nodded.

'Got the report back on those pansies and poppy petals you gave me,' she said, shaking her head. 'They don't match. Whatever Antony Morgan is selling in his florists, they're not from the same location.'

'Or he's done that deliberately,' Anjli suggested.

'Possibly. But, let's be honest, if he was trying to prove his intelligence to us, he would have found other ways,' Doctor Marcos sighed, leaning back on her chair, stretching as she did so, groaning as her back clicked.

'We're just chasing our tails here,' she muttered, 'and I don't know why we're having this game played with us.'

There was a knock on the door and on opening it, Anjli saw Cooper standing there.

'You asked to see me, Guv?'

'We're going to check Kelsey Junior School,' Anjli explained. 'We've worked out their logo is the same one that the cap had.'

As she turned to leave, Doctor Marcos held a hand up.

'Anything more from Crossbone Graveyards?' she asked.

Anjli shook her head.

'Only the camera and the poem,' she replied. 'I was hoping Billy might have found something from the Ring doorbell, but Billy's not looked into it yet.'

'That's because he's not.'

'Sorry?'

'I thought you'd been told,' Doctor Marcos frowned. 'Mile End stepped in and took it off us.'

'You're letting Mile End take on the case?'

'It is their case, Anjli,' Doctor Marcos said quietly. 'Just because we've taken it on doesn't mean it doesn't matter. Detective Superintendent Harris at Mile End made the call. There was nothing we could do.'

'Someone should have told me,' Anjli folded her arms as she faced the divisional surgeon. At this, Cooper stepped back from the door as Doctor Marcos rose from her chair.

'Do you remember the times when Declan has got a little bit too carried away with the case and decided it was much more of a personal attack on him than it was an investigation by a team?' she spoke, her voice emotionless and calm.

Anjli shook her head with annoyance at this.

'If you're going to tell me that this is the lecture I'm supposed to have—'

'This *is* the lecture you're supposed to have,' Doctor

Marcos interrupted. 'Whoever this person is, they're playing with you and I get that. But the question you have to ask is *why now?* Why didn't they play this with you last week, last year? Why didn't they do it the day after the news came out about Declan and the will? Why didn't they do it the moment you were in the paper for saving the Prime Minister and the Queen and all those people? There's a reason this is happening today. And at the moment, we need Billy to find us answers. Checking the Ring doorbell's configuration to work out where it was linking to? That's IT and cyber, but it's something that anyone can do.'

'Do we at least know who's doing it?'

'You'd have to ask Esposito.'

'Fine,' Anjli muttered. 'I'll ask him then when I next see him. That'll be fun.'

As she walked out, Doctor Marcos looked at Cooper.

'It's okay, Doc. I'll keep an eye on her,' Cooper said. 'I'll stop her from being her own worst enemy.'

'You're speaking like someone who's seen it before.'

Cooper grinned.

'Of course I have,' she replied. 'I've worked cases with both DCI Walsh and DI Kapoor. It's second nature now.'

14

DETENTION

'Two detectives in as many days! We are feeling special today,' Miss Linton gave a small smile as she waved Anjli and Cooper into her office.

'Detective Inspector Kapoor, ma'am,' Anjli said. 'And this is PC Cooper. You spoke to my partner, Detective Chief Inspector Walsh, yesterday afternoon?'

'Yes,' Linton closed the door, offering Anjli and Cooper chairs as she went and sat opposite them. Anjli noted that they were sitting opposite across a small coffee table, rather than Miss Linton's desk. She appreciated the gesture, Miss Linton obviously trying her best to make Anjli feel at home.

'I didn't expect to hear from you so fast,' Miss Linton said. 'I only gave you the details yesterday.'

'I know, but something came up, and we wanted to grab some confirmation for it,' Anjli said. 'It's in relation to your school's logo.'

'Our logo?' Miss Linton frowned. 'What about it?'

Anjli pointed at the top of the headed paper that had been passed to her by Billy earlier that day.

'This is the paperwork you gave us with the list of people who worked at your school,' she explained. 'As you can see here, you have an image of a duck. It's very stylised, one line in an outline shape, but it's quite obvious what the animal is.'

Anjli placed her phone onto the coffee table, a screenshot, the image from the website pulled across and uploaded onto her own phone, now visible. On it, Miss Linton looked at the photo of children with baseball caps and teachers beside them, all with the golden duck that was now ingrained in Anjli's mind.

'Okay,' Miss Linton said, looking down at it. 'That's the old design. I still don't get ...'

'Swipe to the left,' Anjli said. 'Then I think you'll understand a little more about what I'm talking about.'

Miss Linton did so, and the CCTV image of Debbie Watson staring up at the stranger was now displayed.

Miss Linton looked up, her eyes wide.

'Is that ...?'

'That's the moment Debbie Watson was taken at the British Museum,' Anjli confirmed. 'Now, I'm not showing this to scare you or cause any kind of reaction, but I want you to notice the baseball cap that the stranger, who we can't make out, is wearing.'

'Okay ...' Linton nodded.

'Swipe again.'

Now the group photo appeared, and in the background, face down, half-hidden from the camera, Miss Linton could see the small gold duck against the navy-blue of the cap was clearly visible.

'The photo's not great,' Anjli said, 'and the subject is moving, but I think we can make a pretty good case that the cap that they're wearing is one of yours.'

Miss Linton nodded, understanding now.

'Good God.'

'So, my question now is who have those caps?' Anjli asked. 'We saw that the website sells them so we don't know if the website has a list of the adults who would have bought them, but we need to know—'

'Wait, hold on ...' Miss Linton held her hand up to pause Anjli. 'Are you asking for people who are *grown up* and wear those hats?'

Anjli frowned as she stared at the headteacher.

'What else would I be asking?'

'It's just that, well, the website ...' Miss Linton leant back. 'Look, I'm sure you're doing your job very well, but I think you're jumping to conclusions here. We don't sell baseball caps for adults on that site.'

'But you do have a website where you can buy baseball caps?' It was Cooper who now asked, looking up from her notes.

'Not for adults. The ones that you found are sold for children.'

'You don't sell the baseball caps as merch?' Cooper insisted.

'We wouldn't make that much if we wanted to,' Miss Linton shook her head. 'It's just an easy portal for people to buy the baseball caps for when the children go on school tours, or days out to, well, places like museums in London.'

She tapped the image on the phone.

'I can see here that Debbie isn't on a school tour because she's not wearing one of the caps. The school's always done it. The children wear the caps so we know that they're part of our school, and any adults who are chaperoning them, if they're teachers or school assistants or parents or whatever, they'll have a cap on as well,' she continued, looking around the office for a cap, and pointing at one on a hook beside the door. ' Like that one. That way, if somebody sees a grown adult walking over to a group of small children and telling them to follow them, they're not going to cause a problem, because they can recognise the cap.'

'I see. When did you change the logo?' It was Anjli's turn to ask now.

Miss Linton looked down at the images.

'When I came here,' she said. 'They'd had the duck logo for about thirty years by that point and it felt a bit dated. We wanted something a bit more stylish and cool. I had a friend who was a graphic designer and he made the logo for us.'

She looked back up at Cooper.

'All the caps that the students now wear have this logo on it, likewise the teachers and helpers.'

Anjli rubbed at her chin.

'When was the last time you saw one of these caps?'

'Honestly? Early on in my first term as headteacher,' Miss Linton said. 'We arranged during the summer holiday to get it changed.'

'Because it was dated? Or because of Sarah?' Cooper asked.

'A little of both, really,' Miss Linton admitted. 'None of the photos shown of Sarah had her wearing a cap, but we knew there were probably a few out there, and we wanted to get away from being associated with such a terrible thing.'

'So it was a concern about bad PR?'

'I suppose. But what can you do? Margaret, my predecessor, had already started the wheels moving.'

Anjli nodded. She understood why the school would want to get away from an image that was linked to such a terrible thing.

'And if somebody wanted to buy one of these ...'

'Check on eBay, maybe. I don't think anybody would want to try and sell one of these though,' Miss Linton replied. 'There might be one or two in the staff room, but again, I haven't seen one in ages.'

Leaning back, Anjli considered what had been said.

'This wasn't the only reason we came to you today,' she said, nodding to Cooper to continue. 'We had a little more excitement, shall we say, about this case yesterday.'

'The list that you gave DCI Walsh,' Cooper leant forwards, tapping the list on the coffee table. 'I'm afraid we now need to know how many of these people would have been in school between the hours of nine o'clock and twelve o'clock yesterday.'

'Yesterday morning?' Miss Linton picked up the list of names, looking down at them. 'Quite a few of them really. I mean, most of the teachers were in, and the dinner ladies would have been preparing for lunch ...'

She looked back over at Anjli.

'Why?' she asked, a suspicious expression on her face. 'I don't mean to interfere, but it seems strangely specific.'

'We have a witness that saw the same person that abducted Debbie, or at least who we *believe* is the same person who abducted Debbie, in Central London between the hours of nine and twelve yesterday morning,' Cooper said, reading from her notes. 'This would mean that anybody who was in school with you yesterday morning could not have been in two places at once, and therefore would not be a viable suspect.'

'Would not be a viable suspect,' Mrs Linton repeated the line. 'I can't even believe that anybody here would be classed as a suspect in the first place. I can't see any of these people doing such a hideous thing.'

'And yet someone did,' Anjli said carefully. 'Now, as my companion here stated, we were looking for people who are on this list and who weren't here yesterday morning. But now I'm also wondering if we can add a little more to that, and find a list of people who weren't here yesterday morning, but were here when the old design was part of the school. So, before your tenure.'

Mrs Linton scratched her head.

'As you say, Detective Inspector, it's before my tenure,' she said. 'I'd have to call in someone.'

She rose from the chair and opened the door.

'Nicola, can you come in for a sec?' she asked, walking back and sitting back down. The receptionist, an old lady with grey curly hair that looked as if it had been added into rollers the night before, wandered in.

'Nicola's been here as long as I know,' Miss Linton said. 'Definitely ten to fifteen years at best.'

Anjli passed Nicola the list of names.

'Is there anybody on here that you know wasn't in school yesterday and has been around for over, say, three years?'

Nicola looked down at the list.

'Ruth, she was around, Rowena, I saw her, Gail, definitely,' she looked up. 'Not many that weren't here, I can ask around if you'd like.'

'Please,' Anjli said, 'that would help us a lot. You were here before Sarah Thompson was taken, right?'

'Terrible thing,' Nicola said, 'absolutely terrible.'

'You met the florist, Thomas Blackthorne?'

'I met him here and there.'

'Do you ever recall Thomas Blackthorne having a cap?' Anjli tapped the image of the navy-blue baseball cap with the old logo of the school on it in gold.

Nicola scrunched her face up as she tried to consider this. Then her eyes opened as she recalled something and nodded.

'The hundred years,' she said.

'The hundred years?'

'Sorry, I mean, when we had the 1918-2018 hundred year anniversary at the end of World War One, we did a big church service. I remember Blackthorne's shop did the flowers.'

'And why would he have had a cap?'

'Because they were around loads of children,' Nicola said, as if it was the most obvious thing in the world. 'The previous headteacher said anybody who was dealing with the children had to wear one of the baseball caps, so that there was nothing that came out in the press that would cause any problems. So Thomas Blackthorne would have had a cap, yes ... but I would have assumed he would have given it back directly after.'

Anjli looked down at the photo. This was something she'd never known three years earlier. More importantly, nobody had ever said that the caps had been worn back then. But if Sarah Thompson had been at the school in 2018, she would have been five years old. That would have been Year One. There was every chance she would have seen Blackthorne with the school cap of trustworthiness on, and then years later, followed him unknowingly to her death.

'Thank you,' she said. 'Please, if you can find us a list of people, that would be appreciated.'

'Oh, don't you worry,' Nicola smiled. 'I've got my finger on the pulse. Few people in this school know much more than I do.'

Anjli smiled and then frowned as a new thought came to mind.

'Actually, on that point, did anybody here contact Stephanie Thompson yesterday?' she asked. 'Sarah Thompson's mother?'

At the question, Miss Linton looked at Nicola with a strange, confused expression on her face.

'How do you mean?' she eventually asked, looking back at Anjli.

'When DCI Walsh left the school after talking to you, he was confronted by Stephanie Thompson,' Anjli explained. 'He didn't understand how she knew he was there, but she said that a friend of hers had told her, and that people talked. I was curious, as you say you know everything around here, Nicola, about who would have told Stephanie that DCI Walsh was in the building, considering the fact that Miss Linton here had made a point of keeping him out of sight, in fear of giving concern to the children.'

It hadn't meant to come out as argumentative, and Anjli worried briefly that she'd gone too far, as Nicola had the same confused expression on her face as she looked at Miss Linton before turning back to face Anjli.

'She wouldn't have been told by anybody,' she said. 'She would have still been around. She hadn't checked out by the time he turned up and I was at reception when I signed him in, so I know that for a fact.'

'Hold on,' Cooper said, holding up her pen, paused in mid-writing. 'Are you saying that Stephanie Thompson was *at the school?*'

'Well, yes,' Nicola nodded. 'She's one of the playground monitors for lunchtime.'

Anjli rose, snatching back the list of names. She didn't mean to do it in a confrontational way, but there was panic in her eyes as she started to flick through the list.

'She's not here,' she said. 'She's not here.'

She looked up almost accusingly at Miss Linton.

'This was supposed to be a list of everybody who was here yesterday who would have known.'

'No, stop,' Miss Linton argued, holding up a hand. 'We were asked to give you a list of people *employed by the school.* Ms Thompson is a volunteer. She just turns up at lunchtimes to do the school playground duty – that's all she really does. She doesn't get paid for it, and she's done it, well, since I've been here.'

'Since Sarah first started at the school,' Nicola agreed. 'She's a volunteer, unpaid. She wouldn't be on this list.'

Anjli leant back in the chair, passing, reluctantly, the list back to Nicola.

'In that case, I need to know any volunteers who should be on here as well,' she said. 'Because if there's people around who are connected, but aren't on this list, then this list is worth nothing.'

She shook her head, realising the enormity of what this meant.

'Cooper, I need you to go speak to Stephanie Thompson once we get out of here. I think we need to have a conversation about what she's been up to.'

This ordered, Anjli narrowed her eyes as she stared back at Nicola.

'She's part of the lunchtime crowd,' she said. 'Playground monitor duty. Lunchtime starts at ...?'

'One pm,' Nicola replied. 'They usually come in about twelve thirty to twelve forty-five.'

'So, Stephanie Thompson arrived around quarter to one yesterday afternoon, and isn't on this list,' Anjli shook her head. 'Would she have worn a cap?'

'Stephanie? Oh absolutely,' Miss Linton said. 'During my time she's definitely worn it and that was after Sarah had gone. Stephanie would definitely have worn one of the new design these days, of course.'

Anjli had a feeling that something momentous had crossed here. Suddenly, she wondered if she was even looking at the right person. Stephanie Thompson had the cap, had the motive and had the opportunity. As somebody who the children saw every lunchtime session, Debbie would have recognised her in the museum, would have likely followed her in the same way that the students would have followed the lunchtime monitors.

She turned back to Cooper.

'Contact De'Geer,' she whispered. 'If he's at Temple Inn still, tell him to speak to Antony Morgan. It shouldn't take long to get to Chancery Lane from the office.'

'Guv, don't you want to go instead?'

'I don't think Morgan will speak to me in person again without a solicitor present,' Anjli said softly. 'And I think we need to have somebody give the fear of God to him right now. A seven-foot Viking police officer might be exactly what we need.'

She scratched at her chin.

'Tell him to ask Morgan if he ever saw Thomas Blackthorne wear a dark baseball cap with a gold duck on it, and if so, does he know where it is?'

'You think he might have kept it?'

'At this moment,' Anjli rose from the chair, nodding to both Miss Linton and Nicola as she finished her comment to Cooper. 'I'm not sure about anything.'

15

OLD ROUTES

De'Geer had been at Temple Inn when the call had come in from Cooper, and he had made his way quickly to Chancery Lane. From Temple Inn, it was no more than a ten-minute walk, especially at the speed he travelled. Chancery Lane was one of the roads that led up from Fleet Street, outside the main entrance to the courts of Temple Inn, and so De'Geer didn't bother taking a car, instead using his own size thirteens to make his way quickly back to the *Green Man* florist.

He couldn't be sure, but it certainly felt like Antony Morgan had been waiting for him. He didn't even seem surprised to see a uniformed officer in his doorway. Although, that said, the fact the officer was seven feet tall may have caused him a bit of a surprise.

'Let me guess,' he said, his accent still a mixture of English and American twang. 'DI Kapoor can't come and see me anymore without me crying for a lawyer, and so she's decided to try to find somebody else to scare me.'

'I'm not here to scare you, sir,' De'Geer said as politely as he could. 'I'm here to actually ask a question. We were hoping you might be able to cast your mind back to the time you worked for Thomas Blackthorne.'

'The time I worked for Thomas Blackthorne? You want me to go back there? Really?' Morgan shook his head. 'I already told her how much of a nightmare that time ended up being for me.'

'You also said you didn't believe he did it,' De'Geer replied coldly. 'This is your opportunity to give us something that could go towards that.'

'Okay, and what's that then?' Morgan muttered.

De'Geer opened up a screenshot on his phone. It was one of the sale photos of the old-style baseball cap. It wasn't great resolution, but it was enough to show a gold duck on a navy-blue cap.

'Did you ever see Thomas Blackthorne wearing this cap?' he asked.

Morgan took the phone, stared at the photo silently for a good thirty seconds before placing it back on the counter between them.

'I'm not sure,' he replied. 'And don't get me wrong, it wasn't because he didn't wear caps. Thomas liked baseball caps. He was losing his hair, and it was a way of hiding that. But I would remember if I saw a duck. No ... wait ... is this the school?'

'What would make you think that?' De'Geer asked in response.

'They've got a similar logo,' Morgan replied at the statement.

De'Geer leant closer.

'And how would you know that, sir?' he asked.

Antony Morgan paled.

'No, no, wait,' he said. 'I wasn't in any way saying—'

'Please, sir, tell me why you asked such a question.'

Morgan sighed, looking around.

'Look, I didn't tell DI Kapoor this, because, between us, I'm pretty pissed off at her,' he said uncomfortably. 'I still to this day do not think that Thomas Blackthorne was competent enough to do the things she claimed he was. I get she had a corrupt boss. I get the entire unit seemed to be on the take. And I'm not casting aspersions. It's just what I heard afterwards. It's just ...'

He swallowed, licking his lips, and De'Geer got the impression this was something that he really didn't want to talk about.

'A few weeks ago, I was at the New Covent Garden flower market, near Battersea. It's where the wholesalers sell, and a lot of florists go there to pick up their stuff. It's where Thomas used to go; it's where he picked up the posy of flowers he then got accused of placing on bodies.'

He bit back his next comment, calming himself down before continuing.

'The wholesaler is still there and they still sell to shops. It's just I won't buy from them anymore.'

'We know, sir,' De'Geer said. 'We checked the petals you gave us.'

Morgan waved at the selection by the side.

'Feel free to take any of them, random samples, check them as you want,' he said. 'I've got nothing to hide. But a couple of weeks back, I noticed someone else there. The mom of the girl who died, Sarah.'

'You saw Stephanie Thompson at the flower wholesaler?'

Morgan nodded.

'Look, loads of people go there. I see them all the time. But I recognised her, you know? I'd done a wedding six months ago. I didn't realise at the time, but it was for Stephanie's sister-in-law. She was helping with the details and we bumped into each other while I was setting up the flowers for the church. She remembered me from years earlier; I'd done a school fete with Thomas for something, and this reunion, well, it wasn't an easy conversation to have. She wanted me removed because of my connection to Thomas, and I understood that. I pointed out that I had nothing to do with it, but she still had me removed. I lost out on a fair chunk of money there because they decided not to pay me, even though I'd provided the flowers and everything. We're still arguing it. It's a pain in the arse and it's going into the small claims courts. But when I was at the flower wholesaler, I saw her, and I never forget a bitch that screws me over, pardon my language.'

'And the cap being connected to the school?'

'Yeah,' Morgan nodded now. 'I remember. They made us wear these caps while we were setting up. We gave them back after, and I pretty much forgot about it.'

As De'Geer noted this down, Morgan pondered the moment, stroking his chin as he did so.

'But when I saw Stephanie, she had a baseball cap on,' he said. 'It was like this, but it had a different design, more like a stylised line drawing of a bird. She had it worn low over her head, as if she was trying not to be seen. But in a way, just walking around with that on made her stand out even more. If you're at the wholesalers, you're shouting things and running around and looking hectic, and anyone who stands at the side folding their arms and glaring at people does kind of get noticed.'

'Do you know what she was doing there?' De'Geer asked. 'Maybe she was planning another wedding.'

'No, the public can't really buy from there,' Morgan shook his head. 'And I know she's not a florist, because if she was, she wouldn't have asked me to do the wedding, even if she constantly said she could do better.'

He scratched at his head now.

'Look, I don't want to say this because it doesn't sound good for her, but she was grabbing samples from people, claiming that she had a school event that she had to get ready for, and she needed to check colours. She wasn't gaining much, just a couple of flowers here or there, but she was near Watkins.'

'Watkins?'

'Watkins and Sons is the wholesaler who has the pansies that linked Thomas to the murders,' Morgan replied bitterly. 'Never saw them being accused though. There are others wholesales that do them, but mine are more violet now, while Watkins keeps them pure. You should—'

'We should keep to the subject at hand, sir.'

'Sure. Whatever. She spoke to a lot of the wholesalers. There's every chance she asked which ones dealt with Blackthorne and then asked for samples, especially Watkins.'

'Why?'

'I've got no idea. Maybe seeing me brought it all back up, and she wanted to try to solve the case herself. I wish I could help more but ...'

De'Geer nodded.

'Thank you,' he said. 'I think you've actually helped us more than you realise.'

Morgan said nothing else, just giving a tight, curt nod as he poured some hand gel onto his fingers and rubbed it in. De'Geer turned and left, heading south, back down to Temple Inn and the Unit.

If Stephanie Thompson had been at the florist wholesaler and had picked up the pansies that morning, then there was every opportunity for her to leave them at the British Museum. Also, based on what Cooper had told him in the phone call when he was asked to visit Morgan, it sounded like Stephanie Thompson hadn't been at school yesterday morning, and had the same cap that the stranger had worn, although in the new style.

Stephanie Thompson, who had demanded that Declan get someone, anyone, to reopen the case to gain closure.

Was this some kind of sick game to her? Could she, by chance, have taken Debbie Watson purely to get the case reopened?

Now with the phone to his ear, he dialled another number.

'Esme,' he said as Cooper answered it. 'Did you say you were going to speak to Stephanie Thompson?'

He nodded as Esme replied with the affirmative.

'Stand down,' he replied. 'I'm coming with you.'

There was a flurry of activity down the line; Esme was annoyed that De'Geer would feel that he had to go to protect her from what was effectively a grieving mother. So, once Cooper had finished, De'Geer took a deep breath and then relayed everything he'd been told by Antony Morgan.

By the end of it, Cooper didn't need to worry about a reason why De'Geer would be turning up with her.

By the end of it, Cooper agreed as well that De'Geer should turn up – if only to stop her strangling the woman.

Declan hadn't returned to Temple Inn directly after speaking to Mama Delcourt. He'd decided it was best to pay a visit to Henry Farrow at Tottenham North Station, even though ever since the Reaper's return, his appearances had been rather less accepted.

In fact, the last time he'd spoken to Henry Farrow, DCI of the unit, he'd been effectively told to curtail his appearances.

It didn't help that his ex-wife was Henry's now current wife. It also didn't help that the last time he'd actually been in the office with Henry properly, he'd been finding a hidden gun from a time he was a military police officer, threatening to use it on a serial killer who was then found dead, having fallen to his death from a roof where Declan was standing.

A serial killer who now, apparently, had left Declan *everything*.

Henry wasn't there, but DI Poole, a young man with a surprisingly bushy scruff of dark-brown beard, was in the office when Declan arrived. Declan had met him a couple of times but never really dealt much with him.

'I understand you went to see the Sisters,' Poole said with a grin.

'And you know this because?'

'Because we have informants watching the Sisters,' Poole shrugged. 'They are people of interest. You would be doing the same, I'm sure, DCI Walsh.'

Poole looked around.

'Look, as much as I'm happy to chat and talk war stories, I don't think DCI Farrow would be happy if he knew you were here.'

'Where is Henry?'

'At home with his wife and your daughter,' Poole replied, and Declan got the distinct impression there was no love lost between Declan and Poole right now, probably as Poole would have had loyalties to Farrow over anyone else. 'He's keeping them safe from maniacs shooting airsoft rifles at them.'

'That's why I'm here, actually,' Declan said. 'We've got an idea of what the bike was.'

'We know,' Poole said. 'We've been given the description from your cyber guy.'

'Oh, good ...' Declan said, but the way he said it was enough to cast doubt on the veracity of his words.

'You knew we had it,' Poole said in realisation. 'You've come here under false pretences, DCI Walsh, haven't you?'

Declan shrugged.

'Honestly, I wanted to see how me and DCI Farrow were right now,' he admitted. 'I'm aware this is my fault, but *isn't* my fault at the same time. And I'm also aware it's going to give him shit. I kind of wanted to smooth things over.'

'Well, I'll let him know you were here,' Poole said. 'Apart from that, I'm afraid you're going to have to leave.'

'No, that's fine,' Declan said. 'Totally agree. Before I go, can I just use your toilet? It's okay, I know the way.'

'I'll get an officer to ...'

'Honestly, I know where it is. I worked here, remember?' Declan laughed. 'And by the time you get the guy here, I'll have been.'

Poole sighed, waving Declan off, and Declan headed down the stairs towards the changing rooms and toilets.

He didn't intend to go to the toilet, however. He'd spent years working with Derek Salmon here, even before Farrow took over the hotseat, and he knew better than most people the back routes through the building. As soon as he was out of sight, he doubled back on himself, heading down a south-facing corridor, up the back stairs and back into the detective's office.

He guessed that Poole would wait around for him at reception; after all, he would be the one on the line if Declan did anything wrong. So, he knew that Poole's computer would be empty for the moment.

There was nobody in the office as he walked in, and Declan was quite glad about this; he hadn't actually considered what to say if somebody else had been there. But quickly and quietly, he slipped down into Poole's seat, opened up his laptop, and brought up *Holmes2.*

Now in the system, and using Poole's ID to do so, Poole stupidly keeping his password on the laptop as a cookie for speed, Declan pulled up the address of Easter Clarke. He had guessed that Easter wouldn't exactly have been an angel in the area, and he wasn't mistaken; seventeen years old and already with a list of offences that would make most criminals blush. At the top of the file was a photo, a description and an address in Tottenham, north-east of Seven Sisters.

Declan quickly took a picture with his phone, closing down *Holmes2* and exiting out of the office as quickly as he could. Then, retracing his steps, he emerged back out into the main reception area where, as expected, DI Poole stood, irritated.

'I thought you were going to be quick,' he muttered.

'Hey, what can I say?' Declan replied. 'I get shy in unfamiliar bathrooms.'

Poole shrugged and pointed at the door.

'DCI Walsh, I'm afraid we're going to have to ask you to disappear now,' he said.

Declan nodded and started towards the door, but then paused, looking back at Poole.

'This attitude you have for me,' he asked, 'is this because of what's happened with your DCI, or is this something more?'

At the question, Poole looked uncomfortable.

'I wasn't here when you were around,' he said. 'But I was here when Derek Salmon came in and admitted to the murder of Angela Martin. You might remember that; you guys turned up and threw your weight around.'

'I do remember,' Declan said. 'And if I remember correctly, I was brought in because Derek wouldn't deal with anybody else.'

'Strange that,' Poole replied. 'You see, this is my problem with you, DCI Walsh. You were trained under a corrupt officer in a department run by an officer who regularly gets accused of corruption.'

'I'm guessing you mean Monroe.'

Poole didn't answer, but it was obvious Declan had hit the mark.

'Since Farrow took over, Tottenham North has been a good station,' Poole eventually spoke. 'Every time we have a problem, it's because you or someone from your department's turned up.'

He shook his head slightly.

'In a way, Declan, I almost wish my boss had never married your ex-wife. Because then, you'd have no reason to turn up here.'

Declan laughed at this.

'Mate, you're not the only one,' he said. 'And trust me, I wasn't happy about this either.'

'Then perhaps you shouldn't cosy up to serial killers?' Poole's face was tight, and Declan could see the suppressed anger in his eyes.

Declan, however, had had enough of this man and his annoying beard, and so turned around and walked up to face Poole. They were only a few inches apart.

'If you think I'm corrupt, Detective Inspector,' he said, 'feel free to get Internal Affairs to have a look into it. Because I can tell you now, whatever Karl Schnitter has done, it was done to get me back, not to provide me with things. And if I hear you state one more time that I'm corrupt, I will have you removed.'

'Of course, you have the power to do that,' Poole snapped back snarkily. 'But don't worry, your Prime Minister friend will go soon as well—'

He stopped as Declan slammed him against the wall, his extendable baton across his throat.

'It's "don't worry, *Detective Chief Inspector,*" or "don't worry, *Guv*",' Declan hissed. 'You don't know me well enough to use my first name so casually, because if you did, you wouldn't pull the shit you're pulling right now.'

Poole's eyes bulged on stalks, as he was probably realising just how far across the line he'd crossed.

'And don't worry,' Declan continued. 'I'll tell DCI Farrow I was here. And how you helped me with my enquiries.'

'I didn't help you.'

'No, I suppose you didn't.' Declan stood there for a long moment and almost considered punching the man, but in the end, he shrugged and stepped back. Returning the baton to its hiding place up his sleeve, he then brushed himself down, flipped Poole the finger casually, turned and walked out.

He didn't need to do anything, really. After all, by the time it came out that the address for Easter Clarke had been searched for at North Tottenham, it would be Poole's computer that showed the access report.

It would be Poole accused of passing information to Declan.

In a way, Declan no longer felt bad about getting the man into any problems, because of his usage of his ID.

Now, however, he had an e-bike riding thug to find.

16

HALF-FILLED ROOMS

'RIGHT THEN, WHAT DO WE HAVE?'

Monroe stood in front of the half-filled briefing room. Declan was missing, as were both De'Geer and Cooper. Doctor Marcos sat beside Anjli. DCI Esposito sat at the back with DS McAlroy, and Billy, as ever, sat at his computer, his laptop to the left.

'And where the hell is Declan?' Monroe grumbled.

'He went to speak to Mama Delcourt,' Anjli spoke. 'I'm guessing it took longer than he thought.'

'Well, as long as he isn't knocked unconscious like he was the first time they met, we should see him later on,' Monroe muttered to himself. 'The Viking and his love?'

'Picking up Stephanie Thompson.'

'Good,' Monroe straightened as he faced the room once more. 'I think we need to have a chat with that woman. There's something more going on there, I reckon.'

He looked at Billy.

'What do we have on her?'

Billy was already working on the laptop as Monroe asked

him, and on the screen behind Monroe, the image of Stephanie Thompson appeared.

'Stephanie Thompson was married to Sean Thompson, but the revelations following the death of her daughter, especially parts of her past, caused the relationship to fall apart. They divorced a year later,' Billy read from his notes. 'She blamed Mile End police, in particular Detective Chief Inspector Ford, for the collapse of her marriage, claiming that it was information about her past that didn't need to become public that caused this, and that DCI Ford had deliberately done this as some kind of retaliation for complaints Stephanie had made about her attitude to her superiors. Obviously, after Blackthorne had died, the case was effectively closed.'

He looked across at Anjli.

'I'm assuming that's correct?'

Anjli nodded tersely, and Billy continued.

'And that's really it. Sean left Stephanie the house, it was already paid for – however they remortgaged half of it before he left to provide him with a deposit for his own new accommodation.'

He carried on scrolling.

'Last year she passed a beautician's exam, looking to start her own business. She claimed in an interview on a beautician blog that she'd taken it up after she realised she had alopecia and looked for ways to hide this. Eventually, she leant into it.'

On the screen, a Facebook page for a beauty clinic appeared.

'It looks bigger than it is,' Billy added. 'From what we can work out, she does afternoon appointments and weekends, mainly from her garage, or maybe a conservatory at her house; something which she's tricked out to cover some basic beauty techniques.'

'Not mornings?' Anjli asked.

Billy shook his head.

'Nothing before two,' he replied. 'Which confirms the story we now have that she still volunteers at the school.'

'Why would she still do that, though?' Esposito asked. 'It has to be hard, going back to where your daughter went, day after day, long after she's gone?'

Billy looked back at him.

'No idea, Guv,' he said. 'Although, looking at some of the reviews on her Facebook page and cross-referencing the names, a lot do seem to be mothers of the students at the school, so with my cynical hat on, it could be purely a case of making sure she's visible at the school, so that the parents of the kids she looks after use her services?'

'Makes sense,' Anjli said. 'An hour a day of lunchtime volunteering to gain yourself a few hundred pounds' worth of sales, and it's probably repeat sales as well.'

She leant back in the chair.

'Must be tough as well. Losing your daughter and your husband in the space of a year. Past should be past, you know. She shouldn't have been judged.'

'The impression we have, though, is that it was your DCI who judged her,' McAlroy added. 'Not saying it was you, but Ford isn't exactly the most tactful of people.'

'Okay, so we know she runs the lunchtime shift, and we know she doesn't do anything in the mornings,' Monroe interjected, pulling the conversation back on track. 'We also know that somebody put together a website with a password and placed a QR code on a pump in the middle of Soho in the middle of the morning.'

He pointed at the photo of the woman behind him on the plasma screen.

'Her build fits the stranger who abducted Debbie Watson, and she could wear any colour wig, holding it down with the cap. We also know now that Debbie would have known Stephanie Thompson from the lunchtime playground times. I think we can say there's enough here to make us consider her as a prime suspect.'

'Motive, sir?'

'She'd blindsided Declan, demanding us to reopen the case,' Anjli suggested to Billy, who'd asked the question. 'Maybe she doesn't believe us when we say Blackthorne was the killer and he won't kill again.'

'Extreme way to get things reopened,' Monroe puffed out his cheeks. 'You sure you don't want to take point on this, Alvaro?'

'I'm fine right here,' Esposito replied. 'We like our cases a little less all over the place. This circus show is definitely one for you guys.'

Monroe laughed. It was a small, almost bitter sound, as if he knew that Esposito was telling the truth rather than making a light-hearted comment. This was turning out to be more than they wanted, or even expected.

'Billy, what else do we know about this woman?' he asked.

'We're looking into her at the moment,' Billy replied. 'Checking if she has any other properties or places that she visits a lot.'

'Well, perhaps if she's got something somewhere that she thinks people haven't thought of, she might have the girl there,' Anjli nodded. 'That, of course, is if it's her.'

'We need to look into it either way,' Monroe said. 'Keep checking into it. What do we know about the boy?'

'Black hair, young, maybe thirteen, fourteen years old,' Cooper read from her notes. 'Scrumpy hadn't paid much attention, said that he was keeping his distance. After she walked off, he walked over to the pump and took a photo, possibly testing the QR code or confirming that it happened.'

'How much are we sure they work together?' Anjli asked.

Cooper frowned.

'Actually, Guv, I'm not sure,' she said. 'He never stated that the two of them walked along together. It could have been that he was following.'

'Hypothetical question,' McAlroy now said. 'We're going along the basis that whoever this abductee is, they have a thirteen or fourteen-year-old boy helping them. But what if this boy is actually playing amateur detective? Maybe *he* is following them?'

'Well, then it'd be good to know who it is, so he could tell us what he's found,' Monroe grumbled. 'Is there anybody who would have a connection to the murders who is of the age?'

'Actually, there is,' Anjli nodded, looking up from her notes. 'Mia Chen had a brother. He was a year, maybe two years older than her. Oliver.'

She looked over at Billy, and she didn't need to say anything as he was already typing in details, pulling up an image onto the plasma screen. It was one photo of Mia Chen, taken before her death three years earlier. She was nine years old; black hair cut in a bob, a fringe high on her forehead above her smiling green eyes. Beside her were her parents, and beside them was another boy. At this point, he was around eleven years old, slim, with jet-black hair cut into a shaggy cut.

'He'd be about the same age, and he has the black hair,'

Monroe nodded. 'Find me an up-to-date photo of him and get Scrumpy to have a look. See if he recognises him.'

He stopped himself from continuing, looking back at the briefing room.

'Actually, hold on that,' he said. 'By the time we get a confirmation, it'd be too late. Maybe we can speak to the parents, ask if we can chat to wee Oliver already? If he's not the boy, then we—'

'That'll be difficult,' Esposito spoke now. 'We had a message about him a few days back. Boy went missing at the start of the week.'

'Wait, so this is another missing kid, from the same time as Debbie, if not shortly before?' Declan looked around. 'Is this now two people we're hunting?'

'Yes, but not in the way you think,' McAlroy answered. 'He left a note, claimed he needed time away; apparently he'd had a fight with them, they'd unfairly blamed him for his sister's death for years, and this wasn't the first time he'd run off. Usually he'd stay at a family friend's for a couple of days and then return.'

'Can we see if we can find this family friend?' Monroe asked.

'Go for it,' Esposito shrugged. 'I hope you do better than we did. The kid's a sodding ghost.'

Monroe considered the response, narrowing his eyes as he worked through the currently unpopular range of options he now had.

'Anjli, go find Scrumpy and check if this is possibly Oliver Chen. McAlroy, as you weren't in Mile End at the time, go and visit the family, as they might be happier to see a new face, rather than someone from a traumatic time. See if you can find any clues as to where Oliver could be.'

He muttered to himself, looking around.

'Where the bloody hell is Declan?'

'Still hasn't come back to us, boss,' Anjli said. 'But currently, I think Jess's attacker is a little bit more important for him.'

'Aye, I suppose there's a lot of us on one case and only him on the other,' Monroe replied.

There was a moment of silence as the room watched Monroe as he paced.

What I can't get into my head is what the game plan is here,' Monroe eventually stated. 'If she wants us to restart the case, then that's fine, but to kidnap a wee bairn ...'

'Maybe she felt we weren't listening,' Billy suggested.

'Aye, I get that,' Monroe replied. 'But what would happen if we didn't solve the case? What would she do with the small girl? More importantly, what would she do once we *did* solve the case and realised, as it looks like we're doing now, that *she's* the person we want to chat to? She throws away everything.'

'Maybe she feels it's more than worth it,' Esposito stated. 'As we said, she's lost her daughter, she's lost her husband, maybe she feels this is a suitable sacrifice.'

'Aye, it just feels something's off,' Monroe said. 'Do we have anything more on this bloody poem as well?'

'No, boss,' Billy shook his head. 'Forensics is still examining Crossbone's graveyard. The four strips of her dress and the lanyard are the only things found.'

Monroe's pencil tapped against his teeth as he stared up at the plasma screen, now showing the next poem.

Place of sweating fever,
Where illness finds deceiver,

Butcher's hook! Butcher's hook!
We all feel ill.

'So, five strands of her hair were found at the pump,' he said, staring up at the words. 'Now four torn parts of her dress, as well as her lanyard, are found at Crossbone's Graveyard. These aren't proofs of life, they are proofs of intent, a way of saying, "I have the girl." So all they're doing is sending us on some kind of wild goose chase.'

He slammed his hand on the desk.

'I just don't get it,' he said.

'Boss,' it was Anjli who spoke this time. 'We'll get them, we always do.'

'Aye,' Monroe said, 'we bloody better. We only have a day left.'

He looked at his watch.

'Somebody find me De'Geer and Cooper, and tell me why the bloody hell it's taken them so long to find this woman, and get me Declan sodding Walsh – because if he's not here, he's out there doing something bloody stupid, and likely career-ending.'

De'Geer hadn't been sure what to expect when he arrived at the house of Stephanie Thompson. With no husband or child living with her anymore, Stephanie lived a lonely life, shown by the quiet, almost bare front garden. There was no car in the driveway and in the window was a Labour Party flyer. There'd been by-elections recently and Stephanie had obviously been involved. On the other side of the windows was another flyer, this one for a beauty services parlour with a telephone number and website.

De'Geer had gone to the front door while Cooper walked around to the back of the house, only to find the side gate had been left open. Banging on the door and ringing the doorbell for good measure, he hoped he wasn't sounding too confrontational as he called out, 'Miss Thompson, are you there? This is the police, we need to speak to you.'

There was no answer. De'Geer tried again.

'Anything?' he shouted out.

'No,' the faint voice of Cooper could be heard. 'If she's here, she's not listening.'

De'Geer, giving up on the front door, now walked around to the back of the house where Cooper was waiting for him.

'The back door's open,' she said. 'Should we go in?'

De'Geer frowned at the question. The last few times they had entered a house with the door opened, they either found dead bodies or, sometimes even worse – but it was too good an opportunity to turn down right now.

'Do we believe her life might be in danger?' he asked.

Cooper shrugged.

'She didn't answer the call,' she said, 'and we know she's been very depressed. Confronting DCI Walsh was enough for that.'

'That's enough for me,' De'Geer said as he opened the door. 'Miss Thompson, it's Sergeant De'Geer of the City of London Police. Are you okay?'

There was no answer and, as De'Geer and Cooper walked around the house, they quickly realised there was no answer because Stephanie Thompson wasn't there.

'We should get out,' De'Geer said. 'There's nothing here.'

However, he paused as he looked down at a coffee table.

On it was a photo taken from a distance; he didn't know the man in the image very well, but he had spoken to him earlier that day and therefore he recognised Antony Morgan the moment he saw him.

'It seems Stephanie Thompson isn't just following DCI Walsh,' he said, picking it up carefully, his latex gloves now on, as he turned it in his hand. 'She's following Blackthorne's old shop assistant.'

He looked up at Cooper.

'But is she doing that because she wants him to join her in her crusade or because she believes he's connected somehow?'

'Maybe she believes he can tell her the truth about Blackthorne.'

De'Geer nodded. He went to carry on, but then paused once more. To the side was a vase, and in the vase was a small collection of pansies and poppies.

Pulling out a clear baggie, he took one, placing it into the bag.

'There's a legality here we should be careful about,' Cooper said.

'We'll discuss the legalities if we find it's more important than we thought,' De'Geer said. 'At the moment, I'm just confirming a lead.'

As he turned, looking back at the living room, he asked, 'does something feel off here?' as he carried on turning in a slow circle.

'How do you mean?' Cooper asked.

'It just feels a little staged,' De'Geer shrugged. 'The door being open, allowing us to come in. The posy of flowers handily being here, beside a picture of the daughter.'

He shook his head.

'It's almost like this is a shrine, like we're supposed to see it.'

He stopped, his voice fading to a mutter as he walked over to the coffee table in the middle of the room.

'Look,' he mumbled. 'There's nothing else on here apart from these two pieces of paper.'

On one piece, printed on headed notepaper from Kelsey Primary School, was a note about school changes for lunch hours. The other was an invoice of some kind, for property.

He read it and looked back at Cooper.

'Apparently, Stephanie Thompson rents a small building,' he said. 'Doesn't say where, though. Short-term lease, one month. I think we need to speak to the Guv right now.'

He looked around the room one last time.

'Our suspect isn't here, but has left us a pretty damning clue to where she could be.'

He found himself staring out of the window from where he stood, almost as if waiting for someone to be seen watching them; he couldn't help believing that someone had made sure they found this, rather than Stephanie herself leaving it by accident.

If that was true, then Stephanie could be as much a victim as Debbie Watson.

17

AVENUES AND ALLEYWAYS

Declan wasn't at the briefing because he was still in North London.

He knew the team could do without him; he wasn't any kind of Poirot-level mentalist who could solve the case without anybody else. Every case they'd solved had always been a team effort, and the team was worthy enough to find Debbie Watson before it was too late; he had no doubt of that.

Of course, this could all have been Declan convincing himself that he wasn't needed, that he could spend the next hour staring at the estate on Lawrence Road, watching for movement, waiting for Easter Clarke to appear. He had no proof Easter was the man who had fired the airsoft rifle; all he had was an address stolen illegally from *Holmes2*, which he was sure he'd have to pay for at some point. But he waited nevertheless, and after twenty minutes of patiently sitting on the side of a wall beside a bus stop, he saw the door to the apartment block open and Easter emerge. He'd seen the photo of Easter on *Holmes2*, and he knew what he looked like;

the suspect was young, recently turned seventeen. Declan would usually have called him a boy, but he was old enough to be arrested, to fight in the army, to get married. Easter Clarke had a wispy moustache above his lip, and more importantly, he'd possibly fired a gun at someone's house. This made him a man, and as far as Declan was concerned, made him a man he could confront.

'Easter,' he shouted, rising and walking towards the man. 'I'd like a word.'

It was around lunchtime by now, and Easter had probably relaxed a little from his previous day's escapades, so he hadn't expected to find Declan walking towards him.

'I don't know who you are, mate,' he said. 'I don't talk to strangers.'

Declan pulled out his warrant card, holding it up.

'Then maybe you'll speak to the police,' he said. 'I'd like to talk to you about your bike, especially about it being used in a drive-by shooting.'

'I don't know what you're talking about.' Easter turned and walked over to the bike, chained up in a secure bike locker. It was a *Cycle Hangar*, a fixed storage locker that looked like a small metal-framed hanger; designed to hold up to six standard-sized bicycles and about the size of one car-parking space. Declan had seen them around, and he knew people could rent a space in a hangar, which could only be accessed by a key they possessed once they hired the spot, a lock that the police also had access to in case of theft. It was a good way to keep an expensive e-bike secure, and Declan could see from Easter's positioning and body language that not only was Easter familiar with the hangar, but as he opened it, unlocking the bike, a familiar looking red and black one, that he was about to run.

Good, he thought. *Let him.*

'I know it was you, Easter,' Declan said. 'Who rode past the house, firing the gun. What was it, a BB gun? Maybe an airsoft pistol? Something that wasn't meant to kill, but was meant to scare. Come on, Easter, who paid you to scare the people in that house?'

'What's it to you?' Easter was now on the bike, trying to start it. Declan knew electric bikes worked from pedal movement, but there was also a battery that needed to be turned on first. And that was where the problem was going to be for the younger man.

'I'm the guy the message was meant for,' Declan carried on towards him. 'And your bike won't work, by the way. The problem with electric bikes is they're really easy to screw up.'

He grinned.

'I already did that. You really should have taken it into your apartment, rather than leaving it outside. Who knows what could happen to it? Or was that the plan? If someone stole it, you could claim they did it *yesterday,* if someone like me came along?'

Easter jumped off the now unmoving bike and didn't reply, instead sprinting off down the side alley between the apartment blocks. Declan had expected this, and in a strange way, Declan had actually *wanted* this. He wanted to hunt down the man who had shot at his daughter, even if indirectly. He'd also been building his cardio in recent months, and had brought his running shoes with him today.

Even though Declan was a runner and in the right attire, Easter Clarke wasn't a slouch. He was a seventeen-year-old boy in the prime of his life, and with adrenaline pumping, he was running for his life. Declan found he was actually struggling to keep up with the boy.

He turned down another alley that led off from Anchor Drive and the Brunswick Road car park, Easter leaping over bins and rubbish bags, as Declan doggedly pursued. Declan wasn't sure if Easter had a game plan here; was there a way that he knew to escape via, or was this purely by instinct? If it was the former, then Declan could be running into a trap. If it was the latter, there was every chance that Easter would find himself in an alleyway with no exit. At that point, Declan could finally have his conversation.

As it was, it seemed to be a mixture of both. After five minutes of intense sprinting, both combatants out of breath, they found themselves at a dead end, Easter turning and pulling a butterfly knife, flipping it open, facing Declan.

'Back off, man!' he shouted.

Declan didn't. In fact, he only slowed down, still walking towards Easter, shaking out his extendable baton from his usual hidden sleeve pocket, clicking it into position.

'I could use a taser on you,' he said, 'but that would spoil the fun, wouldn't it? You see, the person you were told to attack, that was my daughter.'

'I don't know nothing about that.'

'And yet you stand there with a blade raised at me,' Declan shook his head. 'You're not exactly arguing your case.'

Easter backed away, but then ran to the side, banging on one of the doors.

'Styles!' he shouted. 'Styles, get out of here!'

Declan realised with a sinking feeling in his stomach, that this wasn't the dead end that he'd believed it to be. This was gang territory, and the door opened to reveal three burly-looking young black men, all holding weapons of some kind. One held a baseball bat, another what looked to be some kind of wooden kendo stick, the third a kukri knife, which Declan was pretty sure was illegal.

'This isn't anything to do with you guys,' Declan said. 'This is police business.'

'Yeah?' The first man emerging, a large, chunky, older man with the bat in hand, who Declan assumed was the Styles who'd been called out, growled. 'What kind of police business is this?'

'Your boy here fired a gun at my teenage daughter,' Declan said matter-of-factly. 'I'd like to know who paid him.'

'I don't snitch,' Easter replied calmly.

'If you've got a problem—'

'Oh, I've got a problem,' Declan said. And before anyone could say anything, he moved in, slamming down with the baton onto the hand wielding the kukri blade. With a scream, the man wielding the blade dropped it to the floor, and Declan spun to face the next one. He knew in a case like this, he needed to take the most fearsome weapon first. He could take a blow from a kendo stick or a baseball bat, but what he couldn't take was a slash from a blade.

Declan barely had time to catch his breath before Styles, or at least who he believed was Styles swung at him. He ducked, feeling the whoosh of air as the bat missed his head by inches. Without hesitating, Declan jabbed his baton into Styles's ribs, eliciting a grunt of pain. The thug with the kendo stick charged next, thrusting the weapon towards Declan's midsection. Declan parried the blow with his baton, but the force of it sent him stumbling backwards. As Easter backed away, Styles saw his chance and swung again, this time connecting with Declan's shoulder. Pain exploded in his arm, but he gritted his teeth and swung his baton, catching Styles on the jaw and sending him sprawling to the ground.

Ignoring the throbbing pain in his shoulder, Declan turned to face the remaining men. The thug with the kendo stick came at him again, but Declan was ready. He side-stepped the attack, then brought his baton down hard on the man's wrist, disarming him. The man cried out and fell to his knees, clutching his broken wrist. Declan looked up to see that Easter had grabbed the kukri knife from the floor in his free hand, and was charging at him with a wild look in his eyes. Declan ducked under the wild swing of the knife and delivered a swift knee to Easter's stomach, knocking the wind out of him.

'Who's next?' he snarled.

It was as if the fight had gone out of Styles and the others. They slowed, staring at Declan.

'This ain't our fight,' they said, looking at Easter, now crouched as they snatched the kukri blade back off him. 'This ain't normal Fed procedure. Whatever you did, this is on you.'

Declan was surprised. He hadn't expected himself to be such a fearsome foe. But as he glanced down the end of the alleyway, he saw a car had pulled up, and two men were watching. One of them he recognised as an enforcer for Mama Delcourt – it looked like she'd been keeping an eye on him as well.

Or was she making sure that somebody on her turf wasn't giving away an answer she didn't like?

Either way, Styles wanted none of it.

'Styles, you can't, you gotta let me ...' Easter started, his voice turning into a yelp of pain as Declan slapped away his butterfly knife with his extendable baton, pushing him against the wall.

'Who paid you?' Declan demanded.

'I don't know what you mean—'

'Who paid you!'

'I don't have anything to say,' Easter stammered.

Declan slammed the hilt of the extendable baton against the wall, an inch from the side of Easter's head.

'It was my daughter,' he hissed. 'This isn't some random person who I'm solving a crime for. It. Was. My. *Daughter.*'

He leaned closer, so close that his nose was touching the tip of Easter's as he stared into the terrified boy's eyes.

'Do you think I'll stop here?'

The boy looked down the alleyway and saw the car still waiting.

'Okay, okay, I can tell you what I know,' he said.

'That's a start,' Declan replied. 'Who paid you to do this?'

'James paid me.'

'Who's James?'

'He's a fixer in Wandsworth.'

'So this fixer paid you to do this, why?'

'Said he'd been asked to pass a message, nothing major, just to put the scares up you, you know?'

'And were you connected to the Hurley message?'

'What's a Hurley?' Easter frowned. 'Look, man, I was paid to fire an airsoft pistol at a window, that was all that I was told to do.'

'Where do I find James the fixer in Wandsworth?' Declan asked.

'You don't, he finds you—' Again, Easter's voice was cut off, this time, however, by Declan's forearm resting against his throat.

'If I push harder,' he said, 'you will lose consciousness and collapse to the floor. If I add more pressure, I'll crush your windpipe. Shall we start again?'

'I can give you a number,' Easter choked out. 'Please, it's all I've got. He just said the bitch wanted to …'

'The bitch?' Declan paused. 'Tell me more about the bitch.'

'She's the one who gave James the job. All I know is that he didn't like her, but he'd worked with her before, and he owed her.'

Declan leant back.

'But you don't know if she was anything to do with Hurley.'

'Mate, I don't even know what a Hurley is.'

Declan stared at the teenage boy who had gone to kill his daughter …

No, he hadn't gone to kill his daughter. He'd been sent to scare her.

That wasn't the point. The point was his family had been attacked and he …

No, it wasn't his family anymore. Jess was his daughter, but Liz was married. They were Henry's family now.

Declan's eyes narrowed in anger. And seeing the expression, Easter shook his head, trying to push himself into the very bricks behind him, convinced he was about to be hurt, and hurt badly.

'I'm going to give you a message of my own,' Declan said, stepping back and picking up the fallen butterfly knife. 'I'm going to make sure you never do this again.'

'Dad, stop!' The voice came out of nowhere and Declan turned to see Jess Walsh standing there, at the end of the alley, beside the car, horrified at what she was watching. 'Dad, what are you doing?'

'Jess.' Declan paused. 'You shouldn't be here.'

'No, Dad. It looks like I really should,' Jess replied. 'Tell me you weren't going to hurt the man.'

'Why do you care?' Declan asked almost suddenly. 'This is the man who—'

'I know what he did, Dad,' Jess interrupted. 'I heard what he said. Someone hired him to scare me. It's a message being thrown to you. I get that. You scared him enough.'

She looked down the alleyway.

'And those men there have done the job as well.'

Declan let Easter go, and before he could say anything, Easter sprinted off down the alleyway, past the car at the end. It was as if all the anger, all the adrenaline, tumbled out of Declan, and he felt bone tired and weary, slumping against the wall as he realised what he'd almost done.

'Jess, how did you—'

'How do you think?' Jess replied, tapping her phone. 'I always know where you are, Dad.'

'How do—'

'I use Billy's tracker, the one you put on all your phones,' Jess gave a weak smile. 'I've sat next to Billy on several cases. Did you think I wouldn't be able to hack into his system? I don't use it that much, but it helps if I'm worried about you.'

She looked around,

'Like if I see you down an alleyway near the Seven Sisters.'

Declan gave a weak smile in response, matching his daughter's one.

'You shouldn't be here,' he said. 'You should be somewhere safe.'

'What if that's what they're trying to do?' Jess asked. 'Seriously, Dad, they had a guy firing an airsoft pistol at us – that's not attempted murder. They *want* us to leave. They want you distracted from the case.'

'I'm not—'

'Why are you here, Dad? Like, right now? Why aren't you trying to solve the case?'

Declan felt like he was being admonished, and he felt a little belligerent.

'You're my daughter and I wanted to—'

'No, Dad, don't give me that,' Jess snapped back. 'There's a girl missing and you're here attacking seventeen-year-old kids. What the bloody hell?'

Declan nodded as the enormity of what he was doing finally washed over him.

'As ever, you're the intelligent one,' he said reluctantly. But he added nothing else, and Jess watched as he closed up his extendable baton and started towards the car.

The man sitting in the passenger seat watched him approach.

'Mama Delcourt told us to keep an eye on you while you were in our manor,' he said. 'She thought you'd probably do something stupid.'

'Tell her I owe her,' Declan smiled. 'Tell her I know it wasn't her who did this.'

He paused.

'Do you know a James in Wandsworth?'

'Everybody knows James in Wandsworth.' The man smiled. With this, he passed a piece of folded paper.

'When he started screaming it, I wrote the details down for you. Class this as a favour fulfilled.'

'What favour would that be?'

'I don't know.' The man shrugged. 'But as far as Mama

Delcourt's concerned, she doesn't owe you anything anymore, DCI. So take the win.'

18

GAIN THE SCOOP

Ian Trent was never one of the lucky ones. For over fifteen years now he'd been at the forefront of four, count them, *four* potential career-making stories – and every single one had been lost to someone else. It was never his fault, of course. He was always the second on site, the third to file the story, the last to work it out.

His editor wasn't angry with him. He was a solid worker and always brought in the goods. It's just that Ian felt he could do better. He was due bigger stories.

He'd been trying to push to take over the Declan Walsh story for the last couple of days. Serial killers and police corruption; there was something there. Maybe a book down the line.

He'd even read the advance copy sent to the paper, the one by Malcolm Gladwell, and that alone was explosive stuff – until Gladwell took it off sale and pulped all copies.

Trent knew this wasn't a light decision to make.

Gladwell had been *got to*. It was the only option.

But Ian's editor at *The Individual*, Sean Ashby, had some kind of connection with Declan, probably because of a dead journalist by the name of Kendis Taylor. Ian had never met Kendis, but he'd heard the stories.

She was an excellent journalist, and unlike Trent, Kendis was always first on the scene.

If he was being brutally honest, Ian Trent had hated everything about Kendis Taylor from the moment he heard about her. There was a line in journalism, that the "luckiest people got the best stories, but the harder you worked at it, the luckier you got." But Ian had worked hard and he still wasn't being lucky.

Kendis, however, had walked into every job she could find – before dying, that was. Again, a death connected to then-DI Declan Walsh.

Or, as Ian Trent liked to say, "the subject of my Times Bestseller."

Ian Trent was a man on a mission to find that story, something that he could use to be first on the scene, to be number one once more. He didn't expect it to come in the form of a phone call.

No one else was on the desk at the time, and Ian, if he was being honest, hadn't even realised he was manning the desk, having just sat down there to eat his lunch. It was only just past noon, but he hadn't eaten breakfast and he was starving, the thought of his BLT sandwich from the Co-op taking over his waking thoughts, which was a quite depressing situation to be in.

'The Individual, news desk,' he mumbled, answering the phone.

'Hi, I'd like to speak to a journalist,' the voice was slightly American. It sounded nervous.

'You're speaking to one,' Ian replied. 'What's happened?' He gave the tone of a man who didn't expect *much* to have happened. This was probably somebody annoyed at their neighbour.

'The missing girl, Debbie Watson. I think I know where she is.'

This was *not* a neighbour complaining.

Ian sat up, dropping the Robert Heinlein book that he'd been reading, leaning closer to the phone even though the receiver was to his ear.

'What do you mean?' he questioned.

'I mean, I think I know where the child is being kept,' the voice continued. 'My name is Antony Morgan. I run a florist on Chancery Lane and, well, I've been talking to the police connected to this. There's a Detective Inspector named Anjli Kapoor who, well, she's not been very nice to me.'

Ian was shaking his head, grabbing paper and pen urgently.

'Now, wait, back up. What has this got to do with the story?'

The voice, this apparent Antony Morgan, paused.

'I'm sorry,' he muttered. 'It's just information has come to my attention that the person who abducted Debbie Watson has them in a lock-up near Smithfield. They've been playing games with the police, including DI Kapoor.'

'So speak to DI Kapoor.' Ian was frowning now. There was a part of him that wanted the story, but another part that wanted the police to be involved here. 'Why haven't you contacted the police?'

'Because they don't believe me, Mister Trent,' Morgan replied down the phone. 'They think I'm connected. My boss back in the day was Thomas Blackthorne, who they reckoned was the killer. They forced him to commit murder. Now, years later, someone's doing it again. I'd started checking into it because I never believed my employer could have done such a thing.'

'So who did this?'

'I'll tell you everything,' Morgan said, and for a moment, for the first time, Ian Trent felt that there was triumph in the voice. No longer nervous, almost as if this was what he'd been waiting for. 'If you want the scoop of the century, Mister Trent, then you really need to come meet me now. I'll give you the address. Find the girl. Let's break this case before the police do. Let's prove that my old boss wasn't the murderer. How's that for a story?'

Ian Trent liked the sound of that. And after Antony Morgan gave him the details, he wrote them down before sending a text to a photographer to meet him downstairs. Then, grabbing his coat, he left the offices of *The Individual* at a run. He would, by some random luck, by being the man on the phone, be the first on site.

Once more, the line about being lucky came into his head. He had been lucky here, but he was damn sure he was going to take that luck and work on it.

In fact, he was so focused on this that he never asked how Antony Morgan knew his name.

WHEN DECLAN ARRIVED AT THE TEMPLE INN OFFICES WITH Jess in tow, he found the place a hive of activity.

De'Geer and Cooper were back, Billy was on the computers, and Anjli was leaning over his shoulder like a mother hen pointing at screens, as if showing Billy things he was missing.

Billy, obviously irritated by this, kept snapping back at her.

Monroe, seeing Declan enter through the windows of his office, walked out.

'You, my office, now.'

Declan had known this was coming, and so he turned to Jess and motioned for her to stay with Billy, who, seeing her arrive, gave a smile and pointed for a laptop beside him to be opened; if she was going to be here, she could start working.

Walking into Monroe's office, Declan felt a coldness he hadn't felt for a while, emanating from the man behind the desk.

'Where the bloody hell have you been?' Monroe barked, looking up at him. 'Do you know what's been going on here?'

'I'm sorry, Guv,' Declan murmured. 'I found the man who shot—'

'I don't care what you found,' Monroe interjected. 'We've possibly found where the bloody bairn is. And you're the DCI in charge of the case.'

'Hold on a minute, that's not the situation here,' Declan interrupted. 'Esposito is the DCI in charge of this, and Anjli is assisting him. This isn't my case, Guv. And you were the one who told me I needed to keep away from it.'

Monroe grumbled to himself and then nodded, and Declan saw this suppressed anger wasn't aimed at Declan, but at the current situation.

'Look, we need to get moving fast,' he said. 'It looks like Stephanie Thompson took Debbie Watson. Why, we don't know, but she's left us clues to find our way there – and I need you, laddie – right here, on the team.'

Monroe's face did not look as delighted as he should have been about the clues, and Declan frowned.

'I'm guessing you don't think the clues were left by Stephanie,' he ventured.

'There are too many things going on here,' Monroe replied pensively. 'We know Ford and Hart are playing their stupid bloody games. We know there's something more going on with Antony Morgan and we still haven't found Mia Chen's brother. But with luck, in the next half hour, we'll be picking up a lost child and arresting a kidnapper. I'll get Billy to fill you in, as that happened while you were out gallivanting around bloody London ... I'd like you to be there if there's nothing else too pressing for you?'

He sighed, rubbing at his eyes.

'Sorry. Long day, and it's not even tea time. Is Jess okay?'

'She is,' Declan smiled. 'Actually stopped me battering the crap out of the gunman. Who claims he was paid by a fixer named James in Wandsworth. That's all I know.'

Monroe's eyes narrowed.

'James Taplow?'

'Maybe.' Declan shrugged.

Monroe nodded.

'James Taplow, worked for Johnny Lucas for a long time, back when he was the Twins. Now outsources for anyone with money and a need, but ...'

He shook his head angrily.

'I know he worked several times with Marie Ford, and probably her bloody Mini-Me, Hart,' he finished. 'If someone told him to do this ...'

Declan nodded, understanding. Ford was playing with him again, poking at him through his family.

'We'll sort James from sodding Wandsworth out later,'

Monroe muttered as he walked from behind the desk, and Declan followed the Scottish Detective Superintendent out into the main room.

'Come on, come on,' Monroe shouted, 'what do we have?'

'I've spoken to the agency that rented Stephanie Thompson a warehouse space,' Billy said, looking up. 'It was done anonymously online. It's an old recording studio in Smithfield.'

'Bloody recording studios,' Declan muttered. 'Why is it always bloody recording studios?'

'Because they're soundproofed,' Anjli spoke up. 'Think about it, a small child screaming, you're going to want to make sure that nobody can hear you.'

'I get it. And from the looks of things, the address is quite industrial,' Billy said, writing something out and passing it across to De'Geer standing beside him. 'Lots of Monday to Friday, nine till five-ers working around there.'

Declan frowned.

'Where have I heard Smithfield mentioned?' he said.

'No idea,' Monroe mumbled.

'I'm sure we had somebody mention Smithfield. Or was it when I was ...'

Declan trailed off.

'Anjli, the poem.'

Anjli paused, looking back.

'Declan, we don't *need* the poem now. We've got an address.'

'But we could be running into a trap. Tell me the poem.'

'Place of sweating fever—' Anjli started the poem once more, but stopped after the first line as Declan slammed his fist on the table.

'Sweating fever,' he said. 'That's connected to Smithfield Market, I'm sure I heard that somewhere.'

Billy was already typing.

'I think it was one of many suggestions last night,' he said. 'The market was involved in the sweating sickness but it was never proven, so I think we moved on.'

'But if it *is* the Market, why would Stephanie lead you directly to this location, after writing out a poem?'

'Maybe the game plan's over now,' Billy suggested. 'Stephanie Thompson must have known we would have worked it out by now. She was playing a game to get us chasing around and looking. The chances were Debbie Watson was never in danger.'

'How so?'

Declan looked back to Monroe, who had asked the question.

'Stephanie Thompson wanted the case reopened. She wanted justice for her daughter. She didn't believe that Blackthorne was the killer.'

He glanced across at Anjli.

'That wasn't anything against you,' he said. 'We know Ford and Hart have been contacting people. It's every chance that Ford got hold of Stephanie, convinced her to restart this. Claimed she was the innocent victim, and that you'd somehow screwed her over.'

'Makes sense. But how does this affect Antony?'

'Same thing,' Declan said. 'Maybe they played Antony Morgan as well, said that he should be working with her, or they told her to follow him, I don't know. But there's something more going on here than just finding a random piece of paper.'

'Oh, we know that, sir,' Cooper said from the door. 'The

place had been left for us to find this, but at the end of the day, we're not going to look a gift horse in the mouth.'

Declan nodded.

'Do we have the address?'

'We do,' Monroe said, looking at Billy for confirmation before continuing. 'Send it to Esposito.'

'Sir?' Declan's eyes became saucers as he looked at his commanding officer. 'Guv, you just said we should go there now.'

'We will go there now, but Esposito needs to be there first,' Monroe snapped back. 'It's his case, Declan. We're helping, remember? We were never going to be the ones taking the win here. If we lost, it fell on us. If we won, it landed on Mile End. The whole point of this was to make sure Anjli got closure.'

He looked back at Anjli.

'I'm sorry, lassie, but he has to be the one to get this. No matter what he's done or not done in this case, we have to give that to him.'

Anjli sighed loudly, grabbing her jacket. But then, as she was pulling on one sleeve, it was almost as if someone turned her off, held in place, one arm stretched out, the coat halfway on her.

'He knew,' she said. 'Morgan knew.'

'What do you mean?'

'The flowers he gave me the first time I met him. He told me they were flowers that were used in sweating sickness, and that we'd probably all be sweating a little bit. I thought he was making a joke about us being against the clock, but what if he was subtly saying, way back then, where she was, hinting at the third poem?'

Monroe frowned.

'Lassie, it's got to be a coincidence.'

'Or, he *is* working with Stephanie.'

'We'll ask them both when we arrest her.' Monroe sighed. 'Let's get going.'

19

RESOLUTION

In the middle of Cowcross Yard, slightly north of Smithfield Market and between the market and Farringdon Station was indeed some kind of abandoned half-completed music studio in a recently renovated warehouse, work vans still in the area. There was acoustic dampening on the walls and Declan had seen from a website Billy had found, based on the building of the studios three years earlier, that the entire inside of the space had been soundproofed. However, as he arrived – the lights on his Audi flashing as his siren went off, followed in turn by Monroe in Anjli's car and De'Geer in a police squad car with Doctor Marcos sat beside him – Declan frowned as he pulled up to the police cordon tape.

'What's going on?' he muttered, climbing out of the car.

'We've got a problem, sir,' the female officer standing there explained.

'Sanford, isn't it?' Monroe asked as he walked over. 'We met yesterday?'

'Yes, Guv.'

'Would you like to let us through so we can have a …'

'I'm afraid I can't let you through, sir.'

'I'm sorry, what?'

'DCI Esposito said that if anybody from the Temple Inn unit turned up, they were not to be allowed in,' Sanford shrugged. 'I'm sorry, sir. This is unorthodox, to say the least, but he told me to tell you that this is a Mile End case and …'

'Now you listen to me, lassie!' Monroe started shouting. 'I won't be kept away from something we've been looking into. We gave you the address of this location. We …'

He paused, smiling, and suddenly his entire demeanour changed.

'You might want to check behind you,' he said.

Sanford wasn't new to the force, and she knew how the ranks worked. A Detective Superintendent chewing her out wasn't going to be great for her career, and so she did what he said, confused at why he would have such a sudden personality shift – until she realised that while he was talking, distracting her, the divisional surgeon for Temple Inn, Doctor Marcos, had gone under the cordon and walked over to a suited officer standing to the side. She didn't know Commander Bradbury, but she knew from the pips on his epaulettes that he was very important. Doctor Marcos was talking to him like they were old friends, and the moment he heard what she was saying, pointing back at Sanford, his face darkened, and he waved for her to let them all in.

'Commanders trump DCIs,' Monroe grumbled as he pushed past.

'Guv, I'm sorry,' Sanford said. 'But, for the record, even though the DCI commanded it, it was Detective Superintendent Harris that ordered it. I just do what I'm told, sir.'

Declan saw the muscles in Monroe's face twitch. He'd

heard of Harris, but Monroe would have worked with him back in the day. Harris had also been in the room when Anjli had originally been called, and he'd been the one to pull the Ring camera from Temple Inn.

Was Harris working with Ford? He would have known her back then, even if he wasn't her boss at the time ...

'And the kid?' Declan asked.

'She's here. She was found. But it's a bit of a circus,' Sanford nodded.

'How so?' Declan looked out after Monroe, already storming off towards the entrance of the building.

'The press were here when we arrived,' Sanford said. 'You'd have to ask the DCI.'

'Oh, don't worry, we will be,' Anjli now marched past, having waited to hear what Sanford had to say. DCI Esposito had walked out of the building, but paused, wincing as he saw Monroe and Anjli storming towards him, their faces both matched in their anger.

'It wasn't my call, Alex,' he said. 'Harris said so.'

'Harris doesn't even work at your office half the time,' Monroe muttered. 'He's like Bullman, comes and goes when he bloody well pleases.'

'I know,' Esposito replied. 'The problem is Harris had a phone call from the press.'

'What kind of phone call?'

'A phone call asking whether we would attend a specific location where they believed Debbie Watson was being held.'

At this, Monroe looked around in confusion.

'I don't get it,' he said. '*We* only just found the address.'

'Apparently the journalist was given it by Antony Morgan,' Esposito nodded to the side, where, with a camera crew around him, Antony Morgan was talking to a journalist with bushy red hair.

Declan narrowed his eyes.

'He works for *The Individual*,' he said. 'I recognise him. Ian Trent. Works with Sean Ashby.'

'Well, apparently Morgan phoned him, saying he'd been given information from a source that said Debbie Watson would be here,' Esposito replied. 'Wouldn't say the source's name, but did say that he didn't trust telling the police because DS Anjli Kapoor had threatened him, and he didn't feel comfortable for his safety after a seven-foot-tall Viking had strong-armed him.'

'I did no such thing,' De'Geer said.

'Doesn't matter,' Esposito replied. 'He told the press, the press told Harris, Harris killed all access for you.'

He sighed.

'I called in Bradbury knowing that he could outrank him, but it won't last long before somebody somewhere pulls even more rank.'

'Stephanie Thompson?'

Esposito grimaced, nodding back into the building.

'In there,' he said. 'She committed suicide. Left a note.'

'What kind of note?'

'We're going through it at the moment,' Esposito sighed. 'Look, I'm not a fan of this as much as you are but you have to know one thing, Declan. We found the body at noon.'

Declan felt a shiver run down his spine. *That was the same time that Ford had given him.*

'Well, I think we can pretty much state right now that Ford and Morgan must have been working together.'

'Not so,' Esposito shook his head. 'Because we had ex-DCI Ford in the offices at Mile End at the same time.'

'Why did you have her?' Monroe frowned, before realisation set in. 'Because you'd been running your own case, separately.'

'Of course we'd be running a case,' Esposito replied. 'When McAlroy brought us that Ring doorbell, we located the IP. Took us to Farringdon and a couple of cell towers. We just couldn't narrow it down until you gave us the address.'

'Billy could have narrowed it down, if you'd just left it with us,' Monroe looked around the crime scene as if he wanted to scream. His face was red with anger, but he was impotent in an ability to give it out.

Luckily for him, however, somebody else was happy to make a noise, and suddenly, from inside the building, forensics and police officers came sprinting out at speed, as Doctor Marcos, now wearing a mask, gloves and booties, was screaming at them.

'Get out now,' she said. 'Find me Rajesh Khanna immediately.'

'Doctor Marcos, he isn't here yet,' DCI Esposito said. 'And I would prefer it if you didn't shout at my officers.'

'I'm more than happy not to shout at them,' Doctor Marcos said as she spun round to face Esposito. 'What I was actually telling them to do was to stay away from the hideously toxic plants they were buggering around with!'

She looked up at Monroe.

'Stephanie Thompson committed suicide by poison,' she said. 'It looks like she's taken some kind of wolfsbane or belladonna – something along those lines – shoved it in a Nutriblend, added a bit of water, downed it in one.'

'Wolfsbane's fatal, right?' Declan asked.

'A two milligram dose can kill you in about four hours,' Doctor Marcos nodded. 'Usually, that is. However, it doesn't often work to kill someone, because people will realise they've been poisoned by it, most likely accidentally, and they'll cough it up or vomit it back. There are enough vomit stains over the body to show that at some point she was being sick.'

She shook her head.

'There's a Nutriblend to the side. Just looking at it, I can see there's a damn sight more than two milligrams in there. She downed it in one go and let it take her away, probably quite painfully as well. The problem here, though, is that Wolfsbane as a flower, if you brush past it, if it touches your skin, you could be dead within days.'

She turned to face Esposito now.

'Your officers, DCI Esposito, have been sodding around with the stuff, picking it up, sniffing it. God, if they've been watching the movies, they might even have been trying to tap it to their tongue to see what happens. I need every single officer who's been anywhere near it to be tested; or else you're going to have a mass recruitment drive once they all start dying.'

She glared at Declan, and he hoped it was more residual anger at the situation than at him.

'The girl's fine. She didn't even realise she'd been kidnapped, she thought it was a game. She's known Stephanie Thompson for years. Stephanie said it was a trick on her friend, the one with the birthday party. She's been sitting in a second room, watching as much TV as she wants, eating cake and ice cream and pretty much living the life of a queen. She even has a nice new lanyard, minus the air tag, of course.'

She looked back at Esposito.

'You don't need us here, apparently,' she said, 'so we're

going to leave you to it. But just know now, Alvaro, not only did we solve your sodding case for you when you obviously didn't want it, I've also saved your officers' lives.'

This stated, Doctor Marcos stormed off.

Esposito gave out a long-held breath, looking back at Monroe.

'I'm sorry,' he said simply. 'All I can do is promise that you'll be updated with everything that we get. You'll see everything we have.'

'Aye, we'd better,' Monroe said. 'Because if it *is* Stephanie Thompson, and there *is* some kind of message, then I can bet you any money it's being aimed at Anjli.'

He looked at the vans.

'Oh, and something else for free,' he said. 'That company, *Masons?* They're also helping to renovate the British Museum, and probably rebuilt Antony Morgan's sodding shop. So maybe you could do some police work there, too. Seems too good a coincidence.'

He was going to speak some more, but paused as the reporter, the one who had been talking to Antony Morgan, now started making his way over.

'Detective Superintendent Monroe,' he said. 'Ian Trent, *The Individual.* How is it that a florist is able to solve a mystery that you weren't able to?'

'This wasn't our case,' Monroe said, with the slightest of smiles. 'We were assisting a fellow DCI, and if you have questions about that, perhaps you should ask him.'

'And what about the fact that the amateur detective who solved the case through his own work would prefer to come to a newspaper journalist than an officer, because of fear for his own life?'

Declan had had enough and stepped forward.

'How exactly was he an amateur detective?'

'Antony Morgan saw Stephanie Thompson at a wedding, and remembered her,' Trent explained. 'But, when they spoke, he realised she hadn't moved on, and she was still bitter about the death of her daughter, claiming something would happen soon, something that could change everything. He decided to keep an eye on her, and that led him into making alliances with people who could assist, even at a distance.'

'What people?'

Ian Trent didn't reply, and so Declan, taking a break to calm himself, replied for him.

'The man in question has a history with one of our detectives and worked for the original killer, Thomas Blackthorne.'

He looked across at Antony Morgan, now watching him across the courtyard. He'd never met the man, but he knew the type.

'Mister Morgan is dissatisfied with what happened after his boss killed himself three years ago. As for how he knew, this case is still ongoing and we do not talk about active crime investigations.'

'How is it still active?' Trent asked, looking around, confused. 'The girl's safe. The killer committed suicide.'

He stopped as Anjli grabbed his arm, holding the microphone, the Dictaphone steady.

'Stephanie Thompson wasn't a murderer,' she hissed into it. 'Debbie Watson isn't dead, which doesn't fit the MO of the Posies Killer.'

'She wasn't dead *yet*,' Trent replied, pulling his hand violently away from Anjli's. 'Stephanie Thompson was around when both Mia Chen and Sarah Thompson were murdered. Surely you have to reopen the case now, Detective

Inspector Kapoor, and harbour the possibility that Stephanie Thompson killed her own daughter. Crazier things have happened.'

Anjli went to say something else and Declan, in his mind's eye, saw the same fight that he'd had years earlier – the one that had had him find his way to the Last Chance Saloon – about to happen again.

'As I've said,' he interrupted. 'We don't talk about active investigations.'

This stated, he pulled Anjli, still about to start another argument, away from the location.

'This is bullshit,' she said. 'Blackthorne's the killer and now they're going to reopen it and throw everything onto Stephanie Thompson. She lost her kid, she lost her husband, she lost everything.'

'And we don't know what the letter she left says,' Declan said. 'It could explain everything as well, remember? Until we hear what happened there, we have to sit back.'

He turned to face her.

'But that's not the only case we're working on here, remember? We're also trying to work out what Ford and Hart's game in this is.'

He looked back at Ian Trent.

'I'm pretty sure we're going to learn that very soon.'

20

AFTERSHOCKS

'So, let me get this right,' Peter Morris said, facing across the makeshift studio from onetime Detective Chief Inspector Marie Ford. She was not in her prison gear of joggers and sweatshirt. Instead, she was wearing a dark-blue suit and white shirt, her short hair styled and with make-up on her usually plain face, while Morris, currently not in his traditional seat on the set of *Peter Morris in the Afternoon*, better known as *PM in the PM*, smiled at her, his greying hair still worn in a stylish side-parting that was decades too young for him. 'If I can be blunt, here, Miss Ford?'

'Please,' Ford replied. 'Ask anything you need to know. And please, call me Marie. It's my name, after all.'

'Okay then, Marie. Why didn't you go to the police?'

Ford considered this and then looked back at Morris.

'I was a serving officer all of my career,' she explained, almost wistfully. 'I was an accredited and decorated officer all of my career, but my allure corrupted me. I'll admit it, it turned me into somebody that I wasn't meant to be. I found myself with a gambling addiction that I couldn't stop and it killed my career and took away the one thing I loved.'

She looked at the camera, directly through the television set.

'Being a police officer, solving crimes, making the guilty pay,' she sat back in her chair. 'How could I let the guilty pay when I was one of the guilty myself?'

Peter nodded at this, looking back at the audience, who, as this was being filmed in a prison, weren't there.

'But Anjli Kapoor worked for you,' he said. 'Surely, Kapoor—'

'Works for the same DCI that put me away,' Ford interjected. 'Detective Chief Inspector Declan Walsh. Added to that his father Patrick Walsh had been a mentor to me when I was younger; someone I'd known very well in fact. He'd even recommended that Declan work with me at one point. How could I go back to them, people who had seen me at my lowest, and convince them I had information that was worth seeing?'

She wiped a tear, or at least what looked to be a tear.

'That wee little bitch,' Monroe growled as he watched the television show in the main office. 'She's playing him like a bloody violin.'

On the screen, Peter Morris hadn't finished.

'And so what made you decide to speak to Antony Morgan, a simple florist?'

'Morgan had worked for Thomas Blackthorne,' Ford explained. 'Blackthorne was the prime suspect for the previous set of cases and I'd never been too sure if it was him or not. Some of the evidence wasn't really fitting the case, and I didn't feel that we'd gone deep enough into it.'

'You cow!' Anjli shouted at the TV. '*You* were the one doing that!'

Unable to hear Anjli through the set, Ford continued.

'The problem was, as I said, I'd fallen down a dark hole. I was in hock to gamblers and East End crime bosses were telling me what to do.'

'Bosses like Johnny Lucas, the current MP for Bethnal Green and Bow?'

'Yes, but it was more his brother, Jackie,' Ford was playing the game now. 'I was distracted. I trusted my detective sergeant, and I let her run the case. The problem was, she was overzealous and, well, we already know what happened then. The suspect, Thomas Blackthorne, had been pushed to the edge by her harassment and, well, kidnapped a child, demanding that we stop what we were doing.'

'But surely that must be classed as antisocial behaviour?'

'Yes, I agree,' Ford replied. 'But it was also the actions of a desperate man, a man who had no other way to stop this from happening, and having been in that position, I now understand how he felt.'

She shook her head sadly.

'I never thought I'd say that, that I'd feel the same way as a convicted murderer did, but maybe he wasn't the killer,' she shrugged. 'Anyway, while in prison, I'd spoken to somebody with a connection with the school, and with the girls. Through contacts, they had spoken to Stephanie Thompson and had gained a concern about whether or not she was telling the truth about her daughter. Stephanie, meanwhile, had fostered a strong fascination with Mister Morgan, and I genuinely believe that she was looking to find a way to frame him for the very murders that she might have done.'

She looked at the camera.

'I say might have, as I can't prove that she killed anyone. I can't prove that she didn't. That's not up to me. That's a job for the police. But I was allowed to speak to my onetime friend and colleague, Sonya Hart, imprisoned for simply being loyal to her superior, and we felt it was our duty to inform Antony Morgan, to let him know that he was being profiled, that everything he knew might have been wrong. We talked, a friendship began, and we shared information. Morgan monitored Stephanie Thompson. When the police wouldn't listen to us, we did our own job.'

'When the police wouldn't listen to us,' Anjli looked mortified. 'That bitch—'

'She's talking her way out of prison,' Declan said. 'You'll find that Sonya Hart will do the same thing next, now she's been outed as another "helper" here.'

'Do you think your time here should be reevaluated?' On screen, Morris asked, as he leant closer.

Surprisingly, Ford shook her head.

'I did terrible things and I should be evaluated on that, not this,' she said. 'But if someone like Johnny Lucas, who you mentioned earlier, can go from East End thug to Member of Parliament, can redeem himself in the population's eyes ... I just want that opportunity, too.'

On the TV Ford said nothing else, mainly because Anjli Kapoor had hurled a smartphone through the screen.

IT HAD BEEN TWO DAYS SINCE DEBBIE WATSON HAD BEEN found, and the preceding forty-eight hours had been nothing but hassle for the team of The Last Chance Saloon. For a start, it had come out immediately that not only had Antony Morgan taken the press to the location before the police themselves arrived, but he'd been working with disgraced ex-DCI Marie Ford in some kind of vigilante civic campaign. It didn't help that even though the police were claiming credit, and Esposito had been lauded as a detective genius, the stink of the Last Chance Saloon was still heavy upon them, with several papers claiming that Anjli herself had actively hindered the case and perhaps even caused the wrong person to commit suicide, three years earlier. There was talk that the case would be reopened, that Thomas Blackthorne would be vindicated.

The letter didn't exactly help.

Claimed to have been written by Stephanie Thompson, the letter was a typed-up confession. In it, Stephanie had explained that she had wanted the case to be reopened, and that Anjli had refused to contact her when requested, and that Anjli had also made herself unavailable to meet. Over the years, Anjli, working alone, had effectively pushed Stephanie away from the investigation, causing her the loss of her hair, her husband, her family and eventually her life.

All to make a statement clearing everything, a sacrifice she was willing to pay, a statement explaining that Thomas Blackthorne was not the killer.

Of course, this didn't say that *she'd* killed the other girls, but that wasn't needed here. This would be a discussion for when the case reopened.

Stephanie had ended the letter with the poem:

Ring-a-Ring-a-Roses, a pocketful of posies, ashes, ashes. They all fall down.

It had been pretty damning.

It also came out that she'd been working lunchtimes at the same school as her own daughter, that she'd been having fights with Sarah shortly before Sarah disappeared, and that Mia's parents and Stephanie had had some kind of stand-up row about their son. Stephanie had been convinced that the son, Oliver, had been trying to spy on her while she was in the garden sunbathing.

It had not gone down well.

One of the workmen at the warehouse, Steve Rankin, had explained he was Lily Rhodes' brother-in-law, confirmed his company also worked at the British Museum, and admitted Stephanie had provided them with passes; passes he'd been paid to give to Lily – anonymously – on the condition they invite Debbie Watson.

Now, with the dust finally settling, and Stephanie Thompson already judged by public opinion, the press were getting bored with this case and had started poking once more at the Last Chance Saloon. Because now, as well as having Declan, the man benefiting from a serial killer's will, they had Anjli. The woman who could have sent a man to his death three years earlier, who, because of her own actions, had caused a journalist to discover a killer before the police did, and who was also living with the aforementioned Declan, the man who'd gained something from a serial killer's will.

It had *also* not gone well.

'Right then,' Monroe said, looking at the room as he

turned the now sparking television off, glaring at the embarrassed Anjli. 'Let's get started. What do we have?'

'Everything that we have is taken by Mile End,' Declan said.

'True,' Monroe nodded. 'But Mile End's case, as you can see there, is over, while ours hasn't finished yet.'

'And how do you work that one out, Guv?' Anjli said dejectedly from the corner.

'Hart and Ford? There's a very strong chance they helped with an attack on one of our own's daughter,' Monroe said, looking over at Jess, who'd been sitting in the office in her usual spot beside Billy's bank of monitors. Declan hadn't wanted her there, but ever since the attack, she'd felt more comfortable in Temple Inn, and Henry Farrow had been fine with that, knowing that at least keeping her in one police unit meant she wasn't getting into danger anywhere else.

Declan hadn't worried; after speaking to "James the fixer from Wandsworth", thanks to an introduction from someone in Johnny Lucas's crew, he'd learned the message had been simple; she'd been targeted purely for Declan to be distracted. The only thing he hadn't been told was who sent the message, but he already had a pretty good idea of that answer.

'Do you think we can open a case that gives us everything?' he asked.

'I think so,' Monroe said. 'In fact, I spoke to Bullman this morning, and she reckons that because it was done to distract us, we can look into everything, every communication they made as to *why* this was so.'

He smiled. It wasn't a pleasant one.

'So let's see if we can find out what else Hart and Ford

have been doing; what they've been playing in their little games,' he said. 'Billy.'

Billy looked up from his laptop.

'I've been trying to work out how Sonya Hart was passing messages,' he said. 'She's made a thing about the fact she can't send emails or connect to the internet, and they've found no kind of phone or contraband device on her. She's been a model prisoner, which is understandable, really. She's looking to try to get an early release.'

'Go on.'

'The problem is, people like Hart can't help themselves,' Billy shrugged. 'They want to prove they're cleverer than everybody else. She'd offered her services to help lesser-educated women learn computer skills through a GCSE syllabus, Computer Sciences, and she's been teaching that for the last year and a half.'

He looked around the room.

'It's the only time she gets a computer,' he explained. 'It's specifically blocked from gaining access to the outside world. But it's not air-gapped, like we've had here in the past. It's not blocked from *everything*, because it has to connect to the other computers in the room. And if one of *those* computers is connected to the internet ...'

'She can email out.'

'I asked the person to look into the computer that Sonya Hart used,' Billy nodded. 'They kindly sent it to me. It's a laptop, basic issue, locked away when no one else is using it. Hart had made a point of saying that it had to be the same laptop every time, claiming that she had the course notes on there, and if anybody else was given it, she couldn't trust them to not cheat.'

Declan chuckled at this.

'That's pot calling the kettle black, if ever I heard it,' he said.

Billy shrugged.

'Either way, boss,' he continued, 'once I had a chance to look at the laptop yesterday, I saw she had written a small piece of code, a backdoor into the network. It allowed her to piggyback off one of the other laptops. I also found software hidden deep in the root server.'

'What kind of software?'

'Software that allowed her to check message boards and use automations.'

'Automations?' Declan frowned. 'What, like keyboard macros and stuff?'

'You know what, Guv? I'm actually impressed you knew what I was talking about,' Billy smiled. 'But here, what I mean is quite similar, but not exact. You see, the automations that it looks like Sonya Hart had, meant she could go into one innocuous browser window connected to the GCSE coursework intranet, and by typing in a small line of code before the actual message, she could effectively send *that* message, as an email, to a completely different server, purely by using automations that linked it to some kind of service, like *Make* or *Zapier.*'

'Third party apps?'

'Yes,' Billy nodded. 'Apps which then opened up an entirely new program somewhere far away on a different server. She didn't even have to be in the room to send the email.'

He held up his wrist, showing his Apple Watch.

'It's the same as if you write a little shortcut on your iPhone or Apple Watch that, when you speak to Siri, you can say "remind me to do this", and it does so. The shortcut links to various software to make sure that the reminder is placed in the right app. For hers, her reminders were emails and messages. It would take a matter of seconds to do what she needed to do. She could send dozens of unmonitored emails easily, every hour, while the others worked through the syllabus.'

'Can we track them?'

'Unfortunately not,' Billy shook his head. 'No cache. All we can see is when she sent them. And she sent a lot over the last month.'

Monroe made some kind of guttural growling noise, and Declan had to genuinely check to see if he was okay.

'Do we have anything on the murderer?' he asked. '*Alleged* murderer, I should say. Stephanie Thompson.'

Now it was Doctor Marcos's turn to straighten from the doorway she was leaning against.

'She definitely died of poisoning. Made to look like suicide, although there are two camps to that.'

'What do you mean, two camps?' Declan asked, looking around.

'One camp is that Stephanie Thompson knew she was about to be arrested. She'd made her statement, didn't want to live,' Doctor Marcos suggested, shrugging. 'She'd lost her husband, her child, her hair, her job, her entire life even. This was just one more step. A way to stop the pain.'

'And the other camp?'

'She was murdered, and it was made to look like she'd killed herself,' Doctor Marcos continued, eyes narrowed. 'The more I've looked into this, the more I *know* it's the second.'

There was a silence in the room. Monroe waved for her to continue.

'When we found the body, it looked like she'd drunk some kind of suicide smoothie. She had taken some water and some crushed-up wolfsbane, scrambled it all together and downed it in one. It wasn't a big drink, it was more of a shot and a half. Kind of like when you have an espresso first thing in the morning, and you just want that caffeine to hit you. We know it was wolfsbane because we've examined the residue in the glass. When they checked her stomach in the autopsy, they found it was there as well, so we know for a fact that she drank whatever was in the glass. That part wasn't staged as such.'

'As such?' Declan frowned. 'That sounds leading.'

Doctor Marcos shifted as she stood, looking back at her paperwork.

'To explain what I mean, I have to explain about wolfsbane,' she said. 'Now, I will point out that I wasn't allowed to attend the autopsy due to, well, Harris and Mile End being little bitches. But Rajesh is a friend, and he gave me everything that he found, with some of his own considerations. He too believes that there was a set-up.'

'But, let me guess, Mile End is quite happy to let it stay as it is,' Anjli muttered. 'What a shock.'

'No, from what I can work out, Esposito's got his doubts as well, likely about Harris trying to make sure the ghosts of his past aren't really staying around,' Doctor Marcos shrugged. 'Anyway, he sent me the toxicology reports, and I started looking into it.'

She moved from the doorway now, walking further into the office.

'It's my belief that Stephanie Thompson did ingest the

wolfsbane. But before that, she'd been sedated, probably to an almost comatose state where she was incredibly suggestible to the drink being forced down her throat. Probably couldn't scream, her vocal cords paralysed. There were splatterings of the drink on her clothing as well as vomit. We'd assumed she'd tried to drink it down, struggled, and then thrown up but not managed to eject everything. I now think this was somebody forcing it down her throat ... and her choking.'

Monroe whistled to himself.

'Well, there you go,' he said. 'If Stephanie Thompson didn't kill herself, then somebody had to do it. And if Stephanie Thompson had someone doing it, that means there's somebody else involved.'

He looked around the room.

'We know Sonya Hart had been sending emails,' he said. 'Probably to somebody at Downview Prison, who was passing them on to Marie Ford. There's no way the two of them had a papertrail that led to each of them, everything would have been word-of-mouth, most likely. Ford would then send messages back, which I'm guessing Hart would read during the next lesson she was teaching. But why? The motive that Stephanie Thompson had for getting involved is still valid. She wanted answers, and maybe she was convinced that this was the way to do it, but I don't get where this began.'

He leaned back, looking up at the ceiling.

'I think this could be Morgan,' Anjli said, breaking the silence.

'How so?' Monroe looked back at her. 'I mean, don't get me wrong, lassie, I'm on your side already. Morgan's a piece of work, and I don't quite know what his game plan was here either, but it seemed to be more a case of clearing his boss's name than anything else.'

Anjli shook her head.

'The suicide note,' she replied. 'It ended with the poem.'

'Aye, the same poem that we had written with Debbie—'

'But it's not the same poem that she said to me,' Declan interjected. 'When we spoke, she quoted "Ring a ring of roses, a pocket full of posies, a-tishoo, a-tishoo, we all fall down." But both written messages say "ashes, ashes."'

'We've already worked out that's the same poem, laddie.' Monroe raised an eyebrow. 'Where are you going with this?'

'We know that the term "ashes, ashes" is American,' Declan said, nodding towards De'Geer. 'Our resident folklore expert told us that.'

'We also know,' Anjli added, 'that Antony Morgan is from Philadelphia.'

'You think Morgan being American is the clue we need here?' Monroe shook his head. 'We're going to need a little more than that. He's not the only American in London, I don't know if you've noticed.'

'True, but he's the only American with something to gain here,' Anjli snapped back. 'We also know he was the one who found the body, claiming that he'd been given information by Ford and Hart, who still haven't explained how they knew, in turn claiming mysterious underground sources. We know from his quotes that Stephanie wanted to get answers as well as he did, which explains how they knew each other. He mentioned he'd seen Stephanie at the flower wholesalers. When he spoke to me about it, he said he was convinced she was looking for who sold the original flowers used in the posy; maybe to buy her own ones or solve the case herself. She gave tickets to the workmen at the warehouse, knowing they were at the British Museum, but they were the same ones who renovated his shop. What if there was something else going on?'

'Like what?'

'That I don't know, Guv,' Anjli admitted ruefully. 'At the moment, we have nothing else. Mile End has closed down the case to us—'

She paused as somebody else walked through the doors to the main office; DS Jules McAlroy.

'Hope you don't mind me interrupting,' she said. 'But I needed to talk to you.'

'Lassie, at the moment, Mile End really aren't our favourite people,' Monroe said grumpily.

'I get that,' McAlroy replied. 'So I bring you a gift.'

She opened the door further and from behind her walked a young boy, fourteen years old, with short black hair.

'This is Oliver Chen,' McAlroy said. 'Mia Chen's brother. He's been hiding for the last four days. And he's got something I think you want to hear.'

'Why haven't you passed this to your own DCI?' Declan asked, confused.

McAlroy looked around the room.

'Because as far as Mile End is concerned, this case is over,' she said. 'Me bringing Oliver in doesn't really do anything for it, and in fact, if anything, it starts to throw doubt on what we found.'

She gave a smile.

'I know you're still looking into it; you're all too stubborn to let it go. I thought you could do with a bit of assistance. And besides, I'm with you on this. Somebody at Mile End was passing information to Ford and Hart. There's no other way they could have gained what they knew from their shady underground sources. Which means that if Oliver was to turn up at Mile End, I'd give it a matter of minutes before one of them knew and changed the narrative to the new one.'

'There's a new narrative?'

'Oh, trust me,' McAlroy said, placing a hand around Oliver's shoulder. 'When you hear what Oliver has to say, you'll believe there's a new narrative, too.'

21

RUNAWAYS

Oliver Chen sat nervously on the chair in the canteen, twirling a pen in his hand. After arriving, Monroe had decided it was best to interview him somewhere more comfortable than an interview room; the last thing he wanted was for the poor lad to be shaken from whatever he needed to say, so they'd brought him upstairs, sat him down, and made him a cup of hot chocolate.

Declan sat by the door, Anjli stood nearby while Monroe and DS McAlroy sat in front of him. McAlroy had insisted on staying, mainly because she felt she had a personal reason to look after the boy, having brought him there.

'I understand you ran away, laddie,' Monroe started, keeping his voice gentle. 'Would you like to tell us why?'

'They were watching me,' Oliver said, his voice soft and nervous.

'Who was watching you?'

'I don't know their names,' Oliver said. 'But I saw them following me.'

Monroe nodded. 'And people following you makes you regularly want to run away?'

'No, the phone call did that.'

'Right,' Monroe smiled. 'That makes a bit more sense, doesn't it? Can you tell me about the phone call?'

Oliver nodded, a slight gesture rather than a full-on head bob.

'There was a woman,' he said. 'I never got the name. She phoned my mum and dad. She said she had information on Mia's death.'

'What kind of information?'

'I don't know,' Oliver shook his head. 'I'm sorry, I probably don't have what you need, but I just wanted somebody to understand what I'd been told.'

'Go on, laddie,' Monroe said. 'You're not being judged here.'

Oliver nodded gratefully and sipped at his hot chocolate for a long moment before continuing.

'Look, when Mia died, I was younger,' he said. 'But I was still the older brother, and for years, I blamed myself for her death. I was supposed to be looking after her, and I'd wandered off. My parents ...'

He paused, as if re-evaluating what he wanted to say.

'They were understandably angry.'

'What you are saying is that your parents blamed you for her death,' Monroe stated. It wasn't a question.

Oliver, after looking at him for a long moment, eventually gave another small nod.

'I understood why,' he said. 'If I'd been there for her, she wouldn't be dead.'

'You don't know that,' Declan said from the side. 'Trust

me, you can't spend your life second-guessing, and neither can your parents.'

'Tell *them* that,' Oliver said, before he realised he'd spoken out of line and reddened.

'Go on,' Monroe said. 'There's no wrong answers here.'

Oliver took another deep breath.

'I'd felt there was something wrong about the call,' he said. 'The woman who called, saying that she wanted to look into this again. It didn't sound right.'

'How do you mean?' McAlroy asked.

'She knew stuff. Stuff that only the police officers in the case knew. So I guessed it was something official, but when my parents asked for details, she was vague, wouldn't give them. She wouldn't meet. She just said that she wanted to take down the people who had inaccurately solved the case.'

'Inaccurately,' Anjli said, keeping her voice low. 'You mean the people who got it wrong?'

'That's what she said,' Oliver shook his head. 'But, you see, I don't think they *did* get it wrong. I don't think *you* got it wrong. You see, I knew Michael Ashton, the boy who'd been taken at the end. He told me for ages after that when he was taken by Blackthorne, Blackthorne would walk around the house, muttering to himself, saying he shouldn't have done it, that he couldn't help himself. He effectively confessed, but Michael was a young boy. No one was listening to him.'

'Did he say anything more about what Blackthorne said?'

Oliver shrugged.

'I don't know. And, well, you know, it didn't really matter after he killed himself.'

He leant back in the chair, sipping again at his hot chocolate.

'Anyway, around the time of the phone call, people started appearing, following me. I didn't know what was going on. My mum and Stephanie had argued at this point, and, well …'

'Did your mum know Stephanie Thompson well?'

'No. They'd kind of been thrown together after the case had finished, but … they didn't get on. Mum works in the city. She believes she's better than people.'

'*Is* she better than people?' McAlroy asked, then held up her hand. 'Sorry, I shouldn't ask questions like that.'

'No, you're allowed to,' Oliver softened. 'My mum isn't the best of people. But then I'm a teenage boy, what do I know? You ask anybody, they'll say she's great, and I'm the one who should shut up.'

'You know, you seem to be quite self-assured for a boy of your age,' Monroe said. 'I'm guessing you've lived a lot on your own.'

Oliver nodded.

'Since Mia went, my parents have kind of checked out,' he said. 'They blamed me for the death, and that turned into a disinterest in what I did. They probably don't even realise I haven't been at home.'

'Oh no, they know you haven't been at home,' Anjli replied. 'They've filed a missing person's report for you.'

Oliver seemed surprised at this before accepting it.

'I didn't want to be there because I felt they were in trouble if I was around,' he said. 'When the phone call came, I knew something was wrong, Stephanie had come by to speak to mum, and there was something wrong there, and I decided I needed to check on it myself.'

'Did you speak to your parents about this?'

'They thought I was being silly, that I was going over things that I shouldn't remember. Old wounds that shouldn't be reopened. But I had to do it, you know. I let my sister down.'

'Laddie, you let nobody down.'

'Maybe, but that's not what I feel,' Oliver shifted in his chair. 'The woman phoned again, and I answered the call. And this time I started asking questions. I asked who she was, how they knew these things, and ... she got angry at me. Told me if I didn't shut up, the same thing would happen to me as it did to my sister. I looked out the window, and there was a car parked outside with somebody inside it. It could have been completely random, but it just made me think I was under attack, I was in danger. So I grabbed a bag, filled it up, and ran.'

'Where did you run to?' Monroe asked.

'I've got a cousin who's never got on with my parents. I explained I needed a couple of days' space. He's always been quite cool, and he allowed me to stay for a couple of days while I worked out what I needed to do.'

'And what did you need to do?' Declan asked.

'Solve my sister's murder,' Oliver explained matter-of-factly. 'And I don't mean work out who did it, I mean find out what was going on, and why it'd been reopened.'

He looked at Anjli.

'I started following Stephanie Thompson, and I realised quickly that she was following someone else.'

'Who?'

'The florist, Antony Morgan,' Oliver said. 'Used to be Thomas Blackthorne's assistant.'

'We know him well,' Anjli fought to keep the anger from her voice. 'But Stephanie Thompson was following him?'

Oliver nodded.

'Did you know Antony Morgan?'

'I worked for him.'

'What do you mean, you worked for him?' Declan asked.

'I was a Saturday assistant at his shop,' Oliver shrugged. 'I have been for about six months now.'

'That's convenient,' Declan continued. 'That the man who was the assistant of your sister's potential killer—'

Oliver held up his hand.

'I applied because of that,' he said. 'There was an opportunity to see the man who worked for Blackthorne, to maybe get an answer about whether it had been Blackthorne that did this. It was too good an opportunity to pass up. I turned up, said I'd seen the advert, gave my details, I didn't lie. And Antony never brought it up.'

'Do you think Antony realised you were the brother?'

'He couldn't have *not* known,' Oliver replied coldly. 'I assumed he hired me because he had a sense of guilt as well. Maybe he saw somebody like him who had been left at the side of what had happened, not involved but at the same time cursed by it. I didn't kill my sister, and I wasn't killed by Thomas Blackthorne, but simply being in the orbit changed my life.'

'Okay. What did you learn during these six months?'

Oliver looked uncomfortable.

'Look, if I tell you something, can I say it so it doesn't come back on me?'

'Sure,' Monroe looked around. 'Nobody here is going to judge you. Be as candid as you want.'

'Candid. Yeah. Okay, so the guy was a dickhead,' Oliver replied factually. 'He was so up his own arse, kept going on about how he was going to be the biggest thing in London and how he was going to be a name. One day I pointed out he already was a name because of his previous boss, and that didn't go down too well. Right had the hump on that one. I got the impression that he expected to be bigger than Blackthorne.'

'Can you expand on that?' Anjli asked.

'Oh, I mean, he was annoyed that *he* was also a victim, of sorts, and should have had more press about him. It was quite sad, to be honest. But one day while leaving, I saw Stephanie Thompson. She was watching from across the street. She didn't recognise me – I was just some kid leaving the shop to her – but I recognised her. She's quite visible with, you know, the lack of hair and everything. She wasn't even wearing a wig to try to hide it.'

He took another sip before continuing.

'She looked suspicious, and my mum and her had had a fight, so I wasn't exactly her greatest fan. So, at the end of the day, I realised she was still hanging around, so I hung around as well, making sure she couldn't see me. And I followed her.'

'Followed her where?'

'Honestly? I followed her, and she followed Antony Morgan,' Oliver actually laughed at this scenario. 'As I said, she had a fixation on him. She was going to the wholesalers in the mornings, watching him. I went with him a couple of times, said I wanted to learn about the business, and he took me, probably grateful to have somebody help him with the boxes, but while there I kept an eye out ... and there she was.'

'Do you know why she was following him?'

Oliver nodded.

'I confronted her about a week and a half ago,' he said. 'Said I recognised her, said she'd been sniffing around the shop and I wanted to know why. I didn't say who I was; as far as she was concerned, I was just some shop assistant.'

He chuckled.

'I was the Antony Morgan to his Thomas Blackthorne, in a way.'

'What did she say?'

'She told me I wouldn't understand. That she'd been informed that Antony Morgan was someone she needed to watch, that someone else was targeting him.'

'Someone else?'

Oliver nodded.

'The Posies Killer.'

Monroe looked around the room.

'Blackthorne was the Posies Killer,' he said. 'Or, if you believe the press, so was Stephanie Thompson. Are you saying there's another?'

Oliver shrugged, as if unsure of what to say.

'All I know is she said he was dangerous, and she needed to make sure Antony wasn't in trouble.'

'The "he" being the real killer?' Anjli wasn't sure how to take this.

'She'd apparently seen Antony at a friend's wedding a couple of months earlier and immediately recognised him. She knew she had to keep him safe from ... well, whoever it was.'

'She wanted to make sure Antony Morgan was safe,' Monroe frowned. 'This from the woman who ended up kidnapping a child?'

Oliver shook his head.

'I wasn't there when Debbie Watson was taken. But I can tell you now, neither was Stephanie Thompson, because I was following her. She'd gone back to the flower wholesaler, waiting for Morgan, but he'd gone earlier that day. It was simply a matter of bad timing.'

'What did you do?'

'I waited,' Oliver replied. 'I went back to the shop. It was closed. I didn't understand why. And then I saw a man – well, I think it was a man – leave, climbing into the florist's van Antony drove ... but it didn't look like him.'

'Let me guess,' Monroe said. 'He was wearing a bulky jacket.'

'I saw a bulky jacket, some kind of baseball cap,' Oliver nodded. 'It completely disfigured him, and if I'm being honest, I can't be sure it even was him. Made me think maybe Stephanie was right, yeah? That there was someone else, and now they were framing Antony by stealing his van.'

'And this was when you followed him to Soho,' Declan said. 'Saw him place something on the pump?'

'Yeah,' Oliver nodded. 'I watched him from a distance, then when he left, I walked over and took a picture to see what it was. The QR code opened up a web page, but it asked for a code, and I didn't have it. So I just followed him on.'

'And then what?'

'Then I lost him.'

Declan was writing in his notebook.

'Stephanie told you she saw Morgan at a wedding, and then someone told her to keep an eye on him,' he asked. 'That he was in danger.'

Oliver nodded again as Declan looked back at the others.

'That's almost exactly what Antony Morgan said to us,' he read from his notes. 'He'd seen Stephanie at a wedding and then somebody had told him to keep an eye on her. Although he never mentioned the danger part.'

'Maybe he was arrogant enough to think he wasn't in danger,' McAlroy suggested.

Declan, nodding at this, leant back in his chair.

'What if this isn't the simple hunt we see here? What if this is Ford and Hart playing against each other?'

'What, *battleships* with real people?'

'Maybe,' Declan said. 'Maybe they've got a plan to screw us over or do something else. Get out of prison. Whatever it is they've worked out. But Hart decides she's going to use Antony Morgan as her pawn and Ford uses Stephanie Thompson.'

'But why would Stephanie Thompson kill herself?'

He winced, looking back at Oliver, but the boy was staring off, and probably hadn't even heard him.

'Maybe the two of them buggering around woke up the actual killer,' Monroe spoke softly now, shaking his head at Anjli. 'Blackthorne could still have been involved. Maybe he wasn't solo, lassie.'

He turned back to Oliver, who was listening intently, trying to work out what the hell was going on.

'Is there anything else you can tell us?' Monroe asked. 'Anything from the last couple of days?'

Oliver nodded.

'That place in Smithfield,' he said, 'the one that they found the girl in.'

'What about it?' Monroe asked.

'Antony Morgan was arranging a rental there a couple of months back, claimed it was because he wanted a location he could store flowers. But it was completely the opposite direction from New Covent Garden Market so I didn't quite understand why he would do that. I got the impression he was being forced to do it, like it wasn't his idea. And then he said he had to get the place renovated as it was currently a recording studio.'

Monroe turned to Declan.

'That sounds pretty damning,' he said. 'If we find it wasn't Stephanie Thompson who owned that building, it changes everything.'

'Also, if he's being forced into it as well,' McAlroy said. 'Hypothetical here – could he have been told to do it by Ford or Hart? Or whoever this dangerous third person was? Someone who might even have been there with Blackthorne?'

'Maybe. We should talk to Michael Ashton, perhaps,' Declan said. 'He was the last boy to be taken by Blackthorne. Maybe he can give us a better idea.'

At the name, Oliver looked nervous, glancing around the room. Declan wasn't sure, but this felt a little off, as if Oliver had been comfortable with everything else, but now, with Ashton named, there was something a little "out of comfort zone" going on now.

Oliver looked as if he was about to be sick, but pulled himself together.

'Sorry, as I said, I knew Michael,' he said. 'We were the same age. He wasn't at my school, but we saw each other here and there. When he was kidnapped and then saved, his parents and my parents met a few times. The two of us were left to our own devices to talk. But you won't find him.'

'How do you mean?'

'Because they've gone,' Oliver replied.

22

SLEEPY TIME

MARIE FORD HADN'T EXPECTED TO STAND OUTSIDE THE PRISON, effectively a free woman for another two years at least. She knew that with exemplary behaviour and everything she'd done, her stretch could have been shortened, but not by the amount that it had been. However, her recent help in helping locate the missing child, and the interview she'd been allowed to do, in some small ways, helped both her and Hart in redeeming themselves in the public's eye.

There had been a small outcry to check into their previous convictions, the possibility of mitigating circumstances possibly causing some kind of retrial. Until then, they were allowed out on release under investigation, deemed as no longer a threat to the public.

Marie Ford was now, for the first time in years, in her own clothes, walking out onto the street. She was impressed they still fit.

The press were there, and she smiled and "no commented" as much as she could. She was surprised her solicitor hadn't turned up, although she seemed to recall she'd fired him a while back.

There was a PR company that had contacted her right after the rescue, though; they were the ones who had arranged the TV interviewer to come and talk to her. They had told her earlier that day that a dark van would arrive for her once she was released; a minivan, a seven-seater with black windows to stop the press from being able to take photos of her. They wanted her in the van and out of sight as quickly as possible before they could decide what the next plan was.

As far as Ford was concerned, her next plan was to clear her name and work out how to make money from this. If Declan Walsh was correct, the cryptocurrency she still owned could be worthless. Still, there were ways to change that, and there was always a horse race to bet on.

As she moved through the press, all of them still following her, she saw the van, charcoal-grey, waiting to the side. The PR people had said a familiar face would be there for her, something that would also push for a nice news piece once the following photographers snapped it, so as she arrived at the van, she wasn't surprised to see Antony Morgan emerge from the driver's seat, opening the door for her at the side of the van, ushering her in. The press, seeing Morgan, started shouting out, asking him questions. He "no commented" as well, slamming the door behind him and climbing back into the driver's seat, arranged so that Ford was sitting directly behind him.

Once in the seat, he started to drive; the press moving out of the way, their story now over. Ford leant back in the chair, laughing.

'Oh my god,' she said. 'Did you see them? They all wanted a piece of me.'

'Everybody wants a piece of you, Miss Ford,' Morgan replied, looking back at her. 'Well done for what you did. I didn't have time to thank you. You performed perfectly.'

'Performed?' Ford was going to reply to this, but then shrugged. 'Oh, you mean the interview? I suppose it was a bit of a performance, wasn't it?'

'You've got something on your lip,' Morgan replied, pulling to the side and rummaging in the glove compartment. 'Hold on, I've got a tissue. I can wipe it off for you.'

Ford touched her lip and looked at her hand. There was nothing that came off, but the last thing she wanted was to look bad on camera. As she looked up, Morgan had the tissue in his hand.

'Are we going to pick up Hart at all?' Ford asked. 'I know she worked with you as well. I'd rather be prepared if I'm going to see her again. We haven't had the most cordial of conversations.'

'She's behind you,' Morgan smiled, pointing at the rear seat.

Turning and looking down, Ford saw with surprise that Sonya Hart was indeed lying on the back seat, asleep.

'Laid down, passed out as soon as she got in the van,' Morgan laughed. 'Obviously she hadn't been sleeping for a while.'

'Are you sure she's—'

Ford had turned back to ask, but that was as far as she got, because as she turned to face Antony Morgan, he slammed the handkerchief into her face, and she smelt the sweet cloying smell of chloroform. Ford reckoned herself to be good in a fight; she'd been an East End cop after all. But this had come as a surprise, from a man she trusted, her asset, even. As she struggled to pull it away, she could already feel her strength draining, pushed back into the seat by Morgan's hand as he held it over her mouth …

Before saying anything else, Marie Ford was unconscious in the seat.

Antony Morgan tossed the cloth to the side, leaned over and secured the seat belt on Marie Ford; then, with a whistle and a jaunty tune, shifted back into the driver's seat before he carried on driving.

Declan frowned as he stared at Oliver Chen.

'How do you mean gone?'

'They left about a year ago,' Oliver replied. 'I think their dad won the lottery or something. A seven-figure win. They sold up their house, and they moved.'

'Do we know where?' Declan was noting this down.

'I think it was America.'

'You're kidding?'

'No,' Oliver shook his head, no longer the worried kid he was a moment earlier, warming to the subject. 'I remember Michael telling me about it. He was pissed off that he was gonna have to leave all his friends, but he was excited because, well, you know, America.'

'Do you remember when this was?' Declan asked.

Oliver shook his head.

'Last time I saw him was, start of the year,' he replied. 'Maybe January.'

'So that's what, nine months?' Declan went to text Billy downstairs, but saw Anjli was already doing it.

'We can find a list of lottery winners,' she said.

'It might not have been the lottery,' Oliver replied sheepishly, nervously looking around again, and Declan got the distinct impression he'd either said something he shouldn't, or made up some kind of lie here. He just couldn't explain why he thought this, as the boy continued. 'I just know they came into a lot of money. It could have been an inheritance, it could have been ...'

'How much exactly did they make?' Declan asked, pressing to see what happened. 'Did Michael ever say?'

'No, but he kept saying a million as a ballpark figure.'

Declan considered this, but it was Anjli who spoke first.

'How much money did Antony Morgan inherit?'

'Enough to buy a flower shop,' Declan shrugged.

'Yeah, but what else did he get?' Anjli asked. 'His parents were Philadelphia money, right?'

Billy, at this point, walked into the canteen.

'You texted me, oh mistress,' he said, looking at Anjli and winking at Oliver, doing his best to keep things light.

'Do we know how much Antony Morgan made from his inheritance?'

'It's kept in legal funds and trusts and all that kind of thing, but he was left probably somewhere between one and a half and two million dollars.'

'That's not enough,' Declan said.

'That's not including the properties, though,' Billy added.

'What properties?'

'Well, Morgan's family owned a chunk of real estate in Philadelphia,' Billy said. 'There's every opportunity that he could have sold those and gained, another two, three – who knows – million.'

'Do we know if the houses were sold?' Anjli asked. 'I want to know if a family from Mile End moved into one of them.'

She looked around the canteen.

'Consider it. A million isn't enough to change your life. It's a lot of money, but most families wouldn't move to America for no reason. But a million and a free place to live? A house given as part of the deal, to help someone move on from a traumatic moment? That could do it. A new start. Mummy and Daddy Ashton would have gone to a place where nobody would know about what happened to their son.'

'Check whether they were unhappy where they were,' Monroe said, 'and have a look and see if they now live in Philadelphia.'

He looked around the room.

'How are you feeling, laddie?' he asked.

'I'm good,' Oliver smiled. It was a weak smile, but it was a smile nevertheless, and Monroe leant forward, patting him on the knee.

'Are you good to sit here? We can bring in a police constable, or DS McAlroy could sit with you.'

'Sir, I'd rather stay with you for the moment,' McAlroy replied.

Monroe nodded.

'We'll bring up Cooper, then,' he said. 'She can sit with the lad until we decide our next steps. We all need to have a bit of a chat. Are you good with that?'

Oliver nodded.

'Can you tell my parents I'm okay?' he asked.

'We already have,' Billy smiled. 'They're on their way.'

'Are they unhappy with me?'

'They understand why you ran,' Billy said. 'But if you

manage to completely break this case, I think you'll be the hero of the street.'

He was about to continue, but then paused as his phone beeped. It wasn't the only phone that beeped in the room; Declan, Anjli, and Monroe's phones all beeped at the same time.

Frowning, Monroe stared down at his own phone, reading the text, his eyes darkening.

'Oh, you bloody fools,' he muttered.

He looked up at Anjli and Declan, who had obviously received the same message.

'Have you?'

'Yes, Guv,' Declan replied, his face dark. He looked at McAlroy, the only person who hadn't received a message.

'A judge has freed both Ford and Hart on release under investigation,' he said, 'claiming that their cases need to be looked into, but because of that, they can stay free until the retrial happens.'

He slammed his fist against the table and then held a hand up to stop the now scared Oliver.

'Oliver, I'm sorry,' he said, 'I didn't mean to scare you, it's just we have a history with DCI Ford and DC Hart and knowing they're now on the streets ... just know that will *not* be a good thing.'

'It's also probably the entire game plan from the start,' Anjli growled.

'We need to go to Mile End now,' Monroe was checking a second message on his phone as he spoke. 'I need to make a call first.'

He looked back at McAlroy.

'Do you want to go back there?'

'Not right now,' McAlroy admitted. 'They'll be pissed I came here. I'd rather be out of the firing range right now.'

'Understood. Change of plans, then. You're on babysitting duty,' Monroe replied, nodding to Oliver and leaving the canteen. 'The rest of you, get ready for war.'

As the others went downstairs to prepare, Monroe continued upwards, walking as far from anyone else as he could before making a phone call, waiting patiently for it to answer.

'What?' a gruff voice answered. 'I'm a busy man.'

'I thought I'd give you a heads up,' Monroe said. 'You've got people going after you. I'm not sure if you'll survive this one.'

'I saw the footage,' the voice of Johnny Lucas spoke down the phone. 'Ford thinks she can take me down. That's adorable.'

'You're a Member of Parliament, Johnny,' Monroe replied. 'You might be able to throw a lot of things onto Jackie, but once the screws are in place ...'

'I'll have to resign?' Johnny laughed. 'You're behind the times, Monroe. Haven't you heard? I've already agreed to step down.'

'You have? Why?'

There was a pause.

'Maybe it's a thing about leopards and spots. Maybe it's a thing about not being able to do what *I* wanted to do.'

There was another long pause and then a sigh down the line.

'Alex, I've been in the East End for many years; either

with my family, my brother, or even just by myself, controlling an empire that might have hurt a lot of people, but at the same time also kept a lot of people in line. I became an MP because I realised I had an opportunity to do something bigger. But after all this time in Parliament, I've realised that all I've learned is that I wasn't a big enough *crook*. I think if I want to look after my people, there are easier ways to do it.'

'So what, you're stepping down?'

'I've already announced it,' Johnny said. 'Funny enough, it was your protégé, Ellie Reckless that made me consider it. There'll be a by-election in due process, although they might hold off until the General Election. I can see that happening soon.'

There was a chuckle down the line; possibly at the thought of Charles Baker being deposed.

'I'm sorry, Monroe, what with an election likely kicking Baker out of office, and with me stepping down, you're about to lose a lot of your friends in Parliament.'

'You were never destined for Parliament,' Monroe replied. 'You were more of a ground level general. For what it's worth, I think you're making the right choice.'

'If you start talking about Captain Kirk and how he stopped being an Admiral again, I think I'm going to end up shooting you,' Johnny laughed. 'Anyway, thank you for the heads up. I'm a big boy. I can deal with it myself.'

There was a pause down the line.

'But on that subject,' Johnny continued. 'I'd be remiss if I didn't help you. I've monitored Marie Ford and Sonya Hart. Things that happen in my manor are, well, shall we say, important to me.'

'And Ford still owes you money,' Monroe replied carefully.

'I wrote that debt off years ago,' Johnny replied. 'But listen, when your lad Declan took her out of the game, he didn't take them all, yeah? She has allies, one's still at Mile End. People who speak to her, keep her updated on what's going on. If this is being done to get her out, then they've been keeping her updated on everything that's been going on.'

Monroe nodded, even though he knew that Johnny Lucas wouldn't be able to see the motion.

'It's McAlroy, isn't it?' he said. 'I've got that feeling.'

Johnny laughed.

'McAlroy wasn't even around when Ford was there,' he said. 'If she's corrupt, it's for different reasons. Esposito and McAlroy never dealt with me, apart from in a police sense.'

'Detective Superintendent Harris?'

'Harris ... now Harris is a dodgy bastard, and I wouldn't trust him as far as I could go.'

'So Harris has been talking about us?'

'Harris wouldn't have dealt with Ford,' Johnny replied. 'He's corrupt as hell, but he's an elitist. Ford was just turning DCI when he transferred in. He wouldn't speak down to her and offer to help. She'd have to beg him for assistance. No, I think you're looking more for somebody lower at Mile End who could do this.'

'And do you have a name?' Monroe asked.

'I do indeed,' Johnny replied.

And right before he ended the call, he gave it to Monroe.

MONROE ENTERED THE MAIN OFFICE TO SEE EVERYONE HUDDLED around Billy's monitors.

'Oh Christ,' he moaned. 'What now?'

'Ford and Hart were released, and both got into a minivan driven by Antony Morgan, to be driven to a safe house in Tower Hill,' Billy said as he looked around. 'There're tons of press photos.'

'So why the scrum here?'

'Because they never made it,' Declan replied. 'The van's disappeared, and it looks like the company that arranged it all was paid for and hired by, well, a "Thomas Blackthorne."'

He looked upstairs, as if peering through the ceiling.

'Guv, Oliver ...'

'I know, laddie,' Monroe smiled softly. 'I got it too. But we can ignore it, or let it work in our favour, eh? Now, let's go find some recently released felons and work out how a dead man can hire PR companies, shall we?'

23

RATCATCHER

Mile End was in the middle of a meeting when Monroe, Anjli, De'Geer and Declan walked into the room. DCI Esposito was standing to the side and Detective Superintendent Harris was speaking to the team involving Sanford and a few other uniforms.

'This is a closed meeting, Detective Superintendent Monroe,' Harris said, looking up. 'And I don't think you're welcome here.'

'I'm sorry for interrupting, Harris, but we need to speak to one of your police officers in connection with an investigation we're running,' Monroe replied amicably, ignoring the rank.

'What investigation would that be?' Harris asked.

'Corruption in Mile End,' Declan said. 'I know, what a shock, eh?'

Harris reddened.

'Are you saying that we're corrupt? That *I'm* dirty?'

'We weren't, but we're quite happy to,' Monroe replied. 'We have it literally from the horse's mouth that you've been working with criminal overlords, but on this occasion, we know you're not the one we need to speak to.'

At this, Monroe turned to PC Sanford.

'We understand you're the one who's been keeping in contact with DCI Ford.'

At the comment, Sanford straightened, nervously looking around as Esposito's eyes bored into her.

'Is this true?' he asked. 'Are you the reason DCI Ford and DC Hart could pass the information to everybody?'

Sanford looked as if she was going to lie, but then shook her head, almost as if silently berating herself for considering such a thing.

'I did nothing wrong,' she replied. 'I just passed on messages from mutual friends, did favours here and there.'

'Were you the one passing messages from Ford to Antony Morgan?' Declan asked. 'Maybe you were the one getting the emails from Sonya Hart and passing them back? The go-between, as they told Antony Morgan what to do?'

There was a long, quiet moment in the briefing room.

Harris went to speak but stopped as he saw Monroe glare at him. They might have been the same rank and Harris might have had seniority, but there was a power in Monroe's eyes that basically said *if you say a single word, laddie, I will kick the living shite out of you.*

The silence, however, was broken by Sanford's laughter as she looked around.

'Oh my god,' she chuckled. 'He was right.'

She looked at Anjli.

'This is all your fault, you know,' she said. 'You got the wrong man killed.'

'Blackthorne?'

'I knew him, you know,' Sanford nodded. 'He was a good

man, innocent, quiet. He would never have done the things you said he did.'

'Then why did he kidnap Michael Ashton? Threaten to kill him if we didn't drop the case?'

'He was told to do that,' Sanford laughed. 'He would never have done that off his own cognisance. He *had* to have been told to do that.'

'And who would have told him?'

'The real killer.'

'And who was the real killer?' Declan asked.

'You never found out, did you?' Sanford shrugged.

'Not for want of trying,' Anjli replied icily. 'And not for want of Ford stopping the case the moment he killed himself.'

'Maybe if you'd worked harder at convincing Ford to do her job right, this would never have happened,' Sanford shook her head again. 'You know this wasn't their idea, though, right?'

'What do you mean?' Monroe frowned. 'Whose idea was it?'

'I wasn't passing messages from them to Antony Morgan,' Sanford laughed. 'He was passing messages *to them* through me. He'd realised that Stephanie was the killer, and he wanted to get it fixed. He'd tried to speak to Anjli, but she'd blown him off.'

'That's a lie,' Anjli replied.

Sanford held her hand up to stop Anjli from continuing.

'I don't care what happened between you and Morgan. All I'm telling you is what I was told,' she said. 'Morgan saw Stephanie. She effectively admitted she was going to do terrible things. And Morgan remembered times during the original case, expressions she'd had. He realised that

Stephanie was more guilty than Anjli Kapoor realised, so decided he was going to get DCI Ford and DCI Hart to do your job for you.'

She laughed, taking a long look around the room as she did so.

'And it looks like he did, and in the process they proved they were the police officers they were always believed to be, not the corrupt officials that the DCI there painted them as,' she pointed at Declan as she spoke, the voice harsh now. 'They did good work while they were at Mile End. They put bad people away and the moment that DCI Walsh had them arrested, all of their cases were overturned.'

'That's not true,' Esposito now replied. 'We had to look into them as a matter of course. That doesn't mean that they were all thrown out! Some were, but the authentic cases are still in discussion.'

'They listened to Morgan,' Sanford continued. 'They learned that someone else was involved, a stranger nobody knew of, who was also hunting Morgan.'

'Who?'

Sanford shrugged.

'Ask them.'

Anjli was about to comment on this, but felt a buzzing in her jacket pocket. Pulling out her phone, she saw it was a message from DS McAlroy.

> Find somewhere quiet, and call me now.
> Urgent.

Frowning, she looked at De'Geer.

'McAlroy's just texted,' she whispered. 'Said to call her. I'm just going to pop out and find out what's up.'

De'Geer nodded, and sliding out the back, Anjli walked

out of the office, heading downstairs to a quieter area in the stairwell. Pressing reply, she allowed the number to auto-dial.

After a couple of rings, it was answered.

'Jules?' Anjli asked.

'No,' it was a male voice; nervous. 'It's Oliver. Oliver Chen.'

Anjli frowned.

'Why are you phoning from DS McAlroy's phone?' she asked.

'There's a problem.' Oliver's voice was soft, scared as he spoke now. 'Look. When you left, McAlroy was sitting with me, but then her phone went. She didn't say who she was talking to, but I recognised the voice on the other end. It was Antony Morgan.'

'What did she say to him?'

'She arranged to meet him. Said you were getting closer, and he needed to finish things—'

There was a moment.

'Look. I just ... oh, wait. Shit. Someone's coming.'

'Where are you?' Anjli asked.

'I'm on Fleet Street,' Oliver said, and in the distance, she could hear a car beeping its horn. 'As soon as he called her, I knew I was in trouble. She said she needed to go to the toilet, and when she disappeared I took her phone and I ran. I don't have one myself to call you on and I didn't trust sitting around in case something was going on.'

'I get that,' Anjli said. 'Let me get the others.'

'No, I'm—'

There was a pause, a yelp, what sounded like a rustling and then a fresh voice came onto the phone.

'Hello, Anjli.'

It was the voice of Antony Morgan.

'Mister Morgan,' she tried to keep her voice calm. 'How nice of you to call. We were just talking about you, in Mile End, and ...'

'Lovely,' Morgan replied. 'I'd like to hear what you said. In fact, I'd like to hear what *you personally* said. So how about we meet?'

'Sure,' Anjli replied. 'Let me tell the others, we'll all come by—'

'No, sorry,' Morgan interrupted. 'I didn't say I wanted to speak to the others. I said I wanted to speak to *you*. I have a very special meeting arranged. A very exclusive guest list.'

'Really?' Anjli replied. 'And who's on this list?'

'Currently it's you, DCI Ford and DC Hart,' Morgan continued. 'I'd like you to explain to me once and for all why you chose Blackthorne as your target.'

'Because he was a killer,' Anjli looked around to see if anyone was within waving range.

'No,' Morgan snapped. 'And if you had been paying attention, you'd have realised it couldn't have been him. It was definitely someone else, and maybe if you turn up, I'll tell you who it was.'

Anjli wanted to run up the stairs and tell people that Morgan was on the phone, but something paused her.

'Here's the deal, Miss Kapoor,' Morgan continued. 'Our little friend here made a mistake calling you. I had plans on how to bring you somewhere nice and quiet, but now I'm going to have to change that. I'm going to give you an address, and you're going to come to me right now. If you don't, there'll be another young boy found dead at the hands of the Posies Killer.'

'I thought Stephanie Thompson was the Posies Killer,' Anjli replied. 'And last I saw, she was dead.'

'Come on, Kapoor. Even you're not that stupid,' Morgan snapped. 'I know you've been looking into me, working out what I know. I know Oliver told everyone how there's a third player in the game, someone who could also have done it. Well, if you come along to the address I send you, I'll tell you exactly what I'm doing. But you come *alone*. And I *will* know if you tell anybody, Kapoor; you've already worked out that I have ears in Mile End. And, as you also know now, currently in Temple Inn.'

Anjli wanted to scream, but kept it in, gritting her teeth.

'Send me the address,' she said. 'I'll come to you alone. On the condition that you let the boy go.'

'When you arrive, the boy will be freed and all will be revealed,' Morgan replied. 'Who knows, maybe you'll actually even solve the case. Wouldn't that be nice?'

The call disconnected, and a new text appeared on the screen, an address Anjli recognised instantly.

'Shit,' she muttered to herself, looking up the stairs. She couldn't risk letting them know what was going on so, with a sigh, she headed down the stairs and out of the Mile End Crime Unit.

It was only once in her car that she contacted someone else. It was a risk, and she had to explain the situation ...

But there was no way she was going into this alone.

BACK IN THE OFFICE, SANFORD LAUGHED LOUDLY AND BITTERLY.

'You're a joke, Guv,' she said to Esposito. 'This entire department's a joke. I was gonna leave. Quit. Ask for a transfer. Do anything to get out of here. You've sanitised Mile End. This is a place where gangsters became politicians, for

Christ's sake! We used to fight fire with fire and now we stand there and ask them politely to stop. We're not allowed to use our force in case someone cries out that we're nasty people and we've entered their "personal space". This isn't East End policing.'

She was pacing around the office now; nobody was stopping her, it was as if they were giving her enough rope to hang herself with.

'Antony Morgan gave me an opportunity to solve a case that you guys dropped the ball on and I agreed to help because I saw the faces of the parents,' she continued. 'I saw Blackthorne's face when he was believed to be the killer.'

At this point Declan realised that Sanford truly believed, without any measure of doubt, that she was the true hero here.

'Can you contact Antony Morgan?' Monroe asked, interrupting her diatribe for a moment. 'He seems to be missing, as do Marie Ford and Sonya Hart.'

'What do you mean?' now it was Sanford's turn to frown. 'Hart and Ford were released today.'

'Yes, they were,' Monroe continued. 'But both of them, through a PR agency hired by what looks to be Thomas Blackthorne, picked them up.'

'That's impossible.'

'Aye, it is, but the account was an old one. Can you guess who had access rights? I'll make it easy for you. Antony Morgan. The van that arrived, apparently driven by Morgan, has gone off the grid. Nobody knows where they are. Antony Morgan could have taken them, or they might have all been taken by someone else, a third player Oliver Chen mentioned. Either way, we thought you might have a little chat with him for us, see what his plans are.'

He looked at Harris.

'Unless you still have your briefing to finish.'

Harris's eyes were wide, and Monroe could tell that this was not something he'd been aware of. Harris might have been a corrupt piece of shit at the best of times, but on this occasion, he'd obviously been caught in the dark as much as the others had.

Silently, he nodded to Monroe, allowing him to do what he needed to do.

Esposito walked up to Sanford, holding his hand out.

'Phone. Now,' he commanded.

Sanford quietly pulled out her phone, passing it across to her superior, who passed it to Monroe.

'What name is he under?'

'Antony Morgan,' Sanford replied. 'What else would I put in there? I've got nothing to hide.'

'Or maybe you should have done it better,' Monroe said, scrolling through the phone numbers, finding the relevant one, and pressing call. He put it on speakerphone and held it up.

After three rings, a male voice answered, but it sounded fake, like it was being put through a modulator.

'You're not supposed to call,' the voice said. 'I told you before, they could be listening.'

'Oh laddie, we are listening,' Monroe replied. 'We want to hear exactly what your demands are.'

'Demands?' The voice seemed surprised by the question. 'Why would you think I'd have demands?'

'Because you've kidnapped two previously serving officers,' Monroe replied. 'I'm guessing you have a plan. Please tell me you have a plan. I'd hate for you to have done all this for no apparent reason.'

'Do you think I only have two?' The voice replied defiantly. 'I have three, including Morgan.'

'So you're *not* Antony Morgan?' Monroe raised an eyebrow. Perhaps Oliver Chen hadn't been exaggerating.

There was no response to this; there was a moment where Monroe had even wondered whether the man behind the strange voice, who held Antony Morgan's phone and was, for all intents and purposes likely to be Morgan himself, creating some kind of plausible deniability, had disconnected the phone.

But then the voice returned.

'I have demands,' the voice said. 'They're very important ones.'

'Let me guess, you want Thomas Blackthorne's name cleared?' Monroe replied. 'Well, laddie, or lassie, I don't discriminate against faceless voice-modulated weirdos, and we are unfortunately not miracle workers.'

'Who said it was anything to do with you?' the voice replied with a laugh. 'I've already given my demands to someone else.'

Monroe looked around at Declan and realised, with a sickening feeling, that Anjli Kapoor was no longer in the room.

'Where's Detective Inspector Kapoor?' he asked.

'She took a call from McAlroy, Guv,' De'Geer said, nodding at the main door. 'Popped out there.'

'Go and get her,' Monroe replied.

'Oh, that's okay,' the voice on the phone said. 'Save the lad some legwork. Is he the big chap that came to visit Morgan? I wouldn't want to see him have to run down the stairs. Anjli Kapoor has left. She's come to find me. You see, I wanted to have a chat with Ford, Hart and Kapoor. They were the ones who set up Thomas Blackthorne and made him guilty of a crime he didn't commit.'

'Anjli wouldn't have just left without telling us,' Declan said. 'I think you're lying.'

'She would have if she thought someone was in trouble,' the voice replied. 'As you just heard, the call she got was from DS McAlroy, a trusted source. I think your chickens have come home to roost, and soon everyone will know the truth.'

'And your hostages?'

'Will face justice.'

The call disconnected, and Monroe looked up at the room.

'Is this what you expected?' he asked Sanford, who looked as if she was going to be sick. 'Someone please tell me there's a plan.'

He was going to reply when the door opened, and DS McAlroy entered at a run.

'Little shit stole my phone,' she said in heaving breaths to Monroe, before looking at Esposito and Harris. 'Oh, sorry, Guv. I've ... well ...'

'I think you have a lot to tell us,' Esposito said coldly as he looked at Monroe. 'Alex?'

'I want to hear the lassie,' Monroe replied, and was going to continue when McAlroy showed him a text on her phone.

'How do you have your phone when Oliver stole it?' Declan asked.

'This is Billy Fitzwarren's,' McAlroy explained. 'It's a text he got from Anjli Kapoor. And, as I'm not the bloody snitch, he told me to bring it to you, but not to text in case the *real* snitch learned what was going on.'

She looked at Sanford, nodded to herself, walked over

and then punched the PC square in the face, sending her to the floor.

'I hope you've worked *that* bit out,' she said to Esposito. 'Otherwise I'm in a shit ton of trouble.'

Monroe, meanwhile, was reading the message.

'We have a plan,' he said. 'Let's go.'

'Wait—' Harris held a hand up. 'This is a Mile End case.'

Monroe turned, and was about to kick off, but Harris waved his hands, pointing at Sanford.

'We screwed up,' he admitted. 'Give us a chance to help make it up.'

'Oh, laddie, you'll get that chance,' Monroe grinned. 'You'll get that chance in spades.'

24

SMOOTHIES

THE ADDRESS THAT ANTONY MORGAN HAD GIVEN WAS A familiar one in Leyton, the same house that, three years earlier, Thomas Blackthorne had taken his own life. It had been the house of his friend, but Anjli knew that they'd moved in the last couple of years. She didn't know, however, whether the house was deserted or whether somebody else lived there.

Antony Morgan must have known. Why else would he have used it?

Pulling up in her car, she almost texted a message, but paused. By now McAlroy would have found her way to Mile End, told them what was going on, made up some story about why Oliver had disappeared and maybe even explained a valid reason why Anjli would have disappeared from the office.

It seemed, right now, that Antony Morgan held all the cards.

With a sigh, she climbed out of the car and walked up to the door, only to find it open, left ajar, welcoming.

If she'd been less distracted, she would have seen the 125cc scooter that pulled up down the street, the rider watching her through their tinted helmet visor, before climbing off the scooter and heading to the wall to the side, to make sure they weren't seen by anyone near the house.

But she was distracted, and she didn't see this.

Pushing the door open slightly, she walked into the hallway and looked upstairs.

'Detective Inspector Kapoor,' an American voice spoke from the upper floor, the voice echoing around the walls. 'Come and join us.'

Anjli walked up, checking the place as she did so for anything she could use as a weapon if needed. She had a baton on her, and she knew she could call for help, but she felt strangely weaponless.

At the top, she found that the walls between two of the bedrooms had been smashed through, creating a very large en-suite bedroom. At one end, sitting on two chairs, their hands handcuffed to the arms of each chair, were Marie Ford and Sonya Hart. In front of each of them was a glass with some kind of vile green-looking liquid in it. Anjli recognised the liquid; it was the same as Stephanie Thompson had drunk, the same thing that had killed her. Neither woman was muzzled or gagged, but both were silent.

On either side of them were matching chairs with glasses, holding the same concoction in them. The chairs were both empty, and although Anjli guessed one was for her, she found herself curious who the second empty chair was for. Pondering this, she looked to the side, and saw Oliver Chen standing, a sawn-off shotgun aimed at his head, Antony Morgan behind.

'So glad you could come,' Morgan said.

Anjli nodded to both of her previous colleagues and stepped fully into the room.

'I'm here,' she said. 'You can let Oliver go.'

'Do you hear that, Oliver? You can go,' Morgan replied, lowering his barrels. 'Wouldn't that be nice for you?'

Oliver looked up at Morgan and for a second it felt as if he was about to speak, but Anjli rapped her knuckles against the wall to bring their attention back to her.

'Sorry to interrupt this tender moment,' she said, 'but you can play this as much as you want. I've pretty much worked out that Oliver's not exactly here against his will.'

There was a pause as Oliver turned to face Anjli.

'There's no way you know that,' he said. 'I was brilliant. Everybody believed me.'

'Yeah,' Anjli shook her head. 'Problem you've got, Oliver, is your story just felt a little *too* clean.'

She looked up at Morgan.

'He deliberately kept you out of any potential issues, although still gave a bit of uncertainty about your motives, which not only helped sell the story, but it was something he would have done if he was searching for you. Still played the Stephanie Thompson card to its full extent, too, even though by now we'd moved away from that idea, having worked out that she'd been murdered.'

'She committed suicide,' Morgan said.

'Strange how she managed to do that after somebody stuck belladonna into her, knocking her out,' Anjli replied with a smile. 'Or did you think we'd miss that one? You know, "stupid police" and all that.'

Oliver didn't seem to know what to say and looked back from Morgan to Anjli and back again.

'I'm guessing you weren't hunting Antony Morgan then,' she said, bringing his attention back to her.

Oliver shook his head.

'I was to start with,' he replied. 'I wasn't lying about that. But I was searching for him because I wanted to know the truth, not because I thought he was some kind of sketchy character. And when Antony found me, he gave me a job, and an answer. For the first time, I got to see another side of the story. I got to see what really happened, learned the truth about my mum. What she did. Why she was targeted. He showed me why Thomas couldn't have done it, how Thomas wasn't even around when my sister was murdered.'

Anjli nodded.

'Blackthorne did have an alibi for that day. That didn't necessarily mean he wasn't working with somebody else. We were still investigating him,' she said. 'I hadn't made my final decision. He took his life and stopped me from doing that. I always believed he worked with somebody else.'

She turned and faced Antony Morgan.

'You know, someone like an *assistant*.'

Morgan made a shrugging acceptance face, as if mulling over her suggestion and finding merit.

Anjli wanted to punch him in the teeth.

Oliver, however, seemed to be torn about what to do next, his eyes wide, as if caught in the glare of headlights.

'I didn't—'

'No, you *didn't*.' Anjli stopped him. 'You see, you thought by making out that DS McAlroy had secretly started a conversation with Morgan, that we would think that McAlroy was maybe the mole that we all knew about. The problem was that by the time you did this, we'd already worked out through somebody else that PC Sanford was your primary contact. Or at least the contact that put Mister Morgan here in touch with Ford.'

She now looked over at Morgan.

'We also know that Hart and Ford didn't contact you. In fact, you were the one who contacted Hart.'

She glanced over at Sonya Hart, watching silently.

'Isn't that right?'

Hart nodded, unable to speak, her face a mask of anger.

'I'm guessing you've given them the same thing you gave Stephanie?' Anjli asked conversationally. 'Something that paralyses them from speaking. I'm guessing they can move a little though, hence the restraints?'

'If you believed that I was the killer,' Morgan asked, 'then why did you come here?'

'Believe it or not, I realised I had a duty to look after these two idiots,' Anjli replied. 'When I got the call, and you said where you'd be, I worked out this was going to be the quickest way to sort things out.'

'And yet you came alone,' Morgan shook his head. 'I thought you were cleverer than that.'

'And you assumed I'd *come* alone.' Anjli grinned. 'I assumed *you* would be cleverer than that.'

At the comment, Morgan raised his shotgun.

'I will kill you if anybody turns up.'

'Oh, shut up,' Anjli shook her head. 'There's nobody here. But everything that happens from this point is already expected. Mile End knows I've come to find you. They'd pretty much easily guess it's going to be here in Leyton, based on my last phone's location. I'd be stunned if they're not here within fifteen minutes.'

'Then we'd better be quick,' Morgan smiled. He walked

over to a video camera, turning it on and aiming it at Ford, Hart, and the chair to the right.

'If you'd like to sit beside your two ex-colleagues,' he said, 'I'd like you to tell us the truth about Thomas Blackthorne, including how he was innocent of what you accused him of.'

Anjli nodded, shrugging. She walked over to Ford, who glared at her.

'Don't do this,' Ford said, her voice barely a whisper as she struggled to break whatever drugs were paralysing the throat. 'He's bastardising the force.'

'And you would care because?' Anjli asked, before sitting down comfortably in the chair and looking back at the camera.

'I am Detective Inspector Anjli Kapoor of the City of London Police,' she said. 'Three years ago, I was Detective Sergeant Anjli Kapoor of Mile End. At the time, we were hunting the killer of two children. They'd become known, thanks to the press, as the Posies Killer, due to a posy of rare blue pansies and common red poppies being found on the bodies. And it was believed, because of the evidence, that it was Thomas Blackthorne, a man who, when he realised he was being accused, committed suicide. But today, I'm here to say, I no longer believe it was him.'

Morgan, behind the camera, gave a thumbs up, and Anjli smiled darkly.

'Because the man who did it, Antony Morgan, is currently filming me with a shotgun in his hand,' she said. 'He was the true murderer, and he used the gullibility of his onetime manager to his advantage.'

She looked around, ignoring Morgan's stunned and furious expression.

'I'm stunned you're even happy to be in here,' she said.

'It's dirty. Not as clean as you like it. As clean as, for example, your shop was when I arrived. *Overly* cleaned. Or the place in Smithfield's.'

She frowned for a moment, looking back at the other chair.

'Oh my God,' she laughed, 'I've worked it out. You're going to be in the fourth chair, aren't you? Is that why Oliver's still here? Is he going to film it while you pretend that you two are victims of whoever this is? The mysterious, scary person he *really* made a point of talking about when he came to see us?'

'Shut up,' Morgan snapped.

'It is!' Anjli laughed. 'That's your plan, isn't it? You're going to kill the three of us, force us to drink this liquid, and then drink the first part before the police turn up. Have Oliver run away, so that they think that whoever the real killer is has escaped. You then get to be the sole survivor. That would make the news about *you*, wouldn't it?'

She looked back at Oliver.

'This all relied on you being believed, didn't it?' she asked apologetically. 'I was supposed to do whatever he said, because if I didn't, you'd be killed, the next victim? You thought this was going to help get revenge? Happily helping the man who killed your sister?'

Oliver looked at Morgan, and his eyes narrowed before he returned his gaze to Anjli.

'She was a bitch to me. She deserved it,' Oliver muttered.

'She deserved to die?' Anjli was horrified at the comment.

Oliver looked to the ground, and Anjli glared at Morgan.

'I really have screwed this up for you, haven't I? How exactly are you going to make me drink the poison now? I mean, these two, they're not exactly able to stop you if you're going to pour it down their throats, but me ...'

She gave a dark, vicious smile.

'I will *kick the living shite out of you* if you try.'

Morgan raised the sawn-off shotgun up.

'I'll shoot you,' he said.

'Oh no,' Anjli gave a mock horror expression. 'Do I take the hideously painful poison, vomiting all over myself, giving you the ability to escape your crimes, or do I let you shoot me? A very quick and pretty much painless way to go?'

'I didn't say I'd *kill* you,' Morgan hissed. 'This gun has more than one shot, you know.'

'Oh, it needs to,' Anjli replied casually. 'And you need to be striking a killing shot immediately, because I tell you now, if you fire at me, and you wing me or wound me? I will take that gun off you and I will make you *eat* it. It isn't the one Blackthorne had, is it? You know the trigger on that was a little dodgy, right?'

She looked at the camera.

'Also, you *are* aware this is recording everything, right?'

'Doesn't matter,' Oliver replied. 'I was going to edit it afterwards. Doesn't take long.'

'So, let me get this right,' Anjli said. 'You're going to say that the strange, mysterious killer, this person in the coat with the cap captures you, brings you here – where you find the three of us already dead – but before you can be, what, murdered by the Posies Killer, your loyal subordinate Oliver will come running to the rescue? Maybe bring that journalist again? That'd be good, wouldn't it? And, of course, the police would arrive and find a nice, edited package on the video recorder, explaining how the killer is still at large. And then you would be the hero of the hour. Everyone would want to talk to you.'

This last part was aimed at Morgan.

'While the mysterious Posies Killer would still be at large, having killed the three detectives who tried to take them in. What a story.'

She laughed.

'I will say one thing, though,' she continued. 'I'd like to give you an apology. Because I really got it wrong with Blackthorne, didn't I? Well, partly.'

'What?' Morgan was thrown here, having not expected this.

Shrugging, Anjli continued.

'I mean, I'm aware Ford here wanted to get the case over with quickly. She didn't really want it on her figures and all that, but how long would it have taken us to realise that he wasn't the killer, if you hadn't arranged for him to be killed?'

Morgan's eyes glittered with malice as he glared at the detective in front of him.

'I wasn't the one who got him killed,' he replied. '*You* did that, Kapoor. You did that the moment you brought in Jackie and Johnny Lucas, and got them involved with giving him a shotgun with a hair trigger.'

'That wasn't me,' Anjli replied, shaking her head, her face paling as, somewhere deep inside, she knew that the words he spoke had an aspect of truth to them. She *had* gone to Johnny Lucas, asking for help. *Jackie* Lucas had provided the gun, and she remembered well his comments at the scene.

'I heard the sawn-off shotgun had a bit of a hair trigger. If you were to place it against your chin, for example, and consider killing yourself, you might not get the chance to change your mind.'

Had *she* killed Thomas Blackthorn? Had she killed an innocent man?

Morgan, watching her expression, chuckled.

'Oh my God,' he said. 'You genuinely thought you'd done

the right thing for all these years. Thomas Blackthorne was a clean freak, sure. But he gained that from me, not the other way round. When I started working for him, his flaws were painful. I had to show him how to clean up after himself. He was unclean, and it made me so angry. I wanted to strike out at him, but ...'

'But you found other people to strike out at,' Anjli finished the sentence.

Morgan gave a little bow.

'Stephanie Thompson was the first,' he said. 'I can't remember how I found out. But when I learned what she'd been doing in the past, I was sickened. Back home, she would have been arrested, ostracised. London? Nothing.'

'It was a long time ago,' Anjli said. 'She'd turned over a new leaf.'

'Yeah, the problem with turning over a leaf is that if you turn it back over, whatever it is you wanted to get away from is still there,' Morgan sniffed. 'She was a whore. She was unclean. Her daughter was unclean. I was at a harvest festival, providing flowers with Thomas and I saw her there, saw her daughter and I realised then that she was not a good woman – and her daughter would grow up to be worse than she ever was.'

'You couldn't know that,' Anjli growled.

'Maybe I can't prove it,' Morgan replied, 'but I believe it. People have done way worse for their beliefs. And Mia Chen, her mum was a bitch.'

Morgan nodded across the room at Oliver.

'Ask him, he ran away from his parents. Mia was just as bad; she was a little princess, picked on her brother all the time, blamed him for everything she did. Did you know she actually attacked him with a pair of scissors once, nearly took out an eye? Deranged little bitch. I saw that, realised that she couldn't be left to live as well.'

'Debbie Watson?'

'Debbie was never going to die,' Morgan smiled. 'Debbie was my get-out plan. Her parents were vacuous enough to get away with things. And she'd spent a lot of time with Stephanie Thompson during lunchtime breaks after Stephanie had lost her daughter – nobody wanted to play with her, you see. I felt she was a perfect pawn to be used.'

'Michael Ashton?'

'Michael Ashton wasn't my idea,' Morgan looked unhappy as he spoke now. 'I told Thomas not to worry, that I'd get it fixed. That bloody idiot, he just got scared and ran off.'

'Why?'

'Because he'd gotten involved,' Morgan admitted. 'Sure, he didn't abduct them, but he helped me give them their ... medicine.'

Anjli stared at Morgan. Thomas Blackthorne had been involved. She had been correct. But Morgan wasn't finished.

'Thomas was scared, he was falling apart. He knew too much. I tried to reason with him, even shout at him, but I went too far. He ran, and then somebody ...'

He paused, giving an accusing glare at Anjli.

'Someone gave him a sawn-off shotgun. He thought he had power again. Thought if he pleaded with some leverage, he'd pretend that nothing bad had happened.'

He stopped, and for a second Anjli thought from his expression he was going to actually fire the gun.

'You should have believed the boy,' he snarled. 'You should have originally believed what I left with Stephanie's body. That was the plan. You would agree that Stephanie was the killer, and that everything was solved. And then I would have Oliver contact you personally, saying he was in danger. You would come on your own, and *then* we would have done this. So, go on then, how did you know it was me?'

Anjli shrugged.

'Clean fetish was a giveaway,' she said. 'First time I saw you, all you did was wipe your hands and clean down the countertops. Didn't feel right. And then you've got the poem.'

She settled back in the chair, relaxing, as her two ex-companions stared at her, almost surprised at her composure.

'You see, in the UK, "Ring of Roses" has the line "a-tishoo, a-tishoo, we all fall down". In America, it's "ashes, ashes, we all fall down". When Stephanie told it to me, she said "a-tishoo," just like the press used when they covered the original cases. But when Stephanie *wrote* it, she wrote "ashes," something an American would do. You know, like someone from Philadelphia. Then we also know that Michael Ashton's family were given an opportunity for a new life there – and I know you could claim this was a magnanimous gesture you did on their behalf if it had come out – but Oliver had gone off script, didn't he? He wasn't supposed to talk about that. He was supposed to just come in, get us aimed at the "Mile End mole" and this mysterious new killer and then leave, priming me for his call, but he wasn't expecting the Michael Ashton line being asked, and had to improvise.'

She looked at Oliver as she spoke; Oliver wouldn't catch her gaze back.

'And then the trifecta was your arrogance, Antony,' she continued. 'The fact you *had* to be front and centre. You made us think that you'd been contacted by Ford, or Hart, or both, while we know *you* were the one who made the first move.

You *had* to be the one Ian Trent went with to find the body, someone who'd complained on forums that he never gained the scoop, someone who would have done *anything* to be first on scene and had a grudge against DCI Walsh because of a woman who's been dead for years. You *had* to be the one *here* that survives the killer's grasp. Your ego did it.'

She now leant closer, staring directly at Morgan now.

'But it was the part of your ego that gave me flowers for the sweating sickness that clinched it,' she explained. 'Before we'd even received that poem, you just had to try to show your intelligence to me, show that you were ahead of us. And all you did was give us the clues we needed to come here and put you away.'

'You keep saying "we", Morgan sighed. 'But your companions aren't in any state to do anything, and you didn't call Mile End or Temple Inn.'

'Oh, when I say "we" I don't mean these two muppets,' Anjli rose now, taking both Oliver and Morgan's attention with her as she moved. 'I meant Police Constable Esme Cooper.'

Morgan turned and then screamed as the tines of Cooper's X75 taser slammed into him, dropping the gun as he fell to the floor, twitching.

Oliver went to run, but Cooper was ready for that, too, and with a solid grip on the chinstrap, she swung her bike helmet at his knees, taking them out from under him.

'Yeah, that's who I meant,' Anjli smiled. 'And thanks for putting it all on camera for us.'

25

OLD BOSSES, NEW EXCUSES

FOLLOWING MCALROY'S ARRIVAL WITH BILLY'S MESSAGE FROM Anjli, and following Billy's tracking of her phone to Leyton, it hadn't taken the team long to make their way there, followed by half a dozen police cars. Only to find Cooper, beside her moped, waiting for them.

'Keep the noise down,' she said, nodding at the squad vehicles. 'But thanks for keeping the sirens off. DI Kapoor's in the house, doing a Declan.'

'Doing a Declan?' The man in question looked around, confused.

'She means Anjli's in there going all *Poirot*, and getting the killer to confess, while likely under intense danger, while we all wait around outside like third wheels,' Monroe explained politely. 'How does it feel to be on this side of the fence?'

'I don't like it,' Declan muttered, looking back at Cooper. 'Sit rep?'

'I had a peek, but nipped out to wait for you,' Cooper replied. 'Ford and Hart are secured to chairs, DI Kapoor is in another but seems quite comfortable, and Oliver Chen and

Antony Morgan are filming her. Morgan is armed with a sawn-off shotgun, but I don't think he's going to use it.'

'And why's that?'

'Because DI Kapoor said she was going to make him eat it, if he did so.'

'That works,' Declan headed towards the door. 'Cooper, do you have your taser? We can—'

'Guv, I don't mean to tell you how to do your job, especially with so many people here? But the fact there *are* so many people here means they won't be able to *not* hear us, when we arrive up there,' Cooper replied. 'I've scouted the area, I have a plan, and I ask, please, let me sort Morgan and Chen out before DI Kapoor runs out of words?'

Declan nodded.

'Plan?'

'Taser one of them, and hit the other in the bollocks with my bike helmet.'

Declan looked at Monroe.

'Solid plan.'

He turned back to Cooper, but she'd already entered the building.

'By the way, laddie ... you can be the one to tell De'Geer how you sent his girlfriend into harm's way,' Monroe politely suggested.

A moment later there was the sound of a scream, and a crash – likely as Cooper tasered someone, and hit another beneath the belt with a bike helmet. However, a second later, Oliver Chen came stumbling out of the front door, pausing in horror as he faced a dozen angry officers.

'Up there!' he cried out. 'Morgan! He ...'

His voice trailed off as McAlroy emerged from the crowd.

'Got my phone, you little prick?' she asked coldly.

Oliver slumped, leaning against the wall.

'Shit,' he grumbled.

It had been another half an hour before Anjli emerged from the house. By that time Mile End police and forensics had already made their way in, and Declan, deciding that the house was too small for many more people, had sensibly waited outside.

Harris had been first on the scene, playing the role of the hero Detective Superintendent, making sure that any press that arrived later saw him front and centre. DCI Esposito, to his credit, simply sat back and allowed this to happen, rather than causing a fight on national TV. Declan was glad that Monroe was someone who was more likely to enjoy the actual detective work than the showboating; although, to be perfectly honest, it wasn't Monroe that was causing the problems publicly for the Last Chance Saloon of late.

Anjli walked over to him, a large grin on her face.

'You okay?' Declan asked.

Anjli nodded, and Declan realised that the smile on her face was one of relief, more than anything else, but it was bittersweet. A smile of triumph, but with loss.

'All this time I've believed that Thomas Blackthorne did it alone,' she said. 'All this time, the actual killer had been going free – Blackthorne was just a pawn.'

'That wasn't your fault,' Declan replied, placing a hand on her shoulder. 'The man killed himself. And it sounds like he was a willing pawn, not a victim.'

'Would he have though, if Jackie Lucas hadn't given him a

hair-trigger shotgun?' Anjli looked at Declan now. 'A favour that I had asked?'

'You never asked for Jackie Lucas to sort it out *fatally*. You just asked for some help because your own police force wasn't giving it to you.'

Anjli looked up, back at the house, where somewhere inside, Ford and Hart were likely being re-arrested after being checked over by Doctors Marcos and Khanna.

'I was a lot more naïve then,' she said, 'earlier in my career. I'm not using that as an excuse, but I will make a point of doing better.'

'You already do,' Declan said. 'And I won't have you putting yourself down. That's my job.'

'Of course it is, Guv,' Anjli smiled.

As she spoke, De'Geer, carrying a large, clear baggie with a camera inside, the one that Morgan had been filming on, emerged, glaring at Declan.

'I understand you're the one who sent Cooper into the house, Guv,' he stated coldly. Declan felt there was an admonishing tone to it.

'Let me ask you a question, Sergeant,' he replied. 'Do you think that PC Cooper couldn't cope with that?'

De'Geer smiled. He knew that whatever answer he gave; he was damning himself one way or the other, and it was an argument he didn't really want to have.

'I've got the video footage, Ma'am,' he said, looking at Anjli. 'I'm going to take it to Billy.'

'Not Mile End?' Anjli frowned.

'No, because it contains information on both Marie Ford and Sonya Hart,' De'Geer smiled. 'Detective Superintendent Monroe gave a very good argument why we should look at it first. You know, with it involving one of our own. I think

Harris, realising that he's managed to royally shit the bed, pardon my language, decided that he should at least give us something.'

'How damning is the video?' Declan asked as De'Geer walked off.

'Morgan gave me everything,' Anjli explained. 'I "Declan" ed him.'

'Yeah, still not happy with the way this is now a term,' Declan replied.

'What, walking into danger, being faced by a maniac with a gun and getting him to explain everything to you while you act all smart and clever?' Anjli shrugged. 'Tell me it's not what you always do.'

'Sometimes I chase them,' Declan said, a wry tone to his voice.

Now it was time for Anjli to pat him on the shoulder.

'Do you want to wait around?' she asked. 'They'll be bringing out Ford and Hart, but I'm not too sure what state they'll be in. Morgan had given them a paralysis agent. They were starting to break through it ...'

She trailed off as, through the door, Mile End officers were escorting both Marie Ford and Sonya Hart out of the house. They were walking slowly, but they were being assisted, almost as if they'd woken from a deep sleep and were still incredibly groggy.

'I demand to speak to my solicitor,' Ford said. 'We were freed. We shouldn't be going back to prison.'

Declan stepped up, nodding to the officers.

'I'll take over from here,' he said.

The officers on either side of Ford, young men who probably knew stories of her from before their time nodded gratefully and stepped to the side. Ford managed to hold a hand up, resting it against the doorframe.

'I'm free,' she whispered through hoarse lips. 'There's nothing you can do about that.'

'Marie Ford, Sonya Hart,' Declan said. 'I'm afraid you're both under arrest again.'

'For what?' Ford asked. 'We tried to help.'

'No, you engineered a plot that got Stephanie Thompson killed,' Declan said angrily. 'And, let's be honest, if it hadn't been for Anjli, you would have ended with a far more *permanent* sentence for what you did.'

By now, Sonya Hart had been left beside Marie Ford, the two women now leaning against the outside of the house as they regained their strength, the uniformed officers wisely giving Declan space.

'We know you were sending emails,' he said, looking back at Hart. 'We can't say who to or what they were, but we know when you did it. That alone is enough to have you placed back in prison. The fact you were using these emails to contact Ford and create your own narrative, framing Anjli as the bad guy while claiming yourselves as heroes? That was bad enough.'

He stepped to the side as officers now brought out the shaking and crying Antony Morgan, still recovering from his taser wound.

'The fact you'd used the actual killer is beyond stupidity,' he finished as they walked Morgan off to a waiting van.

'It's not what you think,' Ford protested.

'Oh, I can tell you exactly what I think,' Declan snapped back, interrupting her. 'You see, I don't even think this was your idea.'

He looked at Sonya Hart.

'Morgan contacted *you*, didn't he? He realised he had an opportunity to screw Anjli over. Probably saw her in the press. Realised he had an opportunity. But how could he get all three people that he blamed for Blackthorne's death?' Declan shook his head. 'It might not even have been anger at Blackthorne dying. It might have been anger that everything he did, you pinned on someone else. You were so lazy you didn't bother checking.'

'If we're lazy, so was Anjli.'

'I wasn't lazy,' Anjli now stormed over, having overheard that part. 'I was obstructed by you. Wanting this over and done with so that your statistics were as good as you were claiming them to be. You needed bonuses to gain promotions, to find other financial opportunities so you could gain more time to pay off gambling debts. This wasn't a murder case for you. This was an opportunity to gain status to pay off a bookie. Blackthorne was the obvious choice, but if we'd investigated more, maybe we would have realised that Morgan was controlling him.'

Ford stared coldly at Anjli.

'But that's not why we're here,' Declan said. 'The problem was that Morgan came to you, Sonya, and what? Suggested a way of getting back at Anjli? Suggested a way of clearing your name? What was it exactly he wanted to do?'

'He reckoned he could clear our names,' Hart admitted. 'Said he could find a way that the true murderer would be revealed and we could be cleared. Explained how we could be seen as people helping when Anjli wouldn't.'

'And this was when you contacted Ford, yes?'

Hart nodded, not replying.

'So, when did you decide to change the game?' Declan asked. 'I mean, here's Antony Morgan deciding to help you guys go free. And the next thing I hear, you're telling Stephanie Thompson that he's a wrong-un, and she needs to keep an eye on him.'

'We decided that there was a chance Morgan couldn't be trusted,' Ford admitted, her strength slowly returning to her muscles. 'We realised we could play them against each other. We could tell Stephanie Thompson that Antony Morgan was somebody worth watching, while at the same time following on with Antony Morgan's ideas that we should keep an eye on Stephanie Thompson. That way, we would cover all bets.'

'We didn't trust him to start with,' Hart continued. 'We knew him coming to us meant he had his own agenda. By flipping it, we made it ours.'

'And how did that work out for you?' Declan snapped.

'I made contact with Stephanie. She was desperately looking for somebody to blame still, someone to take the fall for her marriage and hair disappearing,' Ford explained. 'She came to visit, under a different name. I had some people arrange it for her.'

'Sanford.'

Ford didn't answer.

'Anyway, I said how I'd been doing some soul searching and knew that it was time to try to find a way of solving the case, now believing it wasn't Blackthorne. I told her to look into it.'

'Meanwhile, you,' Declan looked back at Sonya Hart, 'were telling Morgan what was going on.'

'I kept him informed, yes,' Hart nodded. 'We wanted to see what he would do once he thought Stephanie Thompson was looking into him. We had worked out he was probably the killer. Bringing Stephanie in was our way of stopping whatever he was looking to do.'

'You turned her into your asset.'

'Why not? It's what police do all the time.'

'You're not police,' Anjli snapped. Declan held her back as she moved forward, angrily.

'So, Antony Morgan thinks he's playing you while you're playing him,' Declan continued.

'We didn't realise he'd got the brother of Mia Chen working for him, or started this new narrative about mysterious new killers,' Ford explained. 'That's on us.'

'That's on you,' Anjli almost spat in fury. 'You're claiming that's the only thing?'

She stopped herself, turned and walked off.

'You deal with this,' she said to Declan. 'I'm done with these two.'

Declan stared at them both.

'Here's how I see it,' he said. 'Morgan came to you, claiming he could solve this crime. You decided you were going to do it yourself. You brought Stephanie Thompson in. And, while searching for Morgan, she made herself a target. Morgan didn't realise that you were bringing her in because it wasn't part of his plan. He thought she was genuinely hunting him, and so he decided she needed to be removed. Which one of you suggested the kidnapping?'

'Me,' Ford replied. 'We were getting impatient, we'd get things moving, but the police weren't involved and neither was the press. We had to find a way to connect Anjli to it. We knew she would need to finish her story and she would make a point of bringing the press with her. No offence, Declan, but you're not exactly a magnet for quietness and calm.'

'It's *DCI Walsh* to you.'

'Whatever,' Ford replied, resting her head against the wall as she stared up at the sky. 'We said we needed to move things along. Morgan told us he'd contacted Stephanie. Explained to her what needed to be done, and the two of them had come up with a plan.'

'Morgan said she was hunting him?'

'Yes,' Ford smiled. 'We suggested he befriend her. And that's what he did.'

'Did Stephanie cooperate with this?'

'No idea, we never spoke to her again,' Ford admitted. 'It was difficult enough calling her, anyway. It was decided that if we were discovered to have called her so close to whatever they had planned, it would have caused problems with our narrative.'

'Your narrative?' Declan almost laughed at the comment. 'So, what? Stephanie was supposed to take the girl?'

'We picked Debbie Watson because she was someone Stephanie knew,' Ford admitted. 'Morgan told us that Stephanie was going to pick up Debbie, take her to a location he'd managed to rent through a shell company somewhere in Smithfield. They would lead you on a merry dance to two or three places, each one giving you a little more of what was going on, forcing you to investigate the case again. And then we ...'

Ford paused, looking over at Hart, who was glaring at her.

'*I* would say that we could find her. Morgan would contact the press, find the building, and Debbie would be found safe and sound, having spent a day or two watching TV, being looked after *by* Stephanie. The whole point was to prove you failed, where we succeeded. I wasn't there at the end, but I think Stephanie was happy to go to prison for it. She had nothing else to live for. She reckoned she could make a case at trial about how she had PTSD, and this had made her do such a thing. Morgan would obviously be seen as a hero for finding her, the case would have to be reopened, and that's what we wanted.'

'But that's not what happened, was it?' Declan asked.

'No,' it was Hart who spoke now, glaring across at Ford. 'You see, Marie here decided she was going to do this herself. She didn't tell me about it. I was planning something else.'

'Yeah, we'll get to that in a minute,' Declan snarled.

Hart gave a half shrug, as if accepting the comment.

'We hadn't realised that Morgan was the killer,' she said. 'That's on us.'

'That's on us,' Declan mocked. 'How kind of you to take responsibility. I'm guessing you hadn't realised that he was going to be the one framing and murdering Stephanie Thompson.'

Ford shook her head.

'He'd spoken to us that morning. Told us that Stephanie was losing it a little. She felt the statement wasn't going to be big enough, wanted to do something more.'

'So, when she was found having committed suicide, you happily let that become the answer to your problems, in they way you always do,' Declan replied.

At the comment, the two women said nothing.

Declan now looked back at Hart.

'But he got you out of prison, didn't he?' he said. 'You got to say how you beat the police. Got picked up by a PR agency. One, by the way, that was booked by Morgan using Blackthorne's old account.'

'We know that now,' Hart snapped.

'Tell me, did you realise it before or *after* he knocked you unconscious and strapped you to a chair to take a suicide concoction?'

Again, there was no response.

'You're going to go to prison again,' he said. 'They're not going to overturn your cases. And in fact, I'd expect to find them lengthened, considering the fact that you'd used illegal means to not only contact the outside world, but you also effectively helped plan a murder.'

'We were nothing to do with Stephanie Thompson's murder.'

Declan shook his head.

'You know better than anyone, Marie. There's no black and white here.'

He looked back at Hart.

'Beep, beep, bang, bang,' he said. 'Do you want to explain that one?'

'It wasn't personal,' Hart said. 'Well, maybe a little personal. I mean, it *was* your daughter who found me out with the cyber scam. Clever little bitch.'

She shrugged.

'We needed Anjli focused on this, but we knew that you, being the DCI, would be the one that took the case. We needed to take your eye off the ball a little. Having you hunting someone who was targeting your daughter seemed a good idea.'

She gave a mock humility smile.

'At the start, we weren't sure how to do it, but then your serial killer friend giving you everything in his will gave us the perfect opportunity. We knew this was something that had affected you. We'd heard how you were trying to give everything away – very noble, by the way – and knew that your weak spot has always been your family. So, having someone target them, connected to something you did, would distract you with your family, with your guilt, and give us more time with Anjli alone.'

'And so you conscripted James the fixer from Wandsworth,' Declan said, watching Hart's eyes widen.

'Oh, you have been working hard,' she said. 'I'm guessing he told you I did?'

Declan said nothing. In fact, James from Wandsworth hadn't really confirmed anything, but sometimes silence was all you needed, and Hart simply shrugged, believing the game was up.

'I'd worked with him a couple of times when I was at Mile End,' she said. 'He was a fixer who could provide things. I needed two people to take on two tasks. The first was to take a zoom lens shot of you and your daughter in Hurley. That was easy enough to do. I just had someone from Maidenhead come and follow you.'

'Maidenhead police?'

'What, you think they're all squeaky clean as well?' Hart laughed. 'Don't get me wrong. Freeman's a straight arrow, but there was a copper there that owed me a favour. I had him take the photograph and then one night, burn a couple of holes in her eyes and nail it to the remains of the garage.'

She paused, frowning.

'Was that you, by the way, burning it down? Nice touch. Anyway, he then made sure it got to Freeman, told him they'd had a call saying to be there for six. This way, it went directly to him and not through anybody else. Freeman saw it, immediately contacted you because he's a big girl's blouse and needs to speak to Daddy Declan. And then, once the ball had started rolling, we needed to keep it going.'

'James the fixer from Wandsworth,' Declan nodded. 'He then contacted Easter Clarke, got him to turn up and pop an airsoft pistol round at the window, enough to break it, cause a shock.'

'Did the job though, didn't it?' Hart replied with the slightest of sneers. 'Took your mind right off the case, meant we didn't have to have one of your big speeches.'

She looked across at Ford.

'Although I suppose we're getting one right now.'

As she said this, Declan shrugged, turning and walking off.

'Hey,' Hart said, 'you can't just leave us here, we can't walk properly yet.'

'Not my problem,' Declan said. 'You're a Mile End issue, but don't worry, I'll make sure they know everything you just said.'

As Hart and Ford shouted after him, Declan walked over to Anjli.

'I'm done here,' he said. 'You?'

'I could eat,' Anjli said.

Declan smiled.

'Then let's get out of here before we have to do some work,' he said, as the two of them, nodding to Monroe, currently talking to De'Geer, left the front garden and headed towards Anjli's car.

The Mile End officers, realising Hart and Ford were once again their problem, moved in to re-arrest them.

EPILOGUE

In the week that followed, the entire house of cards fell down.

Everything Ford and Hart had said was corroborated. Morgan, now gaining the fifteen minutes of fame he had so desperately wanted, was happy to explain everything. In his mind, he was a serial killer worthy of the greats, even if he'd had to wait years for two of them to even be acknowledged. Ford and Hart had been portrayed as nothing more than pawns in his game, needy criminals desperate to find their own limelight. By the time the next day's papers came out, public opinion had completely turned against them. Peter Morris even released an apology for considering that ex-DCI Ford could have been innocent in any way.

Ford was sent back to Downview, a ton of new crimes being landed on her doorstep, whereas Hart was immediately taken off the GCSE syllabus at East Sutton Park. There was no way she would use computers anytime soon, not even as part of an educational supplement.

Declan had decided not to press charges about the

gunshot and had paid for the replacement windows himself. It was *his* problem, after all. Liz had appreciated it and, strangely, had been quite warm to him when he explained what had happened. Declan assumed it was because she'd realised how much he'd had to deal with, but possibly it was because Jess had mentioned to her mother that Declan had almost killed the guy who did it, which in Liz Farrow's book was likely a good thing.

Easter Clarke was released on vandalism charges, again with nothing placed on him from Declan. All he could do was live his life in fear of Declan turning up one day to finish the job. Declan wasn't that worried. That Mama Delcourt knew him and had sent men to watch meant that Easter Clarke would probably be on the straight and narrow for quite a while before he fell off.

Thomas Blackthorne was posthumously charged with aiding and abetting, even though Anjli was still convinced he'd been involved with more, regardless of what Morgan said. DCI Esposito had reopened the case and, with DS McAlroy happily arresting Sanford for her role in the whole damn thing, could finally close it. Oliver Chen, claiming PTSD from his sister's death, was given community service. Declan knew Chen was somebody he'd have to monitor.

As for Anjli, she hadn't really won anything. Sure, the case had been solved, the killer caught, and Ford and Hart, who had tried to discredit her, shown to be liars, but there was still the fact that, for three years, the wrong man had been accused of murder, having paid for this with his death, while Antony Morgan had walked free.

Declan knew how she was feeling, but also knew she was strong enough to get through this. All he had to do was be there beside her as she did so.

The Ashton family had been found living in Philadelphia; Nigel Ashton, the father, had moved jobs shortly after receiving a million dollars and a brand new house. Once they were discovered, they happily explained how Michael, while being held by Blackthorne, had heard an argument between Blackthorne and Morgan, where the former accused the latter of the murders. It would have been enough to bring doubt to the trial, and once he realised that by not offering this, what he had done was allowed murderer to go free, before taking a bribe from them, Nigel decided they'd rather stay in America than come back and face any music for it.

Declan didn't blame them. He'd been impressed, in a way, with Morgan's finale. If they hadn't worked it out, and believed that Stephanie Thompson *had* been the Posies Killer, to suddenly find that the killer was still out there – someone who had not only killed Ford, Hart, and Kapoor but almost killed Morgan before Oliver Chen had bravely leapt in to save him, leaving this mysterious stranger out in the wild – Morgan could have dined out on that forever, written his book, gotten away with everything.

And this time, he would have been happy not to have been named as the killer, for the "killer would still be out there", and Morgan would have been able to kill again.

Unluckily for him, Anjli Kapoor had made sure that would never happen.

Mile End took the credit, of course, but Harris – realising most likely he was on thin ice, especially with Monroe commenting on how it was known that he'd been cosying up with the wrong people – credited the Temple Inn Crime Unit in assisting the case, giving Anjli special recognition, and suggesting an award for her.

Anjli, of course, didn't accept it. As far as she was

concerned, she'd fixed a mistake she'd made three years earlier, and Declan wondered if Harris had known that Anjli would do that, making this a more empty gesture than people realised.

Now with Jess safe, her attackers proven to be false, Ford and Hart back in prison, and Morgan joining them, things could move back to normality for the Last Chance Saloon. By normality, Declan knew this meant the same press circus that had been around a week earlier, all asking about Declan's connections to Karl Schnitter. By now, the solicitors had started breaking up the estate, sending it to various auction houses to be sold off. It was sad to say, but serial killers' memorabilia made a lot of money. Declan hadn't wanted to do this, but it had been suggested to him that if somebody wanted to pay a stupid amount of money for a terrible thing, then that extra money could be passed on to the victim support charities. Meanwhile, the person who wanted such an item would have paid out a stupid amount of money.

There was one item, however, that *hadn't* been sold; something Declan had asked for. Found when going through the items, it was a silver East German mark, double-sided. It was likely not the one that Schnitter had used, perhaps a spare in case he lost his usual one. But Declan had decided he wanted to keep it. Not as a keepsake of a man he once thought of as a friend, but as a reminder to himself to *always be alert,* and that even the most innocent-looking person could be two-faced.

The auctions, making money for charity, had helped in a way with Declan. David Bradbury had even come by and pointed out that the higher-ups were softening on what to do with DCI Walsh. But there was still the case of Declan allowing a serial killer to escape that was hanging over his head.

Two weeks after the case had finally ended, and a week after the auction had begun, Declan walked into Monroe's office, a piece of paper in his hand.

'Guv,' he said, as Monroe looked up from his work. 'I need to give you something.'

'Is it a sweetie, laddie?' Monroe asked. 'I'd like a sweetie if you've got one.'

'It's not a sweetie,' Declan replied.

'Aye, I guessed as much,' Monroe said, leaning back in his chair. 'I'm not accepting your resignation.'

He smiled at Declan's surprised expression.

'I've watched you for the last hour, drama-ing your way through writing it,' he said. 'I guessed what you were doing within ten minutes. I thought I'd just let you do it, though. Get it out of your system.'

'This isn't going away,' Declan replied. 'I'm always going to be the DCI that let a serial killer go. You'll have to check the cases I was involved in. Any solicitor worth his salt can tear my evidence apart in any case we now solve. It's best if I just leave. At the least, transfer out. Go somewhere far away where people won't be able to look at this.'

'Aye, and where would that be, then?' Monroe asked. 'Going up north? Scotland maybe? There's enough detectives up there already. Dorset, perhaps? They like to kill people there. You could do a lot of work in Oxford, Midsomer, even.'

He smiled.

'Or you can have a chat with wee Billy.'

'Wee Billy?' Declan frowned.

Monroe nodded out of the window.

'You're so busy paying attention to what you're writing in

your little office, you weren't paying attention to what was going on in the main one,' he said, rising from his chair. 'Come on, laddie, let's have a chat with our cybercrime expert.'

Walking out into the main office, Declan saw that De'Geer and Cooper were now standing beside Billy, reading the monitors with what seemed to be a hushed shock.

'Guv, you want to see this,' Billy said, looking up as Declan glanced over in his direction. 'There's been a statement made by MI5.'

Declan glanced at Monroe, who shrugged.

'Laddie, she said she was going to do it. I didn't believe her, but maybe she's kept her word for a change.'

'Read it out,' Declan asked.

Billy looked at the screen.

'It's a long and politically worded statement,' he said. 'Can I just give you the highlights?'

Declan stared at him silently, and Billy eventually sighed, turned around, and read from the screen.

'MI5 wishes to address recent inquiries regarding the case of Karl Schnitter, also known as the "Red Reaper", and the involvement of Detective Chief Inspector, then-*Detective Inspector* Declan Walsh. In an unusual departure from our standard protocol, we are releasing this statement to clarify the circumstances surrounding this case and to put an end to unwarranted speculation.'

He looked back and raised an eyebrow; this was uncommon indeed.

'Then-DI Walsh and his team at the City of London Police were engaged by MI5 to investigate the Red Reaper case. This decision was made due to then-DI Walsh's personal connection to the case through his late father,

Detective Chief Superintendent Patrick Walsh, and the need for a thorough, by-the-book investigation. During the course of the investigation, it was revealed that Karl Schnitter, the Red Reaper, was a long-term CIA asset with connections to Cold War-era intelligence. Following Schnitter's arrest by then-DI Walsh, he was superseded at the arrest scene by MI5 operatives, and Schnitter was briefly held by MI5 for questioning. Subsequently, Schnitter claimed asylum with the CIA and was relocated to the United States under a new identity.'

De'Geer whistled at this part.

'Schnitter later faked his death and returned to England, where he continued to target now-DCI Walsh and his family. Thanks to the efforts of DCI Walsh and his team, Schnitter's plans were thwarted, resulting in Schnitter's death during an altercation.'

'Altercation,' Monroe muttered. 'He threw himself off a roof rather than be caught.'

'We acknowledge this case has been a source of controversy. However, we want to emphasise that DCI Walsh and his team acted professionally and within the bounds of their authority throughout the investigation. The recent actions attributed to Schnitter's will are believed to be the final machinations of a disturbed individual and should not be misconstrued,' Billy continued. 'MI5 hopes this statement will provide clarity and bring closure to this matter. We urge an end to any unfounded criticism directed at DCI Walsh, his family, or his unit.'

'Bloody hellfire, laddie,' Monroe smiled. 'Helps to have friends in high places.'

Declan just stared at Billy, almost as if believing that Billy had lied about the piece and had just made up the story.

'And that's out there?' he asked.

Billy nodded.

'At least three news agencies have it already,' he said. 'I'd expect by the time we walk out of this office, you'll have press standing outside waiting to talk to you again.'

He shrugged.

'It seems like you've come from being public enemy number one back to public hero again. Let's hope this time it sticks.'

'Bloody hell,' Declan said as he looked back at Monroe. 'Wintergreen really came through on this.'

'Aye, laddie, did you expect anything less?' Monroe said. 'She is, after all, the wee cow that started you on this entire mess, kidnapping you from Hurley and placing this in front of you, tugging on your heartstrings, knowing that you'd have to investigate your father's death.'

His face was dark, even though he was happy with the situation.

'If you ask me, MI5 should have announced this a long time ago.'

'Hey,' Declan laughed. It was like a weight had been lifted off his shoulders. 'I'm just glad they've done it.'

He was about to continue when Anjli Kapoor came storming through the door, having been downstairs with Doctor Marcos.

'Have you seen the news?'

'MI5?'

Anjli nodded.

'Finally,' she said. 'Well, what does that mean for us?'

'What do you mean?' Monroe asked, frowning, as Doctor Marcos followed Anjli in. With Billy at his computer and Monroe beside Declan, it felt like the entire unit was there.

'Well, I'm kind of used to having the press hating us,' Anjli replied. 'They're going to have to be nice to us for a while.'

'No, lassie, I think you're a little bit mistaken there,' Monroe stretched. 'I think you'll find that they'll be nice to *Declan* for a while. The rest of us are fair game.'

'So, what's next, Guv?' Declan asked with a smile, looking back at his mentor and boss.

'Actually, I think *we* might have something for you.'

Declan looked through the doorway to see Detective Chief Superintendent Sophie Bullman arrive.

'How much do you know about rejuvenation?' she asked.

'Well, I feel pretty rejuvenated right now,' Declan laughed.

'Good,' Bullman replied, her eyes cold, and her lips thin. 'Because I've got the next case right here for you.'

Declan frowned; Bullman was usually one for jokes and sarcastic comments, but this was a darker, more series Bullman that stood before him.

'Local?' he asked.

'No, but very, very personal to me,' Bullman replied as she entered the briefing room. 'What do you know about *cryotherapy*...?'

DCI Walsh and the team of the *Last Chance Saloon* will return in their next thriller

CHEATING MY DESTINY

Order Now at Amazon:

www.mybook.to/cheatingmydestiny

ACKNOWLEDGEMENTS

When you write a series of books, you find that there are a ton of people out there who help you, sometimes without even realising, and so I wanted to say thanks.

There are people I need to thank, and they know who they are, including my brother Chris Lee, Jacqueline Beard MBE, who has copyedited all my books since the very beginning, and editor Sian Phillips, all of whom have made my books way better than they have every right to be.

Also, I couldn't have done this without my growing army of ARC and beta readers, who not only show me where I falter, but also raise awareness of me in the social media world, ensuring that other people learn of my books.

But mainly, I tip my hat and thank you. *The reader.* Who once took a chance on an unknown author in a pile of Kindle books, and thought you'd give them a go, and who has carried on this far with them, as well as the spin off books I now release.

I write Declan Walsh for you. He (and his team) solves crimes for you. And with luck, he'll keep on solving them for a very long time.

Jack Gatland / Tony Lee,
London, August 2024

ABOUT THE AUTHOR

Jack Gatland is the pen name of *#1 New York Times Bestselling Author* Tony Lee, who has been writing in all media for thirty-five years, including comics, graphic novels, middle grade books, audio drama, TV and film for *DC Comics, Marvel, BBC, ITV, Random House, Penguin USA, Hachette* and a ton of other publishers and broadcasters.

These have included licences such as ***Doctor Who, Spider Man, X-Men, Star Trek, Battlestar Galactica, MacGyver,*** BBC's ***Doctors, Wallace and Gromit*** and ***Shrek***, as well as work created with musicians such as ***Ozzy Osbourne, Joe Satriani, Beartooth, Pantera, Megadeth, Iron Maiden*** and ***Bruce Dickinson.***

As Tony, he's toured the world talking to reluctant readers with his 'Change The Channel' school tours, and lectures on screenwriting, story craft and comic scripting for festivals and conferences such as *Raindance* in London and both *Author Nation* and *20Books* globally.

An introvert West Londoner by heart, he lives with his wife Tracy and dog Fosco, just outside London.

Locations In The Book

The locations and items I use in my books are real, if altered slightly for dramatic intent.

The British Museum doesn't do earlybird access, to my knowledge, but it is a real place. Founded in 1753, it's one of the world's most renowned museums, and its vast collection of over eight million objects spans two million years of human history, including iconic items like the Rosetta Stone, the Elgin Marbles, and ancient Egyptian mummies. It was established from the collection of Sir Hans Sloane, making it the first national public museum in the world.

A lesser-known fact is that, in the early 19th century, there was a debate about whether the site of the British Museum should instead be used for the construction of Buckingham Palace. Ultimately, the museum retained its home on Great Russell Street, while Buckingham Palace was built elsewhere. Additionally, the museum once housed the British Library collection until 1997, when the library moved to a dedicated building in St. Pancras.

John Snow's Cholera pump located in Soho, London, is a significant historical symbol in the field of public health and epidemiology. In 1854, during a deadly cholera outbreak, Dr. John Snow conducted pioneering research that linked the spread of cholera to contaminated water from a public pump on Broad Street (now Broadwick Street).

By mapping cholera cases and identifying the pump as the source, Snow's work revolutionised how diseases were understood and controlled, eventually leading to the development of modern epidemiology and sanitation practices.

A lesser-known fact is that Snow's efforts faced significant skepticism at the time, as the dominant theory of disease transmission was "miasma," or bad air. It wasn't until after his death that his findings were fully accepted.

A replica of the pump now stands as a monument to his groundbreaking work, just a few feet away from its original location, with the handle famously removed as a symbol of Snow's intervention to stop the outbreak.

Crossbones Graveyard, located in Southwark, London, is an unconsecrated burial ground with a dark and poignant history. It was originally a medieval burial site for "the Winchester Geese," women who worked as prostitutes in the brothels licensed by the Bishop of Winchester. These women, denied burial in consecrated grounds, were interred at Crossbones. Later, it became a graveyard for paupers, with estimates suggesting over 15,000 people were buried there, many in mass graves, during the 18th and 19th centuries. The graveyard was closed in 1853 and lay neglected for decades.

A lesser-known fact is that Crossbones is now a site of modern remembrance and activism. Since the 1990s, it has become a shrine for the forgotten dead, with a memorial gate adorned with ribbons, flowers, and messages for those buried there. Every month, vigils are held to honour their memory. A fun fact is that this graveyard, hidden amidst the bustling city, has inspired ghost stories and legends, adding an eerie mystique to the area.

It's now a symbol of London's forgotten souls and a poignant reminder of those marginalised in life and death.

Smithfield Market, located in the heart of London, is one of the largest and oldest wholesale meat markets in Europe, with over 800 years of history. Its origins date back to medieval times, when it was a livestock market. The current market building, an impressive Victorian structure, was completed in 1868 and still operates today, supplying meat to restaurants and businesses across the city. Over the centuries, Smithfield has seen its share of historical events, including executions, as it was once the site where public punishments took place, most notably the execution of Scottish patriot William Wallace in 1305.

A lesser-known fact about Smithfield is that it almost didn't survive into the modern era. In the 1950s and again in the 1960s, there were plans to demolish the market, but it was saved by preservationists who recognised its historical and architectural importance.

Chancery Lane, located in central London and where I placed Morgan's florist, is a historic street with deep ties to England's legal system. It was originally laid out in the 12th century, and its name comes from the medieval High Court of Chancery, which was once located nearby. The lane became synonymous with the legal profession, as many of London's legal chambers, barristers, and solicitors have historically been based here. The Law Society, the governing body for solicitors in England and Wales, is headquartered on Chancery Lane, further cementing its status as a hub of legal activity.

A lesser-known fact about Chancery Lane is that it was originally home to the Domus Conversorum, a medieval building established by King Henry III in 1232 as a refuge for Jewish converts to Christianity. Another interesting detail is that beneath Chancery Lane runs one of London's deep-level shelters, constructed during World War II as a refuge from air raids, which was later repurposed for secure document storage.

Hurley-Upon-Thames is a real village, and one that I visited many times from the age of 8 until 16, as my parents and I would spend our spring and summer weekends at the local campsite. It's a location that means a lot to me, my second home throughout my childhood, and so I've decided that this should be the 'home base' for Declan. And by the time book four came out, I'd completely destroyed its reputation!

If you're interested in seeing what the *real* locations look like, I occasionally post 'behind the scenes' location images on my Instagram feed. This will continue through all the books, after leaving a suitable amount of time to avoid spoilers, and I suggest you follow it.

In fact, feel free to follow me on all my social media by clicking on the links below. Over time these can be places where we can engage, discuss Declan and put the world to rights.

www.jackgatland.com
www.hoodemanmedia.com

Visit Jack's Reader's Group Page

(Mainly for fans to discuss his books):
https://www.facebook.com/groups/jackgatland

Subscribe to Jack's Readers List:
https://bit.ly/jackgatlandVIP

www.facebook.com/jackgatlandbooks
www.twitter.com/jackgatlandbook
ww.instagram.com/jackgatland

Want more books by Jack Gatland? Turn the page...

Printed in Great Britain
by Amazon

52671178R00199